P9-CCP-236

A GOOD HIGH PLACE

A GOOD HIGH PLACE

L. E. Kimball

SWITCHGRASS BOOKS   NORTHERN ILLINOIS UNIVERSITY PRESS   DeKalb

© 2010 by Northern Illinois University Press
Published by Switchgrass Books, an imprint of Northern Illinois University Press,
DeKalb, Illinois 60115
Manufactured in the United States using postconsumer-recycled, acid-free paper.
All Rights Reserved

Library of Congress Cataloging-in-Publication Data

Kimball, L. E.
A good high place / L.E. Kimball.
    p.   cm.
ISBN 978-0-87580-635-8 (pbk. : alk. paper)
1. Women--Fiction. 2. Michigan--Fiction. 3. Domestic fiction. I. Title.
PS3611.I4573G66 2010
813'.6--dc22

A portion of Chapter 37 was published as "Phrenology" in a slightly different
form by Lynx Eye literary journal in 2005.

For our Joshua
And for my grandmother Luella whose life provided
inspiration for my efforts, literary and otherwise

ACKNOWLEDGMENTS

I have always been fascinated with time, the nonlinear and synchronistic way in which we experience it. The people and events in our lives float up to us much like those Halloween apples we bobbed for in our childhoods, seemingly randomly, yet never quite that, informing and forever changing the direction of our lives, so that at times we don't understand the significance until we're "meant to," and the past, present, and even implied future become part of our realities in ways we could never anticipate. It's fascinating—even mystical—and nothing could be more synchronistic than the people who "bobbed" up through the murky waters of my life and changed me forever.

First, those pointing the way: Jack Driscoll (could there ever be words?), Keith Taylor, John Smolens, Jaimee Wriston Colbert, and Fred Leebron.

My Anishinaabek advisors: Kenny Neganigwane Pheasant, Language Coordinator and Instructor for the Little River Band of Ottawa Indians of the Anishinaabek nation. Kenny teaches the community and in the elementary, middle, and high schools in Manistee, Michigan, and his efforts to preserve the native tongue among the Anishinaabek people make my endeavors pale in comparison. Miigwech, Kenny, for sharing with me a little of the old ways and giving so generously of your time. And Standing Thunder, who not only provided important details for this novel but also healed me of some of my "self-inflicted afflictions."

I'm indebted to Heidi Johnson, photographer-in-residence at Interlochen Center for the Arts for sharing her photography and knowledge of Traverse City Hospital (formerly Northern Michigan Asylum) and for putting up with a plethora of "one more detail" questions about the institution. One of the saddest moments for me was learning she had passed away a month before I received word that this book was to be published.

Thanks to technical expert Dave Leonhard at our local Orvis store in the Grand Traverse Resort for imparting to me his knowledge of all things piscatorial. And to those who provided historical background: Glenn Neumann of the Elk Rapids Historical Society, Chief Percy Anderson of the Grand Traverse Band, and Larry Wakefield, local historian.

I couldn't have accomplished this without my early readers: Kevin Breen, Jeanne Sirotkin Haynes, Amy Sumerton, Keith Hood, and CC workshop. And certainly not without the faith and hard work of those at Switchgrass Books and Northern Illinois University Press: Alex Schwartz, Tracy Schoenle, Linda Manning, Julia Fauci, and Shaun Allshouse. You have my undying gratitude.

Special thanks to Geoff Bowman, my "northern authority," who introduced me to Kenny Neganigwane Pheasant and Dave Leonhard but who also, it seemed, knew nearly everyone pertinent to my project. Many, many thanks.

Thank you Carol Carr, Charmaine Howell, Karen Ksionzek, and Cindy Lepard. You all know why.

Thanks, Mom. You may be gone, but you're in every line of this book; I still have notes of early research in your hand. Special thanks and love to my dad; my husband, Dick; and my children, Joshua, Hilary, and John, without whom there would be nothing.

A GOOD HIGH PLACE

Luella

CHAPTER ONE

1962

The thing about closeness is that you can choose it, or it can happen anyhow. And you don't have to be friends to be close; a murderer has to achieve an approximate closeness to his victim, after all. Ours has been the kind of closeness that results when two people have been taken hostage or suspended indefinitely between floors in an Otis elevator. We got close the first time, Kachina and me, when I slipped on the wet plank schoolroom floor and landed nearly in her lap. I could smell her sweat: a musky, sagey, sweet smell.

And she, no doubt, got an excellent look up my nose.

They say it won't be much longer, Kachina said last week, her voice on the phone sounding absurdly commonplace like this was news you passed along incidentally. She might have been telling me it had rained yesterday. Or maybe snowed, or that she'd burned last night's dinner. That's always been the thing about Kachina.

How *much* longer, I said.

And she said back, Who knows?

Is he in much pain? I asked.

He says not. He says having your liver and kidneys fail is like having a mild case of the flu.

I couldn't imagine anything worse than perpetual flu and wondered what heart disease would be like.

What about Topini? I asked. Are you having trouble taking care of her?

Mary Crowfeather watches her during the day, and she sleeps here at Keane's with me at night, she said, and then she said, When was Topini ever any trouble? She's fifty-eight years old and still playing with that red ball off in the corner.

Kachina was right: Topini hadn't been trouble for years, had never really been *that* kind of trouble.

So, he's at home then? I asked.

You know better than to ask that, Welly.

And I did know better. Keane would have refused to spend even a single night in a hospital. Well, I'm coming, of course, I said.

What about your job?

I quit that last week. Don't you remember?

Christ, that's right. You wrote me you were going to do that. *Retirement?* How will the stiffs get along without you?

Only Kachina would talk about stiffs at a time like this. Are you all right? I asked her.

God, Luella, she said, don't be a stupid fucking Chemokmon. I'll talk to you when you get here. I started to put down the phone, but the sound of her raspy voice made me put the phone back to my ear. Oh, she said, he told me to tell you to bring the fly-tying stuff. He's got a Hendricks he wants to show you.

SO I CAME TO ELK RAPIDS, Michigan, in mid-May. Made a bad decision that morning and wore a light Windbreaker when I should have worn a coat or at least a heavy sweater. There's an iron bench next to the Johnny Rock, and I sat on it, feeling the curlicue pattern etching itself into my ancient backside through my nylon stretch pants. Why in the hell did they move the rock out of the bay and put it here? I imagined some obscene crane hauling out all eight tons of it, dripping water like giant tears, plopping it ignominiously, albeit ceremoniously, into the park.

You couldn't have missed it in 1910.

It sat out a hundred and fifty yards or so, waves slapping sharply against the sides—igneous rock, I think, granite, maybe, with patches of rose quartz on the side facing north, the side that jutted skyward. A five-year-old kid knew he held the world in his hand if he could manage to swim that far through the inky waters of Grand Traverse Bay. It was a casual, nickel wager for kids over ten. Get there first or cough up. Keane and I had that wager more times than I can remember, and it was a toss-up who'd win.

I remember one night near dark. We had no business being out there, the storm hanging offshore a mile or so and the bay heaving four-foot waves in our faces, fighting us every inch of the way. I was close to sixteen that summer, Keane slightly older, and though I was the stronger swimmer, it would be the last race he would lose to me. I remember my hand reaching for the rock seconds before his. His tension over losing the race turned to something else, and I'd fancied, mistakenly, my future flash through his eyes for a second. . . .

But I don't want to get ahead of myself. Let me say that rocks figured into things, for both Kachina and me, this one a good place to look back from, a point of perspective that brought the town into sharp relief.

Today, in mid-May of 1962, there was a boy of about seven or eight at the park with his mother, the only other humans dumb enough to brave the thirty-mile-per-hour winds that ripped off the bay. The boy escaped the grip of his mother's hand, raced over to the Johnny Rock, and kicked it.

It's big, he said, as if anything big must be kicked. He had a runny nose, tired blue pants that were soggy and bilge colored.

A man dressed in gray sweats, a hood pulled up around his ears, walked toward me. As he got closer I realized he was John Mitchell, the local barber. He didn't go back as far as some families, but John had been here, oh, a good thirty years anyway. He must have been close to my age, maybe a few years older. Looked remarkably like Clark Gable—big ears, heavy brow, round face, and dimples, that touch of sophistication. Only thing missing was that twinkle in Gable's eye. Amazing how much personality and expression change a person's looks. John was just a guy with big ears and good taste in clothes.

Good to see you, Luella, he said, and sat down on the bench next to me, reached in his pocket for a butterscotch, offered me one. I took it; butterscotch has grown on me in my old age.

Out for a walk? I asked him. He told me he always liked to squeeze in a walk early in the day. His brother George had no need of walks, he said, and minded the barbershop in his absence. Mondays are slower than molasses, he said. I told him I thought a walk was superb and asked after his family.

Wish you were here under happier circumstances, he said, and I nodded. Mrs. Joslin tells me you bought the old Lamson house and are moving back. That's sure a nice thing. I guess when you love a place, he said, you can never get it out of your bones, eh? I smiled, and we chatted about weather, gossiped about the McLaughlins, who'd once lived next to me, and soon he went on his way, limping a bit as he headed south along the bay shore. Gave me another butterscotch before he left.

What was it he'd said about coming back? It couldn't be that simple, what brought you back to a place. Or what drove you away. I read somewhere that if you understood a place, there was no need to return. Now that's a bit closer to the truth.

It would be a few days before I closed on the house, so I'de been sitting at Kar-O-Lar Inn, writing in my journal and thinking about suitcases. *Suitcases are like dreams: endless possibilities of remote but luminous destinations. Then all at once they are just a sad reminder of the places you'll never go.*

I shared this with Kachina awhile back in a letter. I don't remember why. She wrote back immediately. Holy *shit*, she said, you sound like me. Find a *man*. If you've got one, trade him in for one with less *flaccid* qualities. An anchor is what you need, you know? Merge your backside to the good earth. Your ass is in the clouds.

That's what she said. Seriously. Which reminded me of bugs. Gave me an entomological image of myself impaled like a colorless moth on a piece of white Styrofoam. It was something Kachina would say, of course. At least to me.

To my knowledge Kachina never owned a suitcase. She used to say that we Chemokmon talk nonsense about finding our dreams, as if they're in some other place, removed from ourselves. As if we believe Gizhe Manido hid them from us on the day we were born and sent us off for all eternity looking for them through haystacks and under rocks.

I thought about that a few days ago when I packed, and it wasn't until I'd thrown in my last pair of socks that I realized I wasn't packing: I was moving.

I'm sixty-three years old in *this* place—this place of 1962. But I've been living in another place. A place that lives in my head like some ridiculous old B movie or one of those stubborn, annoying ditties that get stuck there like "You Are My Sunshine." But I've been living in 1911. I'm twelve. . . .

CHAPTER TWO

1911

Something I discovered early is that boat names are not parceled out willy-nilly but rather on a first-come, first-served basis: first daughter, first love, first original (or unoriginal) thought—those kinds of priorities. And names can be confusing. According to Cap, *Mabel* the boat is 54 feet long, 14 feet across the beam, and draws 4 foot 4 inches of water. She is a passenger/light-freight steamer made of solid oak, built by George H. Notter Co., Buffalo, New York, in the year 1893. She weighs nineteen gross register tons and has a single screw rig of fifty indicated horsepower, which might not mean anything to you, but believe me, it meant something to us.

Mabel the person isn't as broad across the beam and doesn't weigh as much as *Mabel* the boat, but then Mabel the person never learned to buck the waves. *Mabel* the boat lists slightly starboard, as if she's cocking her head, considering if you're worth anything. She creaks and complains and demands much of both Cap and me, but she can turn around and rock you gently in her lap, just when you're sure you've had enough of her. I knew a lot about *Mabel* the boat back then and next to nothing about Mabel the person, my sister who was six years older than me.

Today, as on most summer days, I'm leaning back in my wooden folding chair, short wide feet propped against the railing. I hear the easy slapping of waves against the side of the *Mabel* and the rustling of the reeds as we cut through parts of the narrows. The reeds bow to me as they always do, and I imagine myself as the queen of the lakes, the reeds my loyal and willing subjects. When I close my eyes, the smells ambush me. The musty smell of the old steamer mixes with the odor of the scrap wood we burn for fuel, and there's that fish-fowl-fauna smell as well. I wonder if I'm starting to smell musty, and I figure I am from hours of sitting on these side berths. I'll smell like this for the rest of my life, I imagine; I am in my realm here.

It's sunny, but like a polite smile, I don't feel warmed by it. The wind is southwesterly at ten to fifteen knots. Waves today are less than a foot in Grand Traverse Bay, though we're not in the bay. The *Mabel* runs only through the inland waterway, seventy-five miles of connecting lakes and rivers between the villages of Elk Rapids at the south end of the chain and Eastport or Bellaire at the north end. Right now we're running up Torch River headed toward Spencer's Creek.

Why you so lumpy? Keane, Doc Mulcahey's son, asks me. He's said this to me often—I imagine because he liked the look he saw on my face the first time he said it. His voice isn't distinctive, but it crawls inside me whether I like it or not. I don't answer him, but it's the damned pockets that make me lumpy, or rather the stuff in the pockets that forms cumbersome bulges at my hip joints and hard lumps under my backside. There can never be enough pockets in a pair of overalls, and mine are crammed full of an assortment of gear: fly line, a pair of small scissors for trimming knots, fabric tape measure, silk for tying flies, and rags for oiling line. I adjust the lump under my left cheek and ease back in my chair, which is sandwiched between two black trunks and a packing crate of bluing headed to Eastport.

When you leavin'? I ask Keane. I do my best to look through him, but he's standing over me, and though I can't articulate this quite yet, I can smell things leaking through his pores, something like fast-approaching adolescence mixed with an inexplicable disappointment in something.

Do you mean leave the boat or leave you off to yourself? What kind of question is that anyway? he asks.

You know, I say. When *the heck* you gettin' off? I turn my back on him and see to my line.

Fly line has always intrigued me—the fact that you can cast it at all, even oiled. Flimsy, snarled, angry—it has all the potential of a big knot. Yet, according to Cap, in the right hands it becomes an art, a da Vinci sort of concept: composition, perspective, form, mood, light, imagination. And not just visual but musical as well, he says: rhythm, balance, harmony, distance, and velocity. Fly-fishing is science put into pictures and set to music. Gravity, in her mean attempt to drag it all down (according to me), provides the grace and subtlety.

But I know a lot about knots, too. Tight and imperceptible. Turle, blood, surgeon's, and clinch knots. And several kinds of loops.

Keane's fishing over my shoulder so to speak, annoying the hell out of me. He's older by a couple years, has a habit of walking backward, skipping, and tossing something I've always assumed to be money but usually turns out to be pieces of slag from the heaps. Smart-alecky and cocky is how he looks. Like he's got time to waste while I have none. When he does walk forward, he leans into the balls of his feet, braced, as if he's walking against a strong current. Like it's an effort. It occurs to me then that perhaps he walks backward because he doesn't want stuff to end, while I'm always praying for the finish. (Like visits with Aunt Lena, meals containing salt pork (which can happen during visits to Aunt Lena), long winters, reluctant springs that refuse to turn into summers, bad fishing days—and even good fishing days, because I want them to end before they become bad ones—and any conversation with Mrs. McLaughlin next-door.)

Up to this point in my life, or until recently, the hope of a more superior day in the future overshadowed even an exemplary day in the present; you can't overstate the mere *potential* of a thing. But on this day I find myself understanding that desire to look back, or at least to drag my feet, and I feel sick that I'm reduced to that. Sick that my mind is snagged up at all and sick that I've bothered to have thoughts about Keane Mulcahey's reasons for doing anything.

Keane leans toward me, points to a private wooden launch headed into the river behind us. Won't be long, he says, before people will get around these lakes in those, especially if you keep treating folks the way you do. His head is close to mine, closer than it ought to be. Like that boat. An invasion.

A lady dressed in an impractical hobble skirt, an enormous lampshade-style tunic, white gloves, and a ridiculous matching merry-widow bonnet is standing next to her valise with several tapestry satchels under each arm and is eyeing me, as if I can't be trusted with a few lousy suitcases. The woman's skirt wraps so that it opens in front to slightly below the knees and clings so tightly, I'm sure she'll have to hop like a rabbit in order to move. I know all about ladies like her. Her husband, whose upper lip seems to dissolve into his lower, is turning red and patchy under the blistering sun, his face getting soggier by the minute, though he's dressed more sensibly. No doubt they've spent the whole month of *Ju-lah* reclining on some fancy lounge chair at that Rex Terrace place the other side of Elk Lake. In the shade. Resorters started coming as far back as 1875.

Let's sit inside, Loreta, the man says to the woman. I can't hear what Loreta whispers back, but I'm sure it has to do with my lack of trustworthiness. Loreta plops down on the valise, which sighs under her weight. I turn my back on both of them then.

I'm guiding my leader through the reeds, false casting a couple times to avoid them. You can get cleaned out if you're not careful, particularly through Torch River. Keane keeps on about what a heck of a thing it is I've said to him, a paying customer.

We've got all the business we need, I say to him. But in truth there aren't too many people aboard the *Mabel* today. I tell myself this is because it's a Monday, but in my heart I know there's more to it. I point to the launch, still following in our wake. Why don't you see if they'll take you aboard right now? I say.

The small boat cuts through the wake of the *Mabel*, races up on her port side. Keane waves to a hefty red-haired woman trying to hold on a straw bonnet in the wind. The woman waves back, then puts her hands, one on each side of her head, hunched over a bit, like she's trying to hold her head on instead of the hat. I haven't seen her or the man steering before, but I have seen the boat, dockside, in Elk Rapids. Small cabin, gasoline engine, maybe a twenty-five-footer.

Irrelevant, I tell myself. Steamboats have dominated the inland waterway for better than fifty years, and they always will. But the fact is, the launch is looming, threatening to take over everything we know about ourselves, Cap and me, and it's coming full throttle. Keane is looming, too, seeming to personify that launch.

And it's more than that.

A strange thing has been happening ever since Mama died, and though I couldn't have put it into words, I'm aware of a difference in my perception of things. Can feel a host of events lining up, waiting to happen, even though some things have already happened, and it will take no more than my acknowledgment to make them real. Some are on the verge of happening, threatening to sweep me into a future I have no part in, no love for. I know there's danger in being lost, in being driven one direction, dragged another.

I see Keane is holding a small cardboard box that peeps. I've seen him before with boxes that peep, with birds in his hands or on his shoulder. He opens the box and feeds a baby gull something yellow out of an eyedropper.

Why you taking that bird with you everywhere? I ask.

Have to, he answers. Wouldn't dare leave him at the house.

Why the hell not? I say. Why can't you leave the stupid thing at home?

Just wouldn't be a good idea, he says and jerks his head sideways, blinks fast, like someone is about to kick sand in his face. The look comes as a shock because I've never seen anything there but cocky and can't imagine what this new expression has to do with the bird. Or with me. This is the first time Keane Mulcahey has appeared interesting to me, which confuses me even more.

The point here, the true absurdity of the day, has to do with the lunches, not Keane's silly bird. The day was, in so many ways, a typical day for Cap and me aboard the *Mabel* and, in several important ways, not typical. I always hand out the lunches shortly before we dock at Spencer's Creek, which is what we call it, though it was renamed Alden in 1892 after some senator, I think. Mabel the person has made lunches, which she does every day we run, and they consist today of ham sandwiches, potato salad, and a dilled pickle. The boxes are made of heavy white cardboard, like a cigar box, only these are deeper, squarer, and lined with paper. Handy, reusable little boxes. Among other things, they make a perfect fly box. I took one for that purpose some time ago, and when Cap saw I'd done it, he didn't say anything. Maybe because he figured I'd earned it.

Cap swings down from the wheelhouse, grabs the nearest barge pole, and thrusts it impatiently to Keane. Here, son. Lend a hand, eh? The river's damned low.

The *Mabel* always needs to be doted on, as I said before, demanding much of Cap's time and interrupting mine. On Cap's direction, the passengers will gather in the bow. Their weight will lift the stern of the *Mabel* higher in the water and enable us to coax and wheedle her off the sandbar. Backing and filling is what it's called. Waffling they call it sometimes, too.

What is he talking about—"shift to the front"? the lady in white asks me, sour-faced. I'd prefer to remain here, she says. I look over my shoulder to be sure Cap and Keane aren't within hearing distance, then I tell the lady that she might spend all eternity sitting right there, *right there on that suitcase,* if that's how she feels about it, because we need everybody's weight up in the front in order to make it out of the shallows.

As Cap docks the boat, I finish handing out lunches to the five people who ordered them, collect the money, and get ready to do my errands. The lady in white, who decides in the end to move up front and not spend all eternity on her suitcase, has decided that she will eat a box lunch after all. She'll take it with her on the train, she says, so I run back to get one more from the pile.

A few points of knowledge: The *Mabel* leaves the port of Elk Rapids at 6:00 a.m. six days a week, sails up Elk River, through Elk Lake, makes a fifteen-minute stop at Torch River, then arrives at Alden on Torch Lake at approximately eleven o'clock, where we have lunch each day. Cap's partner makes the northern route south from Eastport and arrives in Alden at the same time as the *Mabel,* where the passengers switch boats if they've a mind to. At noon, we leave Alden and reverse the trip back to Elk Rapids, arriving at approximately five o'clock. My uncle George is the local drayman.

We transport people, my family and me.

Every day Cap grills himself a sirloin steak for lunch. One for me, too, if I'm with him. No concern then about calories or fat content or the expense of a thing like that; Cap's lunch can't be compromised or economized. Every day I head for Coy's store and come back with a steak, some baking potatoes, maybe some green beans, usually some fruit or bread, and an entire pound of butter for the potatoes and vegetables—all in a big tin bucket. Cap will loosen the steam valve on the engine and steam the potatoes and beans done as the steak sizzles inside the open fire door, suspended there between two grilling racks on a partial broom handle.

Why don't you stay for lunch? Cap says to Keane. After you run your errands.

Doc Mulcahey still has a patient or two reluctant to switch over to Doc Birnbaum, the new doctor in Spencer's Creek, who is young but already shiny bald. Keane still runs errands and prescriptions around for his father, and he can see I'm not happy about the invitation.

I'll do that, Cap, he says, but he looks at me when he says it, smiles a lopsided smile.

I decide to fish. Or more precisely, practice casting. If you stand at the stern facing out back across the water and lean as far as possible to the starboard side of the steamer while holding the rod in your left hand and perform a cross between a back and a side cast, you have an adequate casting lane in which to practice, provided no one comes out of the cabin and leans over the railing while you're in midcast.

I tie on a piece of red yarn instead of a fly, pull out several feet of line with my right hand, and shake the tip of the bamboo rod until the line works its way to the end. Then, holding the rod at twelve o'clock, I lower my arm quickly and smoothly until the rod stops at nine o'clock and the red yarn shoots out ahead of me in a neat roll cast. I strip more line and recast, this time bringing the rod slightly out to the side and back to one o'clock, holding it until the line floats up behind me. Then I bring my arm down to ten o'clock. A pretty fair back cast, which by now has worked the line out a good forty feet. I cast the way I live: not without finesse but with a tendency to overreach, cast too much line to handle.

Look, says Keane, when he returns. Isn't that Kachina over on the left bank?

It *is* Kachina, and Topini is toddling along behind, a child of no more than three. I notice, not for the first time, that the child shuffles when she walks or walks flat-footed, and I'd noticed on previous occasions that she didn't talk right, either. She has lighter hair than Kachina and doesn't look much like her, but maybe that's because she was born wrong, like Cap says. Kachina looks in my direction, then away. I know, even then, there is something between Kachina and me. Something inescapable. Only I don't know what. Of course Kachina would someday say to me, *You should've known what, for God's sake. You Chemokmon have to speak things out loud before they become real.*

Nice the way she takes care of her little sister all the time, isn't it? Keane says.

I guess so, I say.

Kachina is picking huckleberries along the riverbank. The Indians sell huckleberries and blueberries door-to-door, ten cents a quart. I don't think much about the Indians one way or another. Some of them, like Kachina, live over in Sand Hill in one of those lean-tos along Bass Lake. Some live in Kewadin. Cap never says bad things about them like some people do. He always says, Everybody's got to be somewhere, Welly, and they were here long before we arrived. So that's all I think of them: they're here, and they've always been here. Chippewa, Ottawa, and Pottawattamie Indians live in this northern part of Michigan, but Kachina would shake her head whenever any of these names were used at Oddfellow School, as if they meant nothing to her. We're Anishinaabek, she'd say, pointing to herself, then gesturing in a large circle to indicate that the term means all Indians in the area. *First good people.*

EVEN THOUGH IT'S AFTER THREE THIRTY, the breeze has dropped, and the cloud cover has disappeared. I feel sticky and tired and *pushed* inside, and I wish Keane would head up to the wheelhouse with Cap, who seems conspicuously absent, or that Keane would sit inside the cabin and leave me alone. I tie a stronger leader to the braided silk fly line, one I had rolled in the pocket of my overalls, then retie the red yarn to the end. Keane leans against the side of the *Mabel* and watches me. Any minute now, any second, I think, he'll be offering advice.

That box container makes a pretty good fly box, better than a cigar box, Keane says.

Yep, I say back. I like it.

Why don't you try a dry fly for the heck of it? he says. It's getting to be a good time of day, and you might get lucky and catch something. You've got that cast down good enough, anyway, if that's what you're doin'.

Keane takes a step closer to me as if to take the rod from my hand, but I back away in that same step. I liked distance between us in those days.

I'll lose a decent fly, and there's no point in that, I say.

Keane makes a motion toward my fly box. Put one on, he says. I've got plenty of those at home if you lose it.

Of course I give in because he's egging me on, insinuating I can't catch fish in a barrel if it were full of fourteen-inch browns. I transfer the rod to my right hand, reach down into the fly box with my left.

Instead of the flies I expect to feel there, my fingers run up against something soft and squishy. The thought crosses my mind to close the box and tell Keane to go to hell, say I don't want to fish, but he has a big shit-eating grin on his face, and I can see there'd be no point in that.

You know what you did, don't you? Keane asks.

Sweat trickles into my eyes.

It isn't like I have no sense of humor—that's for certain. A sense of humor is a good way to start off a relationship like the one Keane and I are about to embark upon. And it's not like I can't see that it's funnier than shit that I've just sold my scissors, my oiling rags, several leaders of various sizes, and more than a dozen perfectly good flies to that fancy white-all-over woman in the hobble skirt and doofus hat for a lousy twenty cents. Not to mention a carefully wrapped piece of black licorice I'd been saving for the trip home, all with a pain-in-the-ass audience blessed with a long memory and a big mouth.

Keane leans close to my ear. These trout may get along on ham sandwiches and dill pickles, he says, but I'd like to see that fancy lady sitting on that train, working on those dry flies about now.

ABOUT THE CASTING: most people who are left-handed are born that way. And usually they must fight to remain left-handed in a right-handed world.

But I switched.

From right to left. I was six years old when it occurred to me to do this, my first year as a deckhand.

Never heard anything so crazy in all my born days and never will again, Mama said. Mama was still alive then, and when she realized what I was up to, she raised holy hell. She demanded to know why I would consider doing something so asinine. I thought she was saying "ass and nine," and I had no idea what that meant, so I refused to answer, figuring anything I said would only make matters worse.

But it all started with his breathing.

I'd stand outside Cap's door and listen to him snore, wondering how Mama or even those "people in China" could sleep through it. It sounded like the saws down at the mill when they go real slow, which is, I'm sure, where they got that saying about sawing logs. But then it sounded a lot like Mrs. McLaughlin's prize hog just before he got slopped, too. And it's when I was standing there listening to the cadence that I noticed it: every so often, Cap would stop breathing. Stop completely, which never seemed to affect Mama one way or another. She always seemed unaware, but I knew there was only one thing to be done: *I'd breathe for him.*

Later I forced myself to write left-handed. My Os all had humps in them like camels, and my Ms weren't humped enough and looked more like waves, and sometimes my Qs didn't come out at all. I played baseball left-handed, dusted the house left-handed, opened jars left-handed. Fly-fished left-handed. I forced Reverend Miller to shake my left hand, which sent Mama into a tirade. My teacher thought I was sloppy, most people thought I was clumsy, and everyone who knew me thought I was plain crazy for ever thinking up "such a thing."

What in the world do you make of her doing *such a thing?* Mama would say to Cap. But Cap never answered. I can't imagine why they didn't know. It made perfect sense to me. Cap was right-handed. And I knew, even at age six.

I needed to be left-handed.

CHAPTER THREE

Ken offered to take care of the yard in Birmingham until I could tie up loose ends and get the house sold. A steady, apologetic sort of man, the kind who looks at you long. Older than me by five years or so. Thing is, the only men who interested me after Duke died happened to be younger. Henry, for instance. Good dancer. Great hands—the most telling feature about a person. How coordinated they are, how clean, how creative, how used to hard work, how vain, how relaxed, how generous. How gentle, too. I remember seeing pictures once, painted in the Middle Ages, of the soul leaving the body: The paintings depicted which parts of the body the soul was thought to inhabit while the person was alive. I'm not sure about that, but I've studied more than my share of dead people over the years, and this is what I think: a man with fleshless palms invariably has a soul to match them.

Henry's hands, strong but well shaped, gave me involuntary muscle spasms in my right leg. Got it shaking uncontrollably, something that hadn't happened before and hasn't happened since. He teased me that it was like a dog thumping its foot whenever you found the right spot, a comparison I didn't appreciate. I couldn't make up my mind whether I found his affect on me annoying or wildly erotic. He was thirty at the time to my thirty-eight, and I told myself then I didn't have the nerve, but that wasn't the reason.

The truth is it was too damned hard to slide over the first time.

Some days I wished I could say my husband had been an odious sort of man, a reprobate, that he swilled whiskey and took to beating me on occasion. But Duke was nothing like that. He laughed a lot, wiggled his ears for the kids in the neighborhood. He was a hard worker. I don't remember who started calling him Duke, but it seemed a dubious improvement over Dewey, his given name. We were married seven years. Most of that time he was Oakland County coroner, which was interesting if you could overlook the corpses in the back parlor and the recurrent nightmares he had that he was lying in the back room of his own house, cold, rotting, and devoid of character, one more body he needed to "get to." But nothing like that happened. They took him straight to White Chapel Cemetery instead. Only thirty-five, he died of Hodgkin's disease before we'd gotten to the core of anything—other than having our son, Dick, of course. So my marriage, like everything else about my life, has an arrested quality, like another truly fine but partly digested meal.

CAP ALWAYS SAYS GRASSHOPPERS are best gathered before sunup and put in old cigar boxes. And jars within jars are best for attracting bloodsuckers, baited with great oozing slabs of liver. Minnows and grubs are easy to come by, most anytime, too, though minnows prove to be trouble because the water needs constant changing. And hellgrammites are things I don't even like to think about. Night is best for night crawlers, of course, unless it's raining, as it's doing now—then anytime is good.

We sell bait. Which is fine. Except that I am a fly fisher and I consider a bait fisher the lowest life-form on the planet. Lower than the worms.

Tonight Cap and Uncle George are going at it. I remember the fast staccato jabs Uncle George delivers under the influence of what appears a justified fervor and too much alcohol and the subdued, legato replies of Cap who has, even then, assumed a defensive posture, head turned slightly away and held low. I can't see him from upstairs, but I know how his body looks. The words they say to each other float up to me as if they are lighter than air instead of words with crippling weight to them. Words like *sin* and *responsibility* are spoken often on either side of the fracas.

Goddamn it, Ira, you live in your own damn world, you do, I hear Uncle George say. You do what suits you with no regard for anyone, not even your girls.

Always some reference to Cap's being a lousy father. Cap's reply is mumbled, and I can't make it out except to know that despite Uncle George's drunkenness, Cap seems diminished in the face of it. How can Cap seem at a disadvantage in these arguments? What, I wonder, could be worse than Uncle George's drinking?

The emotional wrestling will continue through the years between the two brothers, a sort of anchor between them.

Quit rubbering around, Mabel says to me, pillow clamped over her head firmly. Sleep is hard to come by for Mabel, who has to be up by four thirty in order to make it over to Morrisons' farm by a quarter to six in the morning. At sixteen years old, she gets paid two dollars a day for milking cows, feeding chickens, cooking, and cleaning. Mabel is gone before dawn and doesn't make it home until six o'clock most evenings. She makes the box lunches, then does the mending while I get supper. There was a time when Cap helped with the cooking but no longer.

Pipe *down,* Mabel says to me again.

Going worming, I answer, getting out of bed. It's raining out.

I head downstairs to the kitchen, grab Cap's Burberry coat, his old navy cap, and a lantern and close the kitchen door quietly behind me. Cap and Uncle George are sitting by the woodstove, still arguing, and don't notice me. I catch a glimpse of Uncle George's face. He's watching Cap with an expression of frustration mixed strangely with pity. I grab the hoe, but it isn't likely I'll need it. In this rain, those night crawlers will jump right into my bucket.

Mrs. McLaughlin's garden, at the corner of Traverse and Spruce, is the best place for worming because the soil under pine trees is not too acidic. Mrs. McLaughlin doesn't mind if I look in her garden; in fact, she seems more than eager to have me do it. That's because she's hoping to make a trade, I think—the earthworms for Cap. I wonder if Mrs. McLaughlin plans to sweeten the pot any or if she considers the worms a fair exchange. Oddly enough, she seems to be bartering with *me* instead of Cap. I see the porch light is on and hope we aren't going to have one of those how's-your-father-makin'-out, anything-I-can-do conversations. Mrs. McLaughlin has planted geraniums out front this year for the first time, which gives her reason to pace up and down the front walk. Which she does now.

I have always thought a Mrs. McLaughlin should have red hair and freckles, a boisterous personality, exaggerated passionate sighs, and, most importantly, she should be oozing superstition. Catholic, of course. Mrs. McLaughlin possesses all these characteristics except the red hair and freckles. Her hair is black and her skin olive, so I make her out to be Italian or Greek—or some kind of wild gypsy. She talks loud, forcing words in her effort to talk fast, waving her hands, her English broken and halting, though it contains hints of an Irish brogue that make it hard not to laugh. Life exudes from her.

Mama couldn't have been more opposite.

I can cook, Mrs. McLaughlin says during the conversation, leaning toward me with a strange glint in her eyes. And I love little girls.

I wonder if she likes them rolled in cinnamon or perhaps fried in animal lard.

Your father, he is pillar. Yes, yes, that is it. Pillar, she says again.

Could be, I think.

Your uncle George, though, he is more of a *pill,* she tells me.

Mr. McLaughlin, a river man for Dexter & Noble, had contracted some horrible form of dysentery a few years back and essentially evaporated before anyone could stop him. There was talk of the whiskey and/or Mrs. McLaughlin's evil eye. There were nine children left behind, three of them girls younger than me. I didn't plan to share what was left of Cap with any of them.

I've thought about Mrs. McLaughlin's significance during the years because although she lived in such close proximity to us, she never really moved into the influence of our lives. Still, she had a view of the house. She was the Watcher. The Listener. Even if she never really got close enough to get the whole picture properly, she converted the story into a whole by simply observing. Otherwise we might have been lost, each of us, like individual echoes down lonely canyons nobody hears.

Worms.

Adam Wexler is one grade ahead of me and looks exactly like a worm. A slimy, segmented, wriggly sort of person. There are days I feel as if I myself am crawling around in the dark, eating dirt, doing my best to survive the flood, days it makes little difference whether I'm coming or going, or, worse, days I wriggle in two directions at once.

I know precisely what it feels like to be Adam Wexler.

I collect them (worms, not boys) in an old aluminum bucket, but I can't find the bucket or even a tin can and am forced to bring along one of the box lunch containers. Mama's sharpest paring knife—the one I got out of the drawer last week and hid so it would be ready— is in my pocket. (Cap's fishing knife is too long and hard to control for what I have in mind.) I set the lantern on a cedar post along the edge of the garden, which gives me good light down the aisle between the knee-high corn and tomato plants, then make several passes down the row, pulling the hoe behind me. Two night crawlers writhe through the earth next to a tomato plant, so I pick them both up. You have to be damned quick.

I've brought along Mama's cutting board, and I position it on a flat rock under the lantern, visibility being essential. I put one of the night crawlers on the board and study it under the lamplight, trying to identify its segments. When I'm reasonably sure, I hold the worm carefully between the fingers of my right hand and make a precise cut between the tenth and eleventh segments, resisting the urge to close my eyes. I can't tell whether anything oozes out, since the rain is coming down harder, splashing mud all over the board. Neither side of the worm seems to be moving, but I figure it's probably in shock and will need time to revive, so I put both halves inside the lunch container filled with damp soil, then prepare to make the cut on the second worm, thinking I might need to adjust the position of the cut slightly forward; perhaps I counted wrong. Nine, ten, eleven . . .

I'm bringing down the paring knife to make the next cut when I hear something behind me, look up to find Keane Mulcahey standing over me. He must have come down the alley next to the McLaughlins' on his way home from God knows where, the downpour apparently drowning the sound of his footsteps. Why couldn't we live in a town with more than four streets to it?

Interesting stuff you're doing there, Welly, he says. I missed part of it. Can't imagine for the life of me what you could be doing. Go ahead. I'll just watch.

I'm startled and strangely pleased that he's called me Welly. Hell might freeze over before I explain anything to him, though. Over the years I've come to realize Keane couldn't really have understood me about those worms anyway, couldn't compartmentalize himself the way they could, the way I could. Didn't have the ability to move off and leave chunks of himself there, squirming and oozing and unnecessary. There's no use explaining anything to him, I decide now.

I begin gathering my worming tools, piling them into the bucket, washing my muddy hands in a large inky puddle next to the alley. All the while he keeps smiling.

Keane's wearing old clothes, completely mud covered. There's dirt on his face, and the rain is running stringy rivers down it, only the rivers can't make it over his mountain of a nose, and they slide down the valleys next to it instead. There is mud caught in the valleys, too, and it extends down into his dimples in long streaks, making him look like he has one of those Chinese mustaches. I wonder if he has any idea he looks such a mess.

He's gotten tall, a good head taller than me. A walnut-brown, wavy mess of hair makes him seem taller yet. He has a lot of forehead for so much hair, and the bones in his face and jaw are big, too. His shoulders are getting wide, though he's still nothing but bones, his clothes hanging long and baggy on him, as if they were on wooden hangers. I can see he'll grow into all those bones like Max, Uncle George's two-year-old gelding. In fact, he looks like Max. There's a strange temporary look about them both.

You sell those worms to Mr. Hancock down at the bait shop, don't you? he asks.

Yeah, some on the *Mabel,* too, I answer.

Makes you stop and think, doesn't it? he says. Keane has a way of looking serious and amused at the same time, sadly amused, though the amused part could be solely on account of me, for all I know. He could be positively morose without me around to keep him grinning. Talking, I'm sure, will please him. So I don't.

Then he starts talking. Tonight, for instance, he says. Nice night, cool. Just right for a ball game if you don't mind getting a little damp. Tom and Nate were fighting and carrying on over whether or not Tom had stepped out of bounds. Wasn't any reasoning with either one, and after gettin' punched twice in the gut, I decided to leave them to it. Sometimes that's all you can do, he says.

All about winning, I imagine, though I have no idea what that has to do with me. Winning I understand, though. Don't *you* ever want to win? I ask. A funny look passes over Keane's face. We've developed a habit of not answering each other, and he changes the subject.

You sure have a lot of uses for those lunch containers, he says. Remind me never to buy one of those on board the *Mabel.*

He tells me my uncle George is going to give him a job helping at the livery and driving the resorters around, and I tell him it sounds like a good job for him since he seems to get around plenty already, but I'm sorry as soon as the words leave my mouth.

I suppose so, he says, and he rubs his hands across his face, smears the mud around.

I've been standing here trying to figure why you'd do something like what you're doing there, he says. And I think I got an idea what you might be up to even if what you're doing makes not a lick of sense. Probably ought to leave you to it like Nate and Tom.

I'm mesmerized by the black mess oozing down the creases in his face and I want to stick my fingers in them. Or maybe my tongue. Lick them clean for him like a cat would do her young. I'm disgusted and yet fascinated by the thought. I wonder again if he has any idea how dirty he is, if my staring might make him self-conscious and cause him to put his hands to his face, but it doesn't. He looks right back at me.

You know I had that biology class down at the school, he says, though I got other plans for the information than what they all expect from me. You learned that earthworms have both sexes in the same worm, right?

Maybe, I say. Keane walks over to the cardboard box and lifts out half of a limp, lifeless worm, holds it up in the lantern light. And I bet you learned that if you cut them in two, they can still live, he says. Keane keeps flexing his fingers on his other hand as he talks, and I notice that the skin is scraped and bleeding on his left arm, and there is blood along the left side of his jaw. I imagine the salty taste mixed with the gritty mud on my tongue, watch it running down the side of his neck. I'm old enough now to expect his eyes to move to my body, expect them to undress me, but our eyes are locked, and that makes me feel even more naked.

I gather up the rest of the worming tools and the lantern and walk back down the alley behind the McLaughlin place, the shortcut home, leaving him standing there with that smile I'm growing used to. I can still hear him shouting, his voice getting fainter as I walk.

Okay, just so you know, if you don't make that cut right, the worm dies—both parts. And if you *do* make it right, only *half* the worm makes it. He's just *shorter.* So, best case, you're selling Mr. Hancock containers half full of dead worms and half full of short worms. And nobody likes to be *short.* His voice is growing fainter but not faint enough. And then he yells louder: I bet those worms would as soon get eaten all at once, rather than have that hatchet job done on them first. Course that's just *my* opinion.

As his last words are sinking in, the hoe becomes tangled in my feet, sending me sprawling. It falls in the mud in front of me, and I drop the lunch box so I can catch myself before I fall flat on my face. But he's still yelling.

One more thing, he says. Even though those worms have both sexes in one body, they still need *another worm* to reproduce. Just in case you were thinking of mating them things!

THE PAST NEVER BECAME the past for me. It pushed me down the years against my will, which is the thing about me and time: it stretches out flat in both directions. Feels now (and it felt then) as if I exist in two places at once, theoretically possible according to some philosophers and writers of time-travel science fiction novels and a thing I believe to be true. It's not as if there's exclusively an old me or exclusively a young me at any time. Keane himself had a habit of imagining himself and other people old. He told me years later that he used to imagine his life over and done with. But this was different. I *was* old. Already. *And* young. Ashes to ashes, both ends of the process, and every particle of me all the same.

My neck is getting stiff. And I need something to eat. It'll be good to cook again when my stuff arrives. Cooking provides such an escape. A roasted quarter-leg of lamb with fresh mint sauce sounds lovely. Or maybe a sautéed pork chop with fennel and garlic, along with parsleyed red potatoes, a cold asparagus salad, a glass of red wine maybe. I'll have to settle for something cold and blue for now.

Like blueberries.

You know, sometime during the 1930s they made the Indians stop the burning needed to produce them. That's the kind of thing we do: save the trees, wipe out a whole civilization.

Not to mention the existence of a halfway decent blueberry.

CHAPTER FOUR

I moved from the Inn to the Lamson house this morning, though it will be a week before my things arrive from downstate. There's a small bathroom mirror here, the modern kind, white metal with an easily accessed and infinitely annoying door that swings on rusty hinges and seems to invite strangers to poke through intimate details of your life. At some point someone replaced the original sink with a round one, sunk the bowl into a vanity made of something I know can't be wood. Someone, too, must have dropped a heavy object into the sink, leaving a large chip that has rusted into the shape of a tear in the bottom of the bowl.

I piled toothpaste, lotion, and bottles of cosmetics on the vanity behind the sink and ran water over my hands, the water dribbling out in little more than a trickle. Looked in the mirror. Don't worry—I'm not going to describe myself except to say that my face appeared different, like it tends to do anytime you change mirrors.

I wonder why that is. The light in the room? The type of glass in the mirror? The angle at which the mirror is hung? A different background reflected around the edges of the face? At home in Birmingham there had been a window behind me so one side of my face was reflected with part of a windowpane through which you could see the brick brownstone next door; the other side of my face was framed with the periwinkle blue terry-cloth towels that my friend Pat had given me. The towel bar was ridiculously high on the wall so the towel showed in the mirror and caused the eye on the periwinkle side to appear deep blue while the window-against-the-brownstone eye is a sort of slate gray; the face on the periwinkle side slightly sallow, the face against the brownstone side a pinker sort of ivory. Like an asymmetrical theatrical mask.

The reflection in my new mirror is framed with a blank and somewhat dingy white wall behind me. My face is a perfectly symmetrical sand color but more yellow and strangely moon shaped. Early this morning as I washed my face, I felt not unhappy with the new countenance but slightly uneasy and disoriented, so I abandoned it, wandered downtown instead. Past Cinema Elk Rapids. The marquee was blank, maybe because it was Tuesday? Though half the buildings stand empty now, there are two filling stations in operation. A young girl dressed in white hip-huggers pulled up in front of the Sinclair station and walked over to Frank's Drugs. While she was away from her car, I saw a greasy young man with blond hair come out and put a note in the handle of her car door, then return to the station. Something came over me, and I pulled the note out as I passed. I love you, it said. Signed, guy at gas station. It was clear the girl didn't live in Elk Rapids and therefore represented any hope the young man had of a significant event happening to him in this town. I put the note back and walked home: I had no wish to see the young woman crumple the boy's hopes and drive off with them.

But there are other things missing here these days besides women. The neighboring towns of Angell, Mabel, French's Landing, Elgin, and Aarwood, all mill towns or lumber camps, disappeared at the end of the lumber boom around the beginning of World War I. Elk Rapids came close to emptying out at the same time, except for a few potato farmers and a handful of fruit growers. The bustling harbor of 1911 I remember has no more than ten usable docks today in 1962. But when I say Elk Rapids was bustling back then, I don't mean friendly. Because even back then, though it possessed a culture of sorts, it sat on the hard edge of things. People were tough and fit, at least those who settled here long. They'd nod to strangers in town, watch slyly from beneath hat brims or between curtain slats to see how well a newcomer would manage the great conspiracy of wind and water and brutal cold. And if they were fit enough, if they could be seen to throw in a hard shoulder, they were welcome enough. There *was* raw energy here, but there was no wasted motion or emotion; Elk Rapids was a town conserving her strength.

No stray dogs roam the streets these days either. And it's tough to spot coyote or wolf or bobcat tracks in the area, though they say they're still around. You can see black bear at dusk or dawn at the Antrim County dump. Or at an area resort guzzling Coca-Cola, twenty-five cents in the Coke machine. The bottle drops down the shoot of a steel cage, the bear tears off the cap with its teeth to the mindless delight of half a dozen resorters, holds the bottle between its paws, and drinks it off—sometimes twenty or more bottles in succession. The resorters arrive starting around Memorial Day, dressed in neon orange or lime green polyester shorts.

Armed with quarters.

Let's see. Other details. This fine Victorian house is not the one I grew up in. I grew up across town on Chippewa Street, nearly alone it seemed at times, in a rather nondescript clapboard-style house that Cap built himself the year I was born.

I don't have to mention I loved Cap desperately. Or that it was getting harder and harder to breathe for him since Mama died. Or that our time was running out. Or that I knew it and Cap knew it, too. I wasn't always sure Cap knew a lot of things back then, but I know he knew *that*.

What else?

What about Uncle George?

When I think of Uncle George, I think of words. I was parched for them back then, from Cap anyway, but they flowed from Uncle George like a waterspout, a wild, racing, abundant stream of them. It was a gift. I know that now.

READ IT, Uncle George says.

So I do:

> While I nodded, nearly napping, suddenly there came a tapping,
> As of someone gently rapping, rapping at my chamber door.
> "'Tis some visitor," I muttered, "tapping at my chamber door—
> Only this, and nothing more."
> Ah, distinctly I remember, . . .

No, no, Uncle George says. He pulls me from the stable floor, where I've been sitting, drags me to the middle of the aisle. I know why. It's the words. They are uninspired noise, like Mr. Jamison pounding on that typewriter down in the newspaper office. Tinny. Monotonous. Flat. Poe, of course, the obvious, according to Uncle George, for any person who wants to learn to recite.

When did I say I wanted to learn to recite?

Now, close your eyes, he says. The words are alive. Remember that. *Alive.* Picture them before you say them. Let them float along the waves inside your head, like snow geese. Then when you can see them clearly, *let them out.* You're drowning them inside your head before they can fly. Open your mouth. All right, go ahead.

I start again, can tell there's no improvement. While I nodded, nearly napping, suddenly there came a tapping, . . .

Go on, says Uncle George.

I can't, I say. I can't remember the words. You made me shut my eyes.

Say the same sentence, then, he says. Go on.

While I nodded, nearly napping, suddenly there came a tapping, . . .

Again, he says.

But inside my head, my mind is a hole, a bottomless well, a stinking cesspool. What does he mean, *drowning* them? Snow geese can certainly swim, can't they? As well as fly. Normally they can, it would seem, but not in *my* mind. They'd become trapped, the black lid of my stuttering self-consciousness shutting down over them like a lid on a great pickle barrel, the snow geese squawking wildly as they disappear beneath the sour green brine of my ineptness. My thoughts seem ludicrous, but I think to myself, Open the lid. Open your mouth.

Come on, he prods me again.

While I nodded nearly napping, suddenly there came a tapping, . . .

No, no, he says. Again.

While I nodded, nearly napping, suddenly there came a tapping, . . .

Snow geese and pickle brine.

Again . . . again . . . again . . .

CHAPTER FIVE

Uncle George gives me two journals for my sixteenth birthday, January 28, 1915. They are made of soft brown leather, and I run my fingers down one silky cover. He says he gave them to me because he figures I must be getting sick of other people's words and might like to write down a few of my own, but I don't write them. Not back then. Instead, I sit at the writing desk, pen poised over the first blank sheet, the emptiness expanding like a stack of colorless somedays.

But I read the books. The books that belong to me in this place of 1915 (the ones Uncle George gave me, the ones with other people's words so essential that I'd fold them over my chest, open, like a shield) are at the back of my wardrobe, under my brown wool sweater where no one will look, even Mabel the person. Books like *A Room With a View* by E.M. Forster, *Comedie Humaine* by Balzac, and Uncle George's favorites, his Russians: *The Double, Crime and Punishment,* and *The Brothers Karamazov* by Dostoevsky; *Ivanoff* by Chekhov.

You've always got a book in your hand, Welly, Keane said to me once in front of Cap. Cap doesn't like the books Uncle George gives me to read, and I know by the look on his face that he thinks it's one of those books.

Just a poetry book Miss Daniels gave me, I tell him.

And it is. Poetry by Emily Dickinson. I love Emily Dickinson, but it is different from the poetry Uncle George gives me to read. Like the volume given to him by Eduard Dietrick, who helped crew the *Albatross II* and who came here last year straight from Germany. He brought the book, coverless, with him, and the watermarked pages and black smudges make it hard to read. Rilke, a German man, wrote it, and Eduard translated it himself, the words hand scribbled on separate yellow, loose-leaf paper. I don't understand it all except it makes me feel prickly and restless and suspended. I know you have to read words like these out loud.

While I'm reading, most kids are trying to keep busy skating or ice fishing, waiting for the spring thaw. I'd seen Keane and Pat along with Nate Anderson "sailing" out on Elk Lake a few days back, something they accomplish by tying a big canvas kite-shaped sail on a piece of driftwood or sometimes on an old scrap door. Keane claims they go forty miles an hour on the ice. I'm not sure if he's right, but I think they're damned lucky to hang on to life and limb when they hit the shore. The conditions are good for skating down fish, as well, since the ice has been like a mirror for the last week. The boys skate over the fish, trying to tire them out, and keep them from swimming into deep water. Eventually they steer them toward a hole they've made in the ice where one fellow spears them. If he's lucky.

But I don't skate and I don't ice-fish.

And I don't talk to Keane.

It's late. I hear Cap come in from working in the lumber camp at Torch River. Dexter & Noble have other camps: one at the south end of Torch Lake, one on Round Lake, one at Alden, and one on Grass River. Once in a while Cap makes a special trip to one of the others if he's needed. He makes $2.50 a day as a scaler, which is a guy who estimates board yield from any given load of logs. If Cap doesn't make it home by seven o'clock, I keep his supper warm on the back of the woodstove until he gets here.

Cap gives me a hug when I come downstairs. Or is that how I want to remember it? He pulls the leather work gloves from his hands and the scarf from around his neck, stiff with matted snow, puts them next to the stove while he warms his hands. The wind has come up, and it's started to snow. Just lake snow, Cap says, but lake snow can be enough to give Elk Rapids its own private blizzard.

Only coffee, Welly, he says. I'm too blame tired to eat anything else just yet.

Dexter & Noble are behind in production, and it won't be long until the rivers open up and the log drives start.

I'm never a popular guy, Cap says, when I tell them how much they've got. Or, more like it, *don't* got.

I pour him a cup of strong coffee, probably too strong, as it's been on since five o'clock. Where's your uncle George? he asks. Has he been here for dinner?

Uncle George has a room here and eats some meals with us but spends most nights asleep in the livery stable, preferring his own company most of the time to Cap's. Uncle George has never married, but they say there was a woman once, many years ago. Her name? Elise. Though Aunt Lena, my mother's sister, insisted it wasn't Elise Uncle George was in love with.

Can't believe this fiasco he's got going now, Cap says, and I know full well what he's referring to but don't want to talk about the clipping from the *Progress,* which is all about Uncle George, so I change the subject.

May go over to Bass Lake after a bit, Cap. They're having a skating party, tobogganing, big bonfire.

Cap says fine, because he's tired, doesn't expect to be fit company.

Cap was tall and straight once and dark, but the last few years he's gone creamy-gray all over like cooked oatmeal. He's acquired a thin accordion quality to him, too, lightly crumpled, as if someone left him hanging too long in an overcrowded wardrobe.

You got to eat, I say.

I pull the pot from the back of the woodstove, ladle the hot ham and limas into the biggest bowl I can find on the shelf, put applesauce on a small plate along with a slice of bread and pour Cap a big glass of milk. As he starts to eat, I put a piece of pie on a tin plate and the plate on the woodstove to heat up. Then I pull up a chair and sit next to him.

I saw Kachina and her mother in the woods today, Cap, I say. Hmm, is all I get from him, but I keep on. They plum hate me. Why do you think that is? Cap moves his chair closer to the stove, and the chair legs scrape on the pine floor. Mama wouldn't have liked that, and I can see he's thinking the same. Through the years, every time Cap doesn't want to talk about things, I hear that chair scrape in my mind.

It's a different way of life, he says. He tells me how some of the Indians want to adopt our ways. Seem quite anxious to, in fact. Others want to hang on to the old ways.

Any help from us threatens them maybe, he says, a funny edge to his voice.

Kachina doesn't treat the other kids at school the way she does me, I say. That's what's strange about it. I wouldn't mind, I tell him, if I thought she just didn't think much of white people, but it seems to be just *me*.

Cap appears more than tired now. Exhaustion lines his face, but he answers me. Well, I wouldn't set much store by it one way or another. You'll find there's always a few people who aren't going to like you. It's more noticeable at your age, but that's pretty much the way it is.

That's what Mama used to say—that there would always be someone happy to point out your failings. There's other things Mama used to say, too, and I seem to be hearing them more and more often. When Mama was alive, Cap mostly let her do the talking. Now that she's gone, I can still hear her. But I know when it's time to *stop* talking because Cap will flat-out disappear on you. He has that look now, but then he surprises me.

Years ago, he says, Kachina's mother was married, or maybe she wasn't married. I'm not sure. But at any rate, she kept time with old Henry Ballan. He was a ship's captain on the *Albatross II* a few years back, and I don't know exactly what went on between her and him, but when he left and went back to Ontario, he asked me to kind of keep an eye on her, so I've tried. Not that she appreciates it much. And the young girl, she never says anything to me, but they talk amongst themselves in a way that makes me think she'd like to have me shot at dawn. So I guess it might be my doing that is causing her to take a dislike to you. Better stay away from her.

Better stay away from her.

These were words that would haunt me, since I tried damned hard to do just that. Sometimes life doesn't cooperate.

Earlier that morning, Kachina and her mother had been collecting sap from the big sugar maples along Elk Lake Road. I'd taken Adam out since Uncle George didn't have much call for the horses this time of year and they needed exercise. Adam is a chestnut gelding standing seventeen hands high, a good size to handle as a saddle horse but calm enough for all that. I prefer to ride him bareback in winter since his blood keeps my legs and butt warm. Cap grumbles some. Just ain't safe, he'd say, but he really doesn't like it when I skip the bridle as well and jump on with only a halter and lead line. But it's quick and easy, and Adam isn't likely to tear off—too much effort for a lazy ten-year-old horse used to hard work.

Lots of clothes: sweaters and long underwear, fur earmuffs, a couple pairs of mittens, and three pairs of socks under my boots. This is March, and riding a horse doesn't do anything to keep blood pumping through those body parts. I ride down next to Elk Lake and that's when I see Kachina and her mother and the child gathering sap from a gnarly old maple. Seems cold for a child to be out. She can't be more than seven or eight and is not as hardy as most children. But the Indians never leave a child behind. Babies are tied to their mothers' backs on boards. Bigger children toddle along behind them.

I wave, and Kachina's mother waves back, perhaps a bit reluctantly, but Kachina ignores me. While the women work, inserting taps and wooden spiles into a row of maple trees, the child, Topini, busies herself watching squirrels and chipmunks scurrying from tree to tree. I wonder what the name Topini means. The women are wearing scruffy hand-me-down boots like the kind I wear myself, but Topini's feet are wrapped in rags and some kind of worn leather, making it harder yet for her to walk in the two-foot-deep snow.

Suddenly she darts after a black squirrel, makes an erratic lunge, and slides down the steep ridge. I can't see for sure if the back of her head hits the rocks jutting up through the snow. I jump off Adam and reach her first, brush the snow from Topini's face, replace a mitten on a bloody hand, but can see no serious injuries in spite of the loud crying. Kachina is at my elbow in seconds.

We'll take care of her, she says. She pulls Topini from my arms, rocks her back and forth, which only makes the child cry harder.

Just wanted to be sure she was all right, I say to Kachina.

Don't bother, she says back. And you can tell your father we don't need his money either. We're fine.

Kachina's mother says something in a sharp tone in Anishinaabemowin, and Kachina answers in the same tone. They continue to argue in words I can't understand. Thank you, the older woman says finally, nodding at me. She gathers Topini into her arms, and the three of them walk back toward the row of trees, leaving me to figure how to get back on Adam without the stool I use at the stable. The child watches me over Izusa's shoulder as she carries her away. Like some kind of little monkey. Adam, sniffing the frozen ground, snorts suddenly and blows snow about in little swirls like stray thoughts inside my head.

There were thoughts left unsaid back then between almost everybody, but somehow those left swirling between Kachina and me would prove the most painful. There was no compassion in her silence, the implication being that I was somehow not worth the words, and, moreover, I should know why this was.

I wander through the snow, heading toward the livery stable, holding Adam's lead line in my frozen right hand, trying to stay far enough ahead to avoid getting stepped on. Kachina and Izusa make their way back toward the dunes settlement, and I watch until they get swept away in the swirling depths of my confusion.

Did I feel it all coming? Did every step I took move me closer to it? I watch the spot on the horizon where Kachina has disappeared into the skyline.

CHAPTER SIX

A party was given last evening for Mrs. Ira Sharp at the home of
Mr. and Mrs. Leslie Ashcraft. Seven tables were called into use as
"500" was played. At the close of the game a handsome silver berry
spoon was presented to Mrs. Sharp who has been one of the active
ladies of Elk Rapids, and deserving of honor since she was a girl of
about sixteen years of age.

—*Elk Rapids Progress,* October 5, 1905

Deserving of honor since she was sixteen or active in Elk Rapids
since she was sixteen? The *Progress* never did let syntax stand in the
way of a good story.

The mahogany desk with the pigeonholes became mine after
Mama died. Mabel had first choice and took Mama's jewelry, or
most of it anyway. And that was fine. She'd be going off to Michigan
Normal College. And later she'd marry that Marshall boy, Sam, and
would have more need of jewelry than me. The desk was all I wanted.
And the clippings that were inside, upsetting to some people, but I
liked them because they said *something,* even if it was about Uncle
George's drinking:

Marshall Green killed one of George Sharp's horses, or I should say one of his skeletons, that was left in a ditch with a broken leg and couldn't get up March 2. George has been a guest of Sherriff Kittle once before and is skating close to the edge of the ice again.

—*Elk Rapids Progress* March 12, 1915

THE DAY OF THE BLIZZARD.

The horses haven't been called to duty. No school. Snow, as we watch from inside the livery stable, pounds the windows in intermittent fury, driving sideways against the glass so that quantities of the stuff squeeze through the cracks around the edges, float several feet into the barn, drift lazily to the straw-covered floor like huge papery dust particles.

We think the struggle is outside ourselves, Uncle George says.

Like the snowstorm, I answer. I wonder what he's getting at because outwardly Uncle George exhibits a decided lack of purpose. It's hard to picture him struggling against anything. There's a deliberateness about this and even a smugness. As if he knows something the rest of humanity doesn't. He goes about life's duties with the same distracted air with which he fills the blue tin pot he uses to boil coffee.

On the days he can hold down coffee.

Too many nights he sends me down to the beer garden with a covered tin pail, ten cents, and a penny. Ten cents will buy two quarts of beer for him—the penny is mine. The day of the blizzard isn't one of his good days, but he tries to make coffee anyway, his gnarly hands shaking, the crippled middle finger on his right hand bent and bloated from the time he'd gotten it caught in old Asar's halter. His joints are swollen; his knees don't bend right. I know I should help him, but something always stops me. Some secret satisfaction I find in his misery.

He gives up trying to get his fingers through the handle, wraps part of a burlap bag around the pot, pours the inky liquid into two silvery tin cups, and hands me one. I didn't like coffee when I first tried it, but now I do. Something Cap and I came to share over the years.

Not the same with Uncle George.

I guess there are a few people who don't live inside themselves, Uncle George says, but I haven't known many. They never complain about circumstances, he says. Never seem to struggle at all.

I don't like it when Uncle George talks this way because I know he's talking specifics. Eventually he'll come to the point, or part of the point. Or worse, he'll leave it hanging there like some invisible, noxious gas. Only thing remaining is for me to guess which one of us he's referring to.

Coffee is dripping down the side of my cup where Uncle George has slopped it, so I wipe my hand in the yellow straw, pick up a piece to suck on, then move closer to the woodstove. Uncle George sits on an old oak kitchen chair, but I sit in the dirt closer to the stove.

Could have used your help today, Uncle George says.

He means with Indigo, a two-year-old filly, part Percheron, which is where she gets her dappled-gray, nearly blue color. Uncle George is training her to harness. I got tired, he says, running behind her, and she's still pivoting in circles a lot. Would have been great to have you pull her from the front or ride up top maybe. She either dragged me through the cornfields or reared in my face most of the afternoon.

I tell him I could have done that. It would have been a nice change from school. I always learn more around Uncle George than anyone else in spite of trying to avoid him.

I'll take that harness home and soap it for you, I tell him. I notice it has gone stiff.

Your hands work so much better than mine, he says.

How's Adam's leg? I ask him.

To my mind, Adam is mine. I'd take a chair into his stall, jump onto his back, and lie full length along it, arms wrapped around his neck, ear pressed into the hollow, feet extended across the top of his croup, nearly touching his tail. His bony withers would press into my breastbone, his chewing a deafening sound inside my head. I'd close my eyes as he shifted in the stall, feel his feet shuffle as if they were my own. He paid me no more mind than if I'd been a fly on his back. I'd stay there, sway with the feel of him, then open my eyes and be surprised I was only me.

His leg's a lot better, Uncle George says. The big Belgian had stepped off into a deep frozen rut in the roadway two days ago and been lame since.

Keane made him a poultice with some horrid-smelling concoction inside it, Uncle George continues, but damned if it didn't ease the stiffness. I'm thinking of wrapping myself in a great big one, he says.

I smile. And wait.

Did your father take you to buy clothes? Uncle George asks.

Now we're getting to it. I don't answer.

I'll take you, he says.

I don't need you to take me, I tell him. I turn my back on Uncle George, hoping that will end the conversation, but it doesn't.

I'll take you tomorrow, he says.

I tell him again I don't need him. Uncle George seems to have no conception of sixteen. The wind howls, whips open the small door at the back of the stable. I run to close it and hear him mumbling about what a damn fool Cap is and how Cap doesn't even talk to me anymore. Nothing I can ever say will change Uncle George's mind. It's the same thing when I talk to Cap about Uncle George. Each has made up his mind about the other.

We talk, I tell Uncle George.

He swirls coffee in his tin mug, his hair dark as Cap's is white but long and billowing around his head, his eyes slightly rheumy. They gleam now with that too vivid glow they get when he has something monumental to say. I walk through the stable door. Fast. Before he can say it. Things have a way of becoming true soon as Uncle George says them.

CHAPTER SEVEN

I woke stiff this morning. Old age is not something I've adjusted to gracefully.

I was out on the front porch sweeping off the dead branches and winter debris when Clark Gable (John Mitchell) happened by, apparently on one of his morning walks. He wanted to chat, but I was in my terry-cloth robe, so I waved and headed for the door. He gave me a quick salute, fingers touching the brim of the flat, plaid wool cap he was wearing.

I don't really consider men anymore in the sense of keeping one. I think of borrowing an evening's companionship, a couple of willing feet to guide me around a dance floor. Anyway, I knew John had been keeping time with Anna Wilson the last five or so years. But seeing John got me thinking about what he'd said about the town and its character.

Elk Rapids imported people like you'd import caviar or two-bit cigars. There were several types. The gamblers (speculators is too directed a word for most of them) arrived first. They were followed by lumbermen of various skills, primarily from Canada or Michigan's Upper Peninsula. But real immigrants as well, men who made their way from places like Ireland, France, Germany, Norway. Primitive men who lived for the moment and the off chance, enticed here by the barest whisper of green gold, as they called it, white pine so abundant that "God must have started stammerin' when he said, 'Let there be p-p-p-pine.'" River men, sawyers, bull whackers, scalers, chore boys, road monkeys—all found their way here. There were no jobs for the fainthearted.

They came because Dexter & Noble Co. was producing between three and four million board feet of lumber annually by 1865. And just after the turn of the century, Elk Rapids had a sawmill, ironworks, a cement plant, a chemical plant, an electric plant, a hardwood-flooring plant, a bowling alley, and a bicycle club. Not to mention more than half a dozen saloons. They arrived with everything they owned wrapped in a bindle, and most of them would leave with exactly that.

Then there were the hold-down-the-forters. The day-to-day types who planned to be in it for the long haul, hoping the lumber boom would last long enough for civilization to catch hold and make a place for them. Bankers, merchants, potato farmers, fruit growers. Doctors, lawyers, Indian chiefs—the Anishinaabek have been holding down the fort since the Stone Age.

And then there was Cap.

Cap's not exactly the rough lumberman type. He's more the kind of guy who rides on his coattails. Originally from Ontario, Cap accompanied his father, a blacksmith by trade, in 1862. Horses never had the draw for Cap that the water did, so he became a boat captain instead: dredged rivers for the lumber trade, hauled light freight for area merchants, and transported the summer trade around the inland waterway—the kind of guy who plans to stay as long as opportunity exists, without plans for when it doesn't.

A tweener.

Everyone in town calls him Cap, as if he's the only one, though there are dozens of boat captains in town. The rest get called Captain French or Captain Hawley or sometimes just by their first names.

I'M NOT THINKING ABOUT TWEENERS this day in 1915 or about gamblers or hold-down-the-forters but instead about creeks. About how I'm hoping not to share this one. At least not today. Yuba Creek originates in the swamps near Williamsburg and empties into

Grand Traverse Bay. It's shrouded in overhanging willows, tamaracks, and cedar sweepers, and is a pretty decent trout stream when it wants to cooperate. Masses of alder thickets protrude into the creek bed, narrowing it and eliminating the possibility of any type of back cast. But the roll cast or a short side cast will suffice most of the time.

August. The drakes are hatching, which makes it too bad I can't get over to Rapid River. Or better, the north branch of the Boardman, a river I fish now and then, though it isn't *my* river. It will never spill over its banks for me or leave me parched in seasonal droughts. Will never coax me through the bends or drag me into sinkholes the way Yuba Creek will. There's something to be said for recognizing your river.

But flies are hatching, something small like a blue-winged olive or a yellowstone, and I feel my blood scoot as several rippling circles widen by a thatch of tag alders. Which means the trout are already rising. No one else is out here so far, either. I start oiling line faster, the paraffin sliding yellow between my fingers and on the oiling rag. I tie a small fly to about six feet of leader. Most fishermen would choose something gaudy, maybe two or three flies at once and flies with plenty of hackle, but I believe in subtlety where fishing is concerned.

I'm heading down the creek once more when I catch sight of Keane Mulcahey up to his waist in the river, paying out line near several good rises. He doesn't see me, and I'm trying to figure out if that's good or bad. Despite the fact that he has worked for Uncle George now for the past four years, I've managed to avoid him mostly. Not because I have any good reason to dislike him but because I have a way of making myself the perfect fool whenever he's around. He's done a good job for Uncle George as far as I can make out, but if I want to take Adam for a ride, I go when I know Keane isn't working.

I'm uncomfortable around him today for a different reason.

It happened a few weeks back, down by the waterfront. I'd stopped to see if any of the old-timers had had any luck fishing off the bridge. There are always a handful of boys hanging around there trying to pick up a little spending money, diving for hooks that get caught on the rocks. I'd done plenty of diving for the old-timers myself. Keane was there that day along with John Newcombe, a whiner, and Tommy Wilcox, younger than me but a good sort.

Keane retrieves a hook for Mr. Samuels, pulls himself up, dripping and gasping for air, to the side of the dock. He's rewarded with what looks like a dime. The going rate is usually a nickel, so that's quite a haul. It will give him something to toss, I think.

Hi, Welly, Keane says to me. Doing any new enterprises? As usual, I say nothing when he's around, but I notice Tommy Wilcox swim up with a hook in his mouth, and Keane's attention suddenly gets focused on him.

Tommy, for God's sake, take that out of your mouth, Keane says. Goes on to say that the first kid who ever died in Elk Rapids swallowed a pin that he was using as a fishhook. Or breathed it into his lungs, whichever it was. But they didn't have doctors back then, he says, and the boy coughed blood and screamed for three weeks before he kicked the bucket. Is that the kind of end you want to put your mama through? he asks the boy. Keane points out that Doc, Keane's own father, would have to gut him like a fish.

Tommy turns green, takes the hook out of his mouth. Was it true? Maybe. But I was getting pretty sick of hearing so much wisdom all the time from Keane Mulcahey. And it must have been time to push things off dead center.

Sounds like one of your tall tales, Keane Mulcahey, I say to him. Which of course makes him say, Want to bet? and I say, What ya got ya can afford to lose? And then it's Keane's newly earned diving dime against my next earnings digging worms. Keane pulls his shirt on, and we head downtown to Doc Mulcahey's office. Keane is confident of winning, so we stop off at the confectionery for a bag of lemon drops Keane is generous enough to share with me on the way. He's making obnoxious sucking noises he claims are necessary or the lemon drops don't taste right. Water is dripping down his legs.

We pass the post office, blue flag flying, which indicates that the weather prediction for the day is hot and fair. A white flag with a black center means rain. Blue and white: fair and cold. Gray and red: hot and overcast.

Nearly six o'clock now as we get to Doc's office. Doc had moved it downtown, a new thing for a doctor or dentist to do back then. They usually had their offices attached to their houses, but Doc Mulcahey likes to think of himself as progressive. He has a small waiting room outside an office with a big desk and an examining room next to that. Mrs. Madison, a petite blonde woman in her early thirties, normally sits at a small desk in the waiting room outside Doc's office, greets people when they arrive, types statements for services rendered. This day, she is nowhere in sight.

Keane's hand turns the brass knob on the mahogany door, and we step into his father's office, me a step or two behind. Keane stops the sucking noises he's been making, but they're replaced by similar noises coming from inside the office, and then what I can't see much of to begin with I can see even less of real soon, because Keane suddenly throws his body in front of mine as if he's protecting me from some assailant. The force of his weight knocks me back into the waiting room, and as our bodies collide, I lose my balance and fall to my knees. Keane is kneeling as well, a soggy arm slung across my back and around my shoulders. I expect to hear someone screaming for us to take cover, but no stray bullets fly past our heads.

A deafening silence fills the office. But no signs of menace anywhere.

What I had seen was what looked like yards and yards of yellow material on the floor behind Doc Mulcahey's desk mixed with strands of buttery hair and maybe some arms and legs even and what sounded like someone moaning.

I feel the weight of Keane's body on top of me, and now I seem to be holding him up. Keane had left the door ajar, and we can see the enormous mahogany desk in front of the large plate-glass window. We watch as a goldfinch, perched on a feeder outside Keane's father's window, frantically eats sunflower seeds.

When we come back out onto River Street, Keane shoves the bag of lemon drops into my hand and tells me he'll be seeing me later.

CHAPTER EIGHT

The day in the doctor's office a few weeks back is on my mind as I watch Keane fish. The river splits around a couple small islands here. It's wider immediately before the fork, and he's standing at the wide spot backcasting. Gracefully. False casting part of the time, stripping out line, casting the exact spot I'd seen the trout rise. He flips his wrist to set the hook, but I can tell from Keane's manner that it's no more than a junior he has on his line. As he starts hauling him in to release him, the resistance becomes much greater. One of those monster browns has decided to have junior for lunch, it appears. Fly fishermen don't fish with live bait, but if providence helps out once in a while, a fisherman is blameless.

I hear the zing then and I know for sure this is no brookie. The fish has run upstream, stripped line out to the backing on the reel, and he'll be hard to turn. It seems forever before Keane does turn him, and I know his wrists will be getting tired and that he'll be tempted to switch hands. If he does, he'll let off the rod tension and lose the fish.

But Keane doesn't switch hands, and the trout turns, takes a run directly at him. Right past him, in fact, heading downstream for high water, Keane stripping in line like a madman. But it isn't fast enough, and when Keane's rod shoots up and stays there, I know the gig's over, even though I never hear the ping.

Keane is shouting words I won't repeat, and then the rod sails toward me into the bush where I'm still standing unobserved. Keane sits down on the creek bed and tosses stones into the river for what I hope is a discreet interval. He says nothing when I sit next to him.

Any luck? I ask him. Wasn't even fishing, he answers, just enjoying the scenery. Nice and quiet out here, or at least it was. He gazes downstream in the direction of the lost brown. His creel and fly vest are sitting beside him on a nearby log, and I wonder how he'll manage to explain them, not to mention the waders he's wearing. Then I see he has no intention of it.

I guess you'd rather do without company, I say, getting to my feet, feeling surprisingly sad.

You're here already, he says. Might as well stay.

I sit back down. My britches are rolled up and I play with a mosquito bite on my left knee, crossing it with my fingernail to get the itch off. I wonder if Keane is uncomfortable because he's worried I'd seen him lose the brown or if he's thinking about that day in Doc's office. Then I realize we both know what the other is thinking. Minutes pass without either of us saying a word, each of us staring at our feet.

I like rivers, Keane says finally. Better than any of the lakes, he says. Doesn't matter what river.

Any would do. Petobeco, Boardman, Jordan—he liked them all, he would tell me over the years.

Maybe, he says, it's because a river *seems* to have direction to it. They twist and turn, he says, even disappear here and there, unlike the big lake or an ocean.

Keane stands and wades out a ways in the riverbed, stepping over logs and rocks as he moves downstream. The river is low for this time of year, and I know what he means about rivers. I can see he belongs not just in the river but *out there*. No safe corners for Keane, no hiding places, no middle ground.

The river taught me something, he says. Taught me I can stand and fight the current, or I can lift my feet and float on downstream. His hand floats out over the stream like I pictured his body doing. He keeps talking. There are times when you have to do one thing and times when you need to do the other. Then he stops talking and sits on one of the logs facing me.

I had this dream, he says, that I had yards and yards of this shiny yellow material I needed to get folded up and put away. I kept folding and folding until it got too big and then I kept folding anyway, he says. Folded all goddamn night long.

We all have dreams like that, I say.

I used to sit up there on his desk, he says. He'd let me do that once in a while. Second floor and all. I'd sit there pretending I was fishing. Fishing was always good out that window. Keane laughs now, and his hand dips in and out of the water like a plane diving from the sky.

We hear a gentle plop upstream, which might mean trout are feeding again, but neither of us moves. He smiles. Glad to see you made the right decision about those worms, he says. Bought some once after that just to check.

Yeah, well I guess nobody likes to be *short,* I say.

Keane tells me he studied my technique for future reference. Though he figured there was probably not much money in worm doctoring, he thought he might branch out into large animals. He was sure there was a need for a veterinarian around these parts.

Pop says it doesn't pay, Keane says.

I say back, No harm checking into it.

How's the fishin' been for you today? Keane asks.

A brookie, I tell him. Maybe twelve-incher. I'm tempted to say, Nothin,' like the brown you just lost, but things have gone okay so far between us, so I tell him I have plans for breakfast.

Let's add to that breakfast, he says. I know a spot up where the Yuba branches off near the old Cribben place. I'll take you there, he says, offering to take me to *his* spot, something a fisherman rarely divulges.

In a minute, I say, and take off my shoes and socks, drop my britches and am about to remove my shirt and underwear when he lets out the first yell.

What in the hell are you doing?

I'm not sure myself what I'm doing, except I'm tired of things happening to me without me having any say about them. And I know I can trust Keane Mulcahey.

This river looks inviting, I tell him. It's hotter than you-know-what, so if you have a problem with that, you better turn around until I'm in. Which he does so fast, he nearly trips on a rock and falls in himself. He tells me he never dreamed I'd do such a thing, and I tell him he isn't much of a dreamer.

You probably don't even dream in color, I tell him. Why don't you join me?

Nope, he says. And I *do* dream in color. Yellow, for instance.

That's right, I say. You do, and I say it slow: yellow.

He tells me he'll have a drink while I'm carrying on with whatever the hell it is I'm doing. I'm not sure what the hell it is I'm doing, but I've learned that if I keep people watching certain things, they'll miss others.

He pulls out his canteen, unscrews the top, and takes a drink. His fingers are knobby. He watches me swim over to him.

I can see every dad-blame part of your sorry carcass, he shouts at me.

Not the first time you've seen one, I shout back. I tell him I overheard Percy Anderson and John Montreaux talking about the three of them visiting a certain establishment over in Aarwood. Doesn't seem possible for Keane's face to get any redder, but it does.

They drug me over there. It's not a place I hang out, he says. I can't believe they'd talk about that in front of you.

Guess they didn't see me, I say. I grab the canteen away from him, raise it to my lips, and take a big gulp before he can stop me.

Hey, he yells as I make my first gasp. My coughing takes up a long minute between us.

That's straight whiskey, I yell at him. Where in the world did you get that?

He tells me it's none of my damned business.

Give me another drink, I say.

Not on your life. He pulls the canteen out of my reach. Too many boozers in your family already, he says.

You're *Irish*, I say back to him and dunk my head under the water, come up sputtering. Everyone knows the Irish are lushes.

Neither of my parents drink, he says.

So you thought you'd do their drinkin' for them, is that it?

Something like that.

I grab the canteen again. He tells me, Just a small one, and I mean it, and I take a sip. A small one.

Then I simply stand up.

Dad-*blast* it, Keane shouts at me. If you don't quit doing that, I'm going home, and when I do I'll be taking all your clothes along with me. We'll see what explanation you got for showing up buck-ass naked.

I tell him to keep his shirt on, and he says he's not the one missing one.

I climb out on the bank and shake myself dry like a great warm puppy while Keane keeps his back to me. My clothes stick to me as I haul them on, but it's been worth it. Keane says he's sorry about what he said about Uncle George being a drunk. He's not like everyone thinks he is, he says.

I know, I say.

The clouds have pulled together to offer the fish some camouflage, and the wind has died some. The day is full of promise and trout again. Keane stands and begins to lead the way upstream, and when I can stand it no longer I say, It'd be a shame to leave that nice fly rod in those bushes for something to happen to it and a further shame for you to walk the four miles back here to pick it up after I'm gone. Nice brown, by the way—interesting fly pattern.

CHAPTER NINE

Why do they call grave markers headstones? A figurative thing, probably, and head rock doesn't have the same ring to it. I can never figure out which side of the stone the people are on anyway. Sometimes, even though the person's head is toward the stone, the marker is on the wrong side of the grave. It would seem that if you're standing at the person's feet, you should be able to read the stone, but that isn't always the case. All the bodies in Elk Rapids Cemetery, for instance, face east, tombstone and Grand Traverse Bay at the back of their decomposing heads.

Which seems a shame.

Elk Rapids Cemetery is up on the hill across the main road from town. You like to think of a cemetery as having good drainage. Shade is nice. And you like to think green, though red and yellow maple leaves have begun to drop and embrace the bottoms of the stones this day. It's as if the dead are somehow sucking the green carpet down through the earth, a blanket for winter. The relentless odor of decay is always here, but even though I'm barely sixteen, I can smell even the decomposition of my own bones. It's hard to perceive growth when life is nothing more than one long process of degeneration, a slow march to the grave.

I don't like to come here. But I do come.

Not because Mama would have wanted it. She liked fresh, clean air, and when I picture her, which is hard, I picture her hovering. *At rest* were not words that suited her, but for whatever reason I think clearer here.

It's not like I talk to Mama. I'd never gotten around to talking to her when she was alive. Seems funny to start now. Instead I imagine she reads my thoughts, knows all about me, as she did when she was alive, only now she knows even more. So I sit here letting her absorb me like a sponge. And sometimes I'll have a stray thought, and that thought, I imagine, must come from her. I wonder if I have any substance of my own or if I exist now as a product of Mama's thoughts?

She and Emily don't have markers yet. It's marked instead with a simple wooden cross, two rocks on either side to support it. I talked to Cap several times about getting the marker finished, but he never gets around to it.

I sit next to Mama's grave and pick up a handful of dirt from the path that runs next to it. The dirt feels like bits of skin, fragments of bones, as I rub it between my fingers. An itchy dampness oozes through my trousers.

So I lean on Irving Madison instead, a largish stone, maybe three feet tall, rectangular and flat topped. Born 1855, died 1904, the stone says—a couple years before Mama. Just R.I.P. under his name. No loving husband and father stuff, no Bible verses, nothing other than the rest in peace. Is it disrespectful to sit on the monument? I don't know, but I pretend Irving doesn't mind, that maybe he enjoys the visit and has offered me a seat. Often I take one of Mama's flowers and lay it against Irving's stone. Today I offer him a red chrysanthemum.

I hear the sound of laughter at the far east side of the cemetery and look up to see Kachina chasing her sister through the blueberry bushes. I'm not sure what they're doing here so late in the season. Topini is naked, so I figure they've been swimming down by the river as Kachina's arms are full of clothing and blankets or towels. She shouts for Topini to stop, but it's obvious the child loves the chase. She's become amazingly fast for a child who'd seemed so unsteady once. How old can she be now? Eight or nine?

The child sees me, rushes toward me, short legs churning, Kachina closing ground behind her. Then she stops.

'Lo, she says to me. Then, 'Lo, again.

Hello, I answer. I hold a chrysanthemum out, and she holds out a hand.

Rehhhd, she says, smiling a semitoothless grin in my direction.

Kachina, breathless, catches her at last, uses a faded orange woolen blanket to wipe the rest of the water from Topini's dripping body, pulls a red dress over her head, straggly wet hair catching along the neckline, making the child grimace. Kachina attempts to tie moccasins on the child's feet, but Topini squirms out of her grasp, reaching for the flower. I pat Irving Madison's stone, and Topini jumps up on the flat top of it, smack-dab on it, taking the flower, tickling herself in the nose with it.

Kachina's face is motionless. She doesn't blink, and even though she should be out of breath, I can't see her breathing. Her silence has nothing to do with me—I can see that. She seems to be listening.

You're sitting on that marker, Kachina says.

I pull the child into my arms and wonder what Kachina would think about me lying on top of Mama's grave like I do sometimes, feeling her spirit move up through the soft grass into my skin. I commune with the dead, and not just with Mama, either. Flashes of sacred Indian burial mounds fill my mind, and I am fairly certain that this is not something Kachina would approve of. The expression on her face is one that says she's also not surprised.

Kachina pulls the child from my arms, the annoyed expression on her face meant only for me. I take the moccasins from Kachina's hand, put them on the child's feet, and wrap the leather ties around them.

Of all the things I might have said, *schools, special schools,* should not have been one of them. A suggestion is all it was, just *an option.*

And this is part of what plays over and over in my head: There are always options, Kachina says, pointing down. Like the one under your backside.

I'd been leaning on Irving's stone all the while, but I move away now; Irving's stone feels cold and inhospitable. Or perhaps too inviting. I lift Topini to the ground, hand her another flower, and watch as the two of them walk away, Kachina extraordinarily rigid, the child clutching the red chrysanthemums in a pudgy, shapeless hand.

CHAPTER TEN

Dampness encroached through the open kitchen window, making short work of my thin flannel robe. A rosebush whipped in the breeze, making scraping noises against the house's clapboard siding. Visible scratches in the white boards had long needed a new coat of paint. I pulled the window shut and felt the stiffness under my right arm, a stiffness I've had since they removed all the lymph nodes ten years ago. A spring morning can be bone-chilling this close to the bay, but maybe it's more about how close these bones are to the surface these days.

I'd been up since dawn. Made myself a cup of coffee using Mama's blue delftware, which had a way of making me feel warm. Coffee was all I was equipped for so far in this house. Not even a refrigerator yet. I'd set up a fold-out cot in the dining room since it seemed silly to open the whole house until everything arrives.

I'd been thinking about the fishing. The fishing was, in many ways, all there was. Everything in life is fished for, isn't it? People have different ideas about fishing—different ideas for doing it in the first place and different ways to go about it. Some are cerebral fishermen, sort of scientific, Cap used to say. They postulate about conditions, uses of certain flies. They carry out elaborate data-recording systems, followed by revised postulates, followed by more data and more postulates.

Other people fish by feel. Intuition. Some look as if they are praying. And they are: offering up their wives (if not their firstborn children) to the fishing gods for a couple good browns, though they'd probably settle for a perch or two. Some have that keyed-up look I've seen on the faces of kids pitching pennies in back alleys. But they all have a certain thing they do, some technique they've developed because that one time the fish god smiled down on them.

Keane made a good fishing partner back then. Number one, he was there. Through the years, I've come to appreciate an experienced opinion on whether a dry fly is a good choice or should you be using a nymph, which everybody frowns on but we all know works on occasion, and, if so, which one? Leader sizes are fun to talk over, as is the best way to cast a Petobeco Creek as opposed to a Rapid River. It's comforting to see someone off in the distance fishing because then you know you'll have someone to walk home with.

I don't know if I have a single theory, but I like fishing because it doesn't spread out on me and overlap. It stays where it is and what it is. At least then it did.

Another thing about fishing: no matter how much you like your partner and how eye to eye you see the whole business, pretty soon he goes one way in the river and you go the other, because after all, you need room to cast, and because there will always be this one stretch in the river with your name on it, a certain hole that makes it necessary for *you* to fish *there*. Fishing, like dying, is a thing you ultimately must do alone, no matter how many people you start off with.

Another point about fishing: you can't always see them. The fish. And that doesn't mean they aren't there. Which makes me think of Mama. Maybe she's not really dead. Even now. I never saw her dead, and that's a pretty strange occurrence around these parts, or so everybody told me. I didn't see the baby dead, either. They named her Emily. No one saw either of them at the funeral, which makes some weird kind of sense if you knew Mama.

She tidied up conversations, neatened up relationships, spruced up her thinking, and picked up her mood. She ironed things.

Clothes, of course, but pillowcases, too. Sheets, bath towels, book pages. She washed windows every day, dusted under beds. Wore one apron over another one *just in case,* she said. Had a piece of slate with a small hole in it hung by the kitchen door, and it was on this piece of slate that Mama chalked out her directives, in block-printed white letters, all caps: LUELLA: PEEL POTATOES, CHURN BUTTER. MABEL: MENDING.

If Mama gave you the day off, the slate would simply be missing.

Cap tells a story about Mama putting her back out of place once and him coming in and seeing her on all fours, hot-water bottle tied to her back with her apron strings. Which he always meant to be a funny story, but I don't think it was. All part of the explanation for why no one ever saw her dead.

I don't, under any circumstances whatsoever, Mama said, want hordes of people staring at me when I got nothing to say over the outcome, not after I got a look at the job Nettie Ryan over at Nelson's Mortuary did on Marion Thompson.

This was all according to Uncle George. But what Uncle George said seemed right. I didn't dare ask Cap anything about any of it.

But what I always think is maybe Mama's not dead. Even now in 1962.

I want to go to Greece, I remember her saying.

Maybe she got up one day and went. Forgot to come back. I like to think sometimes that she's wandering around in her good summer dress, carrying her big straw bonnet, neatening up the ruins. That would be nice, I think. Heaven was always harder to picture than the Acropolis.

I know what people wear in Greece.

CHAPTER ELEVEN

Ever since Uncle George started spending a night now and then over at Town Hall as a guest of Sheriff Kittle, no one seemed to want to talk about him, period. That's what they'd say: I'm not talking about George, *period*. Even before she died, my grandmother would not talk about him, even though he was the one who took care of her for weeks when she tripped carrying the scalding water that burned her face so bad.

The night it all came apart was the night of the town musicale over at Town Hall. Which happened to be the same night that Uncle George was "visiting" out back (the building served both as Town Hall and jailhouse and came to the notice of a good portion of the townsfolk. Which was what got Cap saying he didn't want to talk about George, period. That plus all the stuff about him neglecting his horses. Which started when Marshall Greene had to shoot Jack the night the rig slid down in the ditch behind the saloon. Only I knew what no one else did: Uncle George wasn't driving the rig that night. Sammy Menkin, the hired hand who never was too responsible, was driving. He'd gone off to dinner and never bothered to tie Jack to the post first. When he saw what had happened, he disappeared. Uncle George never said anything because he said Jack was his responsibility, and it served him right for hiring Sammy when he knew he wasn't good for much.

Uncle George didn't spend much time at the house in those days, and no one seemed to care about that. Except maybe me. I never heard Uncle George say some of the nasty things I'd heard those ladies say who belong to Sara's Circle down at the Methodist Church. The ladies down at the library didn't like Uncle George much either, and I'm sure they wondered why someone like him would bother with books. But that's about all he did bother with.

Books and whiskey.

So Cap had no use for Uncle George, but that hadn't always been the case. Uncle George told me a tale about the two of them.

I CAN SEE IT AS IT USED TO *be when we were kids, he said. All by itself at the top of Sanctuary Hill. We'd snowshoe to it. Or swim. Or sometimes we ascended to it out of the surplus of our father's rage and our mother's indifference.* (Uncle George had that poetic side to him. Grandpa Sharp was a blacksmith, and I don't remember any rage that wasn't directed toward some recalcitrant animal.)

There were plenty of ways to arrive at the Tree of Supreme and Ultimate Sacrifice. It was Ira (Cap) who named it, Uncle George said.

You can't name a tree that, I told Ira, but Ira said that he could, too. There was a tree named the Tree of the Sorrowful Night in Mexico City and, anyway, it was his tree.

Then he'd say, Come on, George. Let's do it.

A good climbing tree. A maple with broad, full branches, a big expansive crotch where we'd sit and spit tobacco and think.

That was paramount, the thinking about it, he said.

We'd look at the stars or the sky or the intersecting tentacle-like branches or down at the bugs scurrying about under the tree, but no matter what, we couldn't miss looking at the scars—the gaping purple wounds on the trunk of the tree, oozing bloody black sap where there once had been branches. It made for an extralong stretch of the legs if you were to make any headway. And that was part of the deal. If it hadn't been for the gaping holes, the black oozing blood, and the missing branches,

the tree would have been called the Tree of Supreme and Ultimate
Happiness. Happiness instead of Sacrifice. And then there would have
been nothing to it at all.

Nothing.

At all.

Ira told me this over and over.

It's the scars, he'd say.

Ira was younger than me but somehow seemed older, nearer to the edge
than I could ever be. And that was because Ira could see it. And I couldn't.

Barefoot. We always climbed barefoot.

Come on, George, climb. It's a rehearsal, after all. Not like it's the real
thing, Ira would say. They're only shooting blanks, you know. The blood
isn't real. Ketchup, he'd say. All life is a rehearsal, and there's always take
two or take three or a complete restaging or a change of director if things
don't work out.

You don't know what you're blabbing about, I'd shout up to him.

But he began climbing anyway. Ira would climb, at least for a while, a
branch or two ahead of me. I couldn't see well, but that's because I only
watched Ira's feet. Anytime a foot moved, that meant I must move one,
too, and that took all my concentration.

But he saw. He testified to wondrous and improbable views. You can
see the lighthouse on Old Mission Peninsula, or you can see the Straits
of Mackinac, or you can see all the way to the Hudson River, or clear
to Morocco. Or you can see the beanstalk, Jack's foot disappearing into
the clouds. Or into Wild Widow Jamison's bedroom window (though her
house was across town and completely obstructed from our view by the
sawmill and dozens of deciduous trees).

Ira was several branches ahead of me, calling to me to keep up, so I
tried, my hands grasping branches that seemed compromised beneath our
weight, bending and swaying from the force of it, though I kept my feet close
to the trunk. Ira was several branches ahead and moving farther away,
and that was when I noticed something strange had begun to happen.

When we started to climb the tree, the leaves had been vigorous and
blooming, a bright pubescent bud color, stray branches poking in our ears

and up our noses, obscuring the view. But as I stopped to rest halfway up the tree, I realized the leaves had become dark and maturely green, even beginning to turn saffron red in patches.

I laid a palm against the bark and saw that the crevices in my knuckles matched those of the tree, nails grimy and ragged and yellow. My knees, propped against a limb for balance, had begun to ache, and I couldn't seem to hear clearly. Worse, I had the idea that rings were forming within my brain like those in the tree, causing it to become fixed and rigid within my skull.

It began to rain then, a bone-chilling, drenching rain that made the branches slimy and hard to hold on to. When had it changed? It was the altitude that was doing it. Ira shouted down that the thin air was causing his nose to bleed, and crimson splotches began landing on the withering leaves, splattering my left foot with pulp like someone throwing tomatoes, and that must have been it.

The blood wasn't real, after all.

Don't stop, Ira hollered down. It's worth it, believe me. Keep climbing.

So I did. But the leaves on the tree had all withered and turned brown, were dropping, leaving the branches skeletal and naked. Blinding snow was blowing clumps into my eyes, and the branches were covered with thin, slippery ice. My body had become as brittle as the frozen branches.

I can't go any farther, I hollered up to Ira.

Keep going, Ira hollered back. All you need to do is get through the clouds. You can see all the way then, and the snow and rain stop, too. In fact, it all stops, he said. There's lots of people here, standing on top of the clouds, and everything feels blue. It looks dazzling white, but it feels a deep, warm, inky blue.

He wasn't quite to the top, but he'd always been headed there. I could see that.

Ira was always looking.

ONE OF THESE VIEWS changed Cap somehow back then, Uncle George had said. Cap climbed down one day and never seemed the same. Uncle George said he knew it didn't happen just like the story he told me. But it *had* happened. And though he could never be sure, he said, he didn't think Cap had seen some hideous sight up there that had left him changed forever, no life-altering experience in the sense you would think it.

It was, Uncle George told me, simply that he had made it all the way to the top.

CHAPTER TWELVE

Something I remember about Cap.

We're on the water, headed upriver to do the annual dredging duty.

What's wrong with teaching? he asks me.

This is a conversation we've had before, and I'm ready for him. I tell him it's fine for Mabel. I turn my back and drag the barge pole off the side railing.

What's wrong with teaching? Cap asks again.

So I tell him. To be a good teacher you have to be inspired, need to like children, need to be passionate about imparting some particular gift to eager young minds. I tell him that is what Mr. James, the principal, says about teaching. And Mr. James is also fond of saying that teachers must believe in the potential of all children or they would do teaching a grave injustice.

I think that's an amazing thing to say, I tell Cap, with Jimmy Sullivan sitting square in front of you in the front row. I believe in Jimmy Sullivan's potential to be the most accomplished guttersnipe to ever come out of Elk Rapids school system. And I believe there's lots more like him. And, I tell Cap, I don't believe we should even be teaching kids who couldn't care less if they learn anything, making the kids who do want to learn suffer for it. Mr. James is right, I say. No one should teach with an attitude like mine.

Did you ever *maybe* think about changing your attitude? Cap asks.

I thought of it once or twice, I tell him, on Sundays when Reverend Miller talks about loving everybody and all, but I realized awhile back it was hopeless. I just am not possessed of a charitable nature.

I've seen you do nice things, Cap says and laughs. I saw you taking chicken soup to Mrs. McLaughlin when she broke her ankle that time last summer.

So I tell him how I do something nice every once in a great great while, but I was finding you just couldn't count on that.

I see the smile on Cap's face and am tempted to feel good, but I'm becoming aware that there's something wrong with this conversation. I'm taking advantage of Cap's vagueness. Our roles have begun to reverse. His suggestion for me to teach was not direction. His tone had a wheedling quality to it, a child's plea for consideration from a domineering parent. Somewhere along the line, without me realizing it, Cap has become like the boat and the water. Like the surroundings.

So maybe the best way to picture Cap is to picture *me*—my life there in 1916.

Mabel left in September of 1916 to go to the normal school, and shortly after that she took that teaching job downstate in Oxford. I think it was a relief to her, since she seemed to never belong anyway—maybe because Cap wouldn't let her come home right away after Mama died, thought it would be easier on her to wait at Aunt Lena's. Maybe Mabel could see that *nobody* belonged in our family, and she hoped for a better deal elsewhere.

Uncle George kept to the stables most of the time. And it seemed as if I lived in the old clapboard alone. I arranged and decorated things as I liked them. Not a lot of fuss. A sentimental touch here and there. I ran things on a schedule that appealed to me, cleaned when I was a mind to, slept when I felt like it. The house was a hodgepodge of secondhand furniture, like the pine end table in the parlor, the one that had once belonged to Mama's mama and was the color of a polished chestnut. I didn't understand all this yet, but it seemed as if I'd inherited Mama's life and Cap's sins.

Their house was *my* house.

CHAPTER THIRTEEN

I no longer avoid the stables when Keane is working. In fact, I make a point of going. Sometimes I help him pitch hay or shovel manure, but today I watch. Keane is looking at me crossly as he spreads straw behind Adam's slip stall. Keane is seventeen and still hasn't filled out, but there are bunchy muscles forming in his wide shoulders and along his forearms, and I know it won't be long. His face has begun to make a background for his nose and lips, so they no longer seem to float in space. His eyes, which stand out due to their greenness, have dark bushy eyebrows that arch much of the time and make him look like he's perpetually asking a question. Today there are angry vertical lines between them.

You could help, you know. Or at least talk, he says.

What's there to say? I ask.

You haven't said a word since I mentioned seeing Kachina over by Johnson's Pond. He has eight tin water buckets in front of him, arranged in two tidy rows. He begins pumping water into them.

I don't see why you insist on being friendly to someone who hates my guts, I say. Anyway, I don't know why I should care: she's nothing but an Indian.

Keane pulls the red handle of the pump down with a thump. His words sound like short, fast punches.

I doubt if she hates your guts, he says. How can you know what someone else thinks? And you have nothing against Indians, *and* I'm hardly friendly. I've never even spoken to her.

No answer from me, so Keane keeps talking.

Most of the Indians here seem to have had the life chased out of them. They're trying so hard to be like us. Kachina doesn't try to be like us. Why don't you ask her why she hates you? Maybe you're afraid to ask.

No comment from me.

The livery stable is on West Second Street and takes up half the village block. It's long, half of it two-story. The single-story end has three large box stalls on one side, with five slip stalls on the other, separated by a ten-foot walkway down the middle and a water pump to one side. The middle is used for grooming and has crossties on either side to keep the horses still while they are being curried and having their hooves cleaned, something Uncle George does himself every morning, or perhaps doesn't do too well these days. I come and groom them sometimes at night.

The other end of the stable is two stories. On one side downstairs is another box stall, which is used as a tack room and office. The opposite side has two democrat wagons for transporting luggage and freight from the trains at Williamsburg and Alden. Never could figure out why they called them democrat wagons or why Uncle George would drive one since he was not a Democrat.

One small sleigh and four smaller buggies, which are rented most Saturday nights, are lined up neatly against the wall. In the middle of the barn is a great sliding door big enough to permit the wagons to pass. Tonight we leave the door open to encourage any slight breeze.

Upstairs at this end of the stable is a loft for hay and feed with a ladder up to it, and this is where Uncle George sleeps now. The barn smells of molasses and alfalfa, mixed with the ammonia smell of urine, which is not strong now since Keane has cleaned the stalls and spread lime powder and fresh straw behind the horses.

I'll milk Hannah, I say, heading into her stall. Hannah is a five-year-old bay mare Uncle George has recently purchased in Williamsburg.

She had a foal still nursing, but Cap didn't like the looks of him and wanted only the mare. He'd been born early so weaning was fine, but the mare was testy from the discomfort of full teats. As I lay my hand on her hindquarters, she kicks out, slamming her feet into the manger, barely misses catching me square in the stomach, grazing my hip instead.

Get a lead on that mare before you do that, Keane says. He ties a rope to the mare's halter and ties that to a bar at the top of the stall. I stick my hand down around the mare's haunches and feel the warm silky sack, full and dripping into my palm. Hannah shifts warily, but my touch is gentle, and she doesn't kick. I pull on the teat, being careful not to squeeze tight with my fingers at the same time, allowing the creamy yellow fluid to escape in hot spurts into the clean straw. I am careful to milk Hannah just enough to give her a bit of relief. With too much milking, she won't dry up properly.

I can feel Keane's nearness. The mare shifts again, and Keane shifts with her, his eyes meeting mine over the mare's back but not before I see his eyes drop to my chest. I picture my small breasts bare, Keane pulling on them. He looks away then, and I wonder if the mare can sense the tension between us the way a dog can. She shifts again, and I keep pulling.

When I'm finished, I sit on the dirt floor in the aisle with my back against one of the box stalls. It feels cool and sturdy. I'm watching Keane finish up and am reading Emily Dickinson at the same time. She writes about death and nature and religion a lot. I like the ones about nature but not the ones about death.

> Because I could not stop for Death—
> He kindly stopped for me—

It seems he kindly stopped for Mama.

Keane is finished now and sits next to me. His arm touches mine, and the sweat from his exertion feels cool and sticky against my skin.

Can't imagine why Kachina wouldn't like you, he says, attempting lightness. Any girl who cares about worms like you do can't be all bad. And you can fish. It seems like she'd admire that. Though I think the Indians mostly use nets.

I visualize one, me on one side, Keane and Kachina on the other, the woven netting dividing their bodies into tiny separate squares as I stare through the cubes, see the lines dissecting the girl's face.

I wonder what happened to her face, Keane says. A bear?

A jagged wound had appeared on Kachina's cheek a couple months back. It runs from the outer corner of her right eye to the corner of her mouth. Like a parenthesis. Until she smiles. Then it turns into a question mark. She doesn't hide that side of her face like most people would. She seems instead to make sure you see it. Several shades lighter than the even tone of her skin, it has a pinkish cast to it that turns pinker if she's angry or exerts herself. Strangely, it doesn't make her features hideous or drag down her face. It's an obtrusive piece of debris floating in a sea of perfection. Which makes her seem even more beautiful. Which annoys me. Most annoying of all, she doesn't explain it.

What bear would have the nerve to get near Kachina? I say finally.

I listen to Adam munch on his hay while I look through one of Uncle George's poetry books. I have to keep reading the same page over and over because the patch of skin on my right arm is resting against Keane's, and it feels as if it's burning hot. I think about that day in Doc's office, about what people do sometimes under desks, about the mare's swollen teats, and I know Keane must be thinking, too, because he moves away a fraction. And then close again, his arm burning a hole in the center of me. I think then something that I know later to be the truth: Keane's like me in that he never loans himself to anyone. The part he gives, he gives up. It disappears along with those he loves, like he's some great hill wearing down over time. I feel Keane inside me already, the part he's missing.

But Keane has rules, and the rules seem ludicrous to me. Rules are not things made to protect me from the opinions of others as they are for Keane. Rules will exist in my life only for the purpose of treating others fairly.

Uncle George walks in then. He looks hot and tired and helps himself to water out of a tin cup sitting next to the pump. There's a strong resemblance between Cap and Uncle George, though it seems like Uncle George, dark and florid, is the flesh and blood version of Cap, who has turned white and shadowy. Like people do in film negatives.

I left Rags and Farmer outside, Uncle George says. Keane, maybe you can curry them down before you fly out of here. Amazing lot of people coming from the train today. Must have made six trips from there to the different resorts. Should have had you down there with me instead of back here.

Keane pulls the team inside and backs the democrat wagon into position before unhitching the horses, and Uncle George sits on a bale of straw next to the pump.

You get to find out a lot about resorters, hauling them around, Uncle George says. Most of them seem like a useless lot, but once in a while they surprise me.

They never do me, I say.

Uncle George stretches his knees out straight, slowly, like he thinks they might come unhinged or that they need oiling.

You shouldn't make your mind up so fast, he says. Take this woman today. I could take no more than ten people plus luggage per trip today, and even with Abe Samson from Alden helping, that's all day waiting around for most of these folks. They made sure they let everyone know who was in line and in what order. There was this woman with a little boy about six or seven, but no man with her that I could tell. She waited most of the day and would have been in line for my fourth trip. Plenty of people still in line behind her. Every time I come back, I'd see her waiting, and the boy was getting tired, like anyone his age would. He was trying her patience pretty good. Kept flipping stones at the feet of the horses or toward some of the other passengers, and she kept telling him he'd better stop or she'd take him off behind Coy's and they'd have a *discussion* about his manners. I could see the little guy knew she didn't want to do that on account of losing her place in line or because she wouldn't want to make a scene, and he kept flipping those stones and annoying everyone at the depot. I could see this woman figuring, and I could see how tired she was, face all blotchy with it. Could see her thinking she could deal with the boy once she got where she was going, which I knew would be too late, and I could see she knew it would be, too. I was certain she'd start loading herself into the wagon, when her face takes on the look of concrete. She tells me to take the other people first; she has business that needs doing. After she'd been waiting there all day. And off she goes, dragging the ornery fellow by the ear. She was willing to pay the price. Reminded me of your mama.

I think maybe Aunt Lena is right about Uncle George and how he felt about Mama, because Cap and Uncle George's altercations always seem to have something to do with her.

Or her death. He keeps talking about her.

Never forget the day your pa and I met her. Ira couldn't have been more than eighteen, me twenty. We were helping John French pull the *Ida* out of the water for the winter, and it was already late November and blowing hard. Your ma was in Elk Rapids that day visiting friends, had been to Goldfarb's Clothing Store, I think. She stopped to watch us work. We were using a birch tree as a bar for the capstan, and Charlie Spaulsbury drove up and hitched his horses to the bar with a rope instead of a chain, though we all told him not to. When the horses moved about a third of the way, they swerved off the circle, and that made the rope slip off. The *Ida*'s weight brought that bar back and caught poor Charlie square in the middle of his forehead. Plumb crushed his skull.

When Emma saw what happened, she ran to see if she could help. Though it seemed pretty unlikely *anything* would help, she sat with Charlie's head in her lap until Doc Sawden came and told her it wasn't any use. She didn't seem to notice the blood. She couldn't have been more than sixteen at the time.

Uncle George is pouring himself another drink of water now, using the tin cup that's attached to the pump handle with a string. I wonder when it's been washed last.

Guess what I liked most about Emma, Uncle George talks on, was her voice. We both visited her after that, Cap and me, and she'd read to us. Somewhere along the line, it was clear she preferred your pa to me, and maybe she was right there.

Uncle George goes on to say that I look like Mama, but that it's my voice that really brings her to mind. I think she'd have liked to hear you read the Rilke, Welly. Read me just a little.

I shake my head. I don't feel much like reading. Uncle George's stories about Mama leave me upset. Uncle George recites one he has committed to memory. It's a poem about love, about fields and stars, about his lover's fragrant hands, and when Uncle George gets to the last few lines, Rilke's words burn in my ears.

> I want, as with inner eyelid sheer,
> to close for you all places which appear
> by my tender caresses now.

The reason I like Rilke is that he isn't all wispy impression and air and fluff, like so many poets. His words have weight to them. Blood. I can feel my face flush hot with Keane in the room hearing those words. I watch Keane's strong hands as he rubs down the two big sorrel geldings. I'm relieved when Uncle George changes the subject.

You do have a way with animals, he says. You bring up that vetr'narian business with your pop yet? he asks Keane.

Keane tells him no, he hasn't said anything yet. Tells him there isn't a vet anywhere in the whole Grand Traverse region and says how they need one badly. How it costs the farmers a pretty penny to lose valuable livestock because there's no one to treat them. It won't pay like doctoring people, Keane tells us, but I've made up my mind.

Well, says Uncle George, lots going to be changing soon around these parts, I'm sure. With lumbering winding down, farming is going to be pretty much the only way of life here. They'll have need of a good animal doctor.

What do you mean? I ask him. I tell him lumbering isn't winding down, that Dexter & Noble is busy as ever, that he should take a walk by the sawmill if he doesn't believe me.

Lots of things going to change soon, Welly, he says. You may not have heard, but there's a world war going on these days. And that's going to change plenty, particularly if we get in it. President Wilson says he'll keep us out, but I don't trust him. They're building roads around these lakes and automobiles in new factories, and it will be these fancy automobiles that will be transporting these rich folk to their fancy resorts pretty soon. And private launches. So nobody's going to need to ride on that steamboat of your pa's either. We've about gone through all the white pine in this area, which is going to put more than half this town out of work. And of course those automobiles will put me out of business one of these fine days, as well.

I tell him cars are too expensive and a fine lot of trouble, that I'm sure he's wrong. But I see the look on Keane's face and feel that same cold, unattached feeling I've been feeling every time I'm out on the *Mabel*.

THE DREAM: I can't remember where the path leads. It looks like a regular old path, but when I walk, my feet never fall; the ground jumps up to meet them instead, rising every time I raise a foot so it feels like I'm being lifted to heaven.

Do I believe in heaven?

I smell moldy leaves, followed by the cloying smell of rotten flesh decomposing. Like Aunt Lena's perfume. No, not Aunt Lena's perfume. More like Uncle George's yeasty, stale breath in my face. His breath expands, encroaching, trespassing, then turns abruptly to snow and sleet, crystals of used air swirling around my face, in my eyes, up my nose; it threatens to replace my own breath. A doctor couldn't have made it through breath like that, certainly not in time.

Bodies.

My body feels as if I'd loaned it to someone and they returned it with things missing. Like an arm or leg or even my head. There are other things missing, too.

A noise like a stray cat under my window at night comes from behind the boulder. Cap is there smiling, and I remember him saying, Did you know cats kill their young if they're born wrong? Then there's that sound again, a mournful wailing from behind a rock.

So much like a baby crying.

I take a step toward it. I always take a step toward it.

CHAPTER FOURTEEN

Lot of times we don't talk. Which is okay mostly. Except this night it isn't.

We sit and stare off across Grand Traverse Bay, which, if you look at a map, extends from Lake Michigan like a large molar with two insidious roots into the northwest portion of Michigan's lower peninsula. Elk Rapids sits on the far outside, midway up on the easternmost root, like an insistent cavity. I look off toward Old Mission Point and think about that schooner that went down a few years back, the *Metropolis*. You don't find the bodies because the water is so cold that stomach contents don't ferment and form the gas that sends them to the top.

We sift sand, the two of us, forming hills like tiny Egyptian pyramids between our legs. Until it gets too windy and the approaching storm blows it back in our faces.

Keane has rubbed off on me, and I've gotten into a mind-set of not wanting things to happen. I don't want even good things to happen because then they'll be changed or finished. Or changed and unfinished. So in a way it's okay with me to let it sit. And in a way it isn't. There's still the me that *does* want something to happen. Except that Keane is holding it back.

The wind and the storm building make me aware how events have a life of their own and a reason of their own. And that it's all right to be swept along with them. Might even be something you'd get used to, the momentum. Time to flow along with Keane's river he's always talking about. Funny that Keane doesn't feel it. I'm mad that he doesn't.

He sprinkles sand across my knees in a playful kind of way, and it feels like tiny needles pricking my skin. I know it's his way of saying leave it be. But I don't want to leave it be and I know he knows it, too.

Race you to the rock, he says, because he knows if he doesn't we'll have to do something else. Talk maybe.

I want to tell him what he can do with the rock. Want to ask him why he can't feel the storm coming or, if he can, why he's content to watch it and stay apart from it. How it's swallowing me, whether I want it to or not, and how I want him to be swallowed, too. I want to ask him why he doesn't put his hands on me because I've known for a long time they belonged there. Instead I run for the water as fast as I can go. Can feel him behind me, and I know he doesn't want to lose this time.

The bay is always cold, and my clothes cling to my body. I have shorts and a cotton shirt on, and they're coming between me and the water and the storm. I feel like ripping them off but keep swimming.

We're fighting four-foot waves to the rock, and I can feel Keane close beside me though he does his best not to touch me. There's a constant low rumbling off in the distance. The sky splits apart for an instant, but I'm past caring about danger.

As we near the rock, Keane's body bumps into mine, though he's still slightly behind, and though I want to stop and face him, I keep swimming. He's gaining on me, and I think about slowing down, letting him win.

But I don't.

My hand reaches the rock ahead of Keane's by a fraction of a second, and though it's close, there's no argument from him who's won. I'm still mad and I can see that it's rubbed off on him, though I figure it's because he's lost the race. Then the mad turns to something else.

The light is good enough that I can see the birthmark on his chest, above his left nipple, and though the light is fading, I imagine the patch of silky black hair matted to his chest. He grabs me and pulls me hard up against him. My clothes are in the way again, but not so much that I can miss his heart beating in my own chest.

I want him to kiss me and I know he's thinking about it. For a minute I think he isn't going to, but then he does, and his lips are cold and wet and his mouth isn't closed all the way so I can feel his tongue against my lips, which makes me want to open my mouth, but then he pushes me away and shoves the rock between us. He still has hold of my arms, and I can feel how strong he is as he pulls me on top of it. Still he says nothing, watches me. I can see his eyes in the half-light and they don't look mad anymore. They look sorry, like something's missing. I don't know what it is, but I know it's missing. I see something else there, though. Maybe not what I want, but something.

We call it the Johnny Rock, though I don't know why. The rock has a pattern to it that reminds me of the pattern I see when I close my eyes and push on my eyeballs—a herringbone sort of thing with a purple-gray cast to it all.

CHAPTER FIFTEEN

Kachina came to see me today, at last. Now, 1962.

You're here, she said. Erma Townsend tells me you've bought this house. I don't see anything of you at all, and you've been here how long—a week?

Yeah, pretty much.

I watched her face carefully. She wore that expression that cut you loose, an emotional shove high in the chest. Conflict, though, was what had always kept us together. It takes a willingness to rub up against someone despite that mutual wearing away of the outer calluses. There was nothing new in this. It would seem that by now one of us should have disappeared. Become lesser. Had that happened? And then I thought to myself: She looks tired. Kachina looks tired. And I realized how amazing it was that I'd never before in all these years seen Kachina look tired. Angry, frustrated, disgusted—but never tired. And there was something else I noticed in her face for the first time. Compassion. I'd never seen compassion there and I wondered for whom it was felt. She'd never allowed even a drop of it for herself, but I could see now that she felt it for the rest of us. A result of all that conflict? No, it was tied to the tiredness. She knew how it felt to be defeated by it at last.

But I could see that it hadn't replaced the anger.

Kachina sat next to me on the veranda, in one of two metal lawn chairs I picked up yesterday at the hardware store. She was dressed in jeans and what looked like a man's blue dress shirt, blue-and-red beadwork along the collar and down the front, shirttails slightly wrinkled and hanging to her knees. She had brown sandals on her slim feet, and her black hair was braided down the middle of her back, as always. It was unusually warm this morning, and she pointed to my sleeveless blouse and shorts.

You look more comfortable than me.

She leaned over, pulled the neck of my blouse open and looked carefully at the massive scarring under my left arm where the lymph nodes had been. I can make you a poultice that will soften the scar tissue, give you more mobility in that arm.

That would be nice, I said. And what can I do for you?

Well, it's about *goddamn* time you asked, she said.

I went in the house for a minute, grabbed another glass, and poured Kachina iced tea out of a pitcher that was sitting beside me on the wooden porch floor. I was coming over tomorrow, I said. I checked with Doc Glanville. He said Keane was stable for now. I had something that needed doing.

Kachina shook her head. It's just so *unlike* you not to be over there taking charge, bossing everyone around. From your phone call, I supposed you'd be coming to watch Keane die. I expected you immediately. Instead you don't show up, and I find out you've *moved* here. Not a word about it.

Right, I said. So no rush, then, right? Anyway, that's what I've done my whole life—watch people die. Then I watch them after they're dead. I did that for a living.

Yeah, and it's always *you* that's there. What's different now?

Damned if I know, I said.

Well, maybe he'll hang around long enough for you to show up.

That's what I was counting on, I said. He'd never die without seeing me.

I saw an expression cross Kachina's face then. I was hoping it was jealousy I saw there, but if it was, it was a flash and then gone.

I told Topini you were coming, you know.

Kachina's face always fascinated me, but never more than now. It didn't hold anger anymore, despite the way the words sounded. Curiosity was more like it. Maybe a touch of annoyance. But I was surprised. Really surprised. It was the first time Kachina had brought Topini up. She never mentioned her, let alone with the insinuation that she was my responsibility. She'd always been accusatory in some nebulous kind of way, tolerated my interest in the child, answered any questions I had about her well-being. She'd even appeared resentfully grateful for my help, but never had she actually solicited an actual act of responsibility from me in regard to her, demanded a response from me in this way. So I didn't answer at first, so busy was I analyzing this change in a woman who had, in many ways, stood as an unwilling and uncooperative moral barometer for the days of my life.

How is she? I asked finally.

Watchful, she answered. And her answer reminded me of a tale Kachina had said her grandmother had once told her years ago about why children like Topini existed at all. There had been twice as many stars in the sky, Oneida had said, stars that served as direction markers, like the North Star. But unlike the North Star, these stars pointed the way inward, the most important journey a person could make. The Day, in exasperation, had removed the obvious stars of direction since He said mankind ignored them anyway, and as far as He was concerned we could learn to make our way inward without them. And yet later He'd felt guilty at leaving us so totally bereft and stumblingly blind, so He'd provided hints. The direction markers showed up in particular places as small beacons that could light the way if a sorry soul paid attention, and one of the places he'd hidden the stars were in the eyes of a child like Topini. I remembered the flecks of shiny light in her iris, luminous gray, like little silver spheres.

There were other places you could find small beacons of light to light our way, Oneida, Kachina's grandmother, had said. Always, she said, they arrived in unexpected places. The North Star was merely a distraction and as unreliable as any guiding star whatsoever.

But now I felt resentful myself. Resentful that Kachina had never wanted to acknowledge that I'd been capable of seeing the light all along.

I see it, damn it, I said then, out of the blue, and was gratified to see the tired look intensify on the woman's face, and then I was immediately sorry I'd provoked it. She knew exactly what I meant.

Kachina stood and, despite being sorry, I said nothing, left it there between us. Then she pointed at my journal and said, What's that?

Nothing that would interest you.

Kachina stepped off the porch, walked off in the direction of Keane's island.

See you tomorrow, I called after her.

Don't bother, she called with a backward wave of her hand.

CHAPTER SIXTEEN

But I went, of course. I stayed with Topini and Keane while Kachina went off and did errands so Mary Crowfeather wouldn't have to. I won't remark on how he looked. You know how someone looks who's about to die. And what's the use of talking about *him* dying and how well he'll do it, with all we had to say to each other. There's too much to tell before that part. For instance, other people died long before Keane will. Like Mabel and Cap and Uncle George and even my own son, Dick.

And dying is so anticlimactic.

I'll be dead soon as well. Which maybe makes this whole story even more ridiculous. But for now, you'll have to wait to hear about Keane's death. Even if you've already heard about mine.

Because I'm not done telling this story.

Kachina

CHAPTER SEVENTEEN

1905

The Day beams down on her, squeezes between the slats of the wigwam, kisses her on the cheek. Good, she thinks. If The Day smiles, Hototo will take me fishing with him. The Day tugs her along, coaxes her to an open window where she can see Hototo already down by the lake. Hototo is seven, and that makes Kachina five.

Hototo's stubby arms haul the heavy net loaded with fish onto the shore, and she can hear The Day drumming, win adawege, happy-crazy against the side of the dock. She smiles. It is always nice when The Day sings. Surely Hototo will be pleased by the music, and it seems he is since she can hear him whistling along tunelessly.

But then The Day changes. A shadow passes over her hand, over her heart, and she can feel Him leading her outside toward Hototo. The big water slaps crazy-windigo now at the shoreline, slaps up hard against her chest, the water rising in her throat. Geese swoop close to her head, squawking wildly. Watch out! Watch out! And that's when Kachina sees Makwa move from behind the hemlocks and toward Hototo, who doesn't seem to hear Kachina or The Day speaking to him. What is wrong with him? she wonders. Hototo always listens to The Day. It was Hototo who taught her to listen.

Makwa is moving steadily toward Hototo now, though Hototo has not once looked over his shoulder. Kachina screams a warning and slides down the embankment, placing herself between the looming black bear and the backside of Hototo. The bear lumbers within a few feet of Kachina, snarling and growling, blowing white foam from between ragged teeth, tongue lolling out of a bloody mouth. The tongue is long, like that of a snake. The tongue whips past Kachina and reaches for Hototo, who still does not hear The Day.

But then Kachina sees it isn't Makwa after all but school-man. How he slides from proud Makwa to school-man is something Kachina will never understand. But Kachina knows if Hototo goes to the school in Mount Pleasant, he will learn about the world like the man says, but he will no longer be able to hear The Day. Already he is becoming deaf to Him. Kachina spins four times like she has seen the sacred dancers do, but it does no good at all.

Now she is inside the wigwam, Izusa standing to the side, saying nothing. Saying nothing though the man is cutting Hototo's braid. The braid that in the Anishinaabek way stands for the three things: body, mind, and spirit. The braid that shows how The Day is keeping Hototo in balance. Hototo's black hair separates as soon as it's cut, falls in great piles, like shards of black shiny light, and Kachina scoops it up, tears streaming down her face because Izusa and school-man have decided Hototo must go.

Hototo's net is empty now, though Kachina doesn't know how it got inside the wigwam. Hototo looks from Kachina to Izusa, says nothing. He sets down his net and goes with school-man, who has become Makwa again. Hototo walks backward with him; Makwa drags him from sight. Until the last second, Hototo's eyes never leave Izusa's face.

Just when Kachina thinks Makwa is gone, the days have passed without him, he is back. She knows he is back for her. When she looks at Izusa she can see that it is Izusa's wish that she go along, too. She doesn't like to disobey Izusa, but she knows she must not leave here. The Day has told her as much.

Makwa can't make up his mind and has once again become school-man, but he suddenly looks pathetic, white, and powerless. Kachina is no longer frightened. She can hear The Day talking to her. She steps outside as the man walks toward her with the scissors. She expects to see the sun glint off the cold steel, but that is when she realizes it is night. She squats in front of the fire, which has burned down into orange glowing embers. As the man approaches, she picks up one of the coals, transfers it hand to hand, like babies do when they play with stones. She hums softly, continuing to move the hot coal between her palms. Kachina feels nothing. She sees nothing except the memory of Hototo's face that, since his absence, hangs in front of her eyes like a bodiless moon. She rocks, leaning left then right, humming all the while. Next to the fire is a large gray rock. Kachina drops the coal, moves the rock, and as she does, she sees several black scurrying bodies hurrying away from the firelight. She grabs one, pops it into her mouth with as much relish as she might a huckleberry.

She doesn't look over her shoulder, but she knows school-man is frightened now. He backs away from her, away from the fire. Says a few words to Izusa about waiting a year or two before taking Kachina to the school, but Kachina knows they will not bother her again. That will make The Day happy, and it will make Hototo happy as well. The man leaves quickly, runs away almost. He has seen the power of The Day and is afraid. Kachina looks up and sees the sad look in Izusa's eyes. It is too bad that it must be there.

It is too bad, too, she thinks, that Hototo will not whistle anymore.

CHAPTER EIGHTEEN

1962

Kachina expected that as time dulled her, she would lose her taste for sweet-salty things like sex and food. But it hasn't happened like that; she has an almost constant need. She feeds it with buckwheat cakes or corn bread laced with butter and maple, sometimes with smoked whitefish, dune morels, or crushed hot chestnuts. Once in a while she assuages it with baked rabbit smothered in garlic, green onions, and wild chives, served with sagey skillet-fried potatoes, but occasionally she drops ice cream and even greasy cheeseburgers into the emptiness, food obtained from roadside places in Traverse City on her way to Peshabetown. Surprisingly, her body has filled out only a little; the hunger never leaves.

She wakes sometimes with racing heart and damp skin, aching joints and a soreness between her shoulder blades that her fingers cannot reach to knead away. There is another kind of soreness, an ache she thought she'd never indulge, but had, and there is no longer anyone she wants to relieve it. Her hands have started to stiffen as well. But even that is not what's troubling her. Things feel uneasy today, raw and unfinished, the red road tenuous and uneven beneath her feet. She shuffles slowly, back and forth from the sink to the woodstove, carrying an enamel coffeepot filled with water to which she has added several large scoops of coffee grounds and a few reserved eggshells necessary to settle them.

The uneasiness had started with the herbs: Kachina makes herself a blood purifier every morning, a mixture of goldenseal, nettle, and sassafras. For some reason the mixture has dried to half its normal volume. But it isn't the herbs that are troubling her either. Today is the day she must admit to herself she can no longer hear The Day, though she strains with every fiber in her being to hear. Searches the Sky Vault and the depths of the weekwetonh for the barest echo of Him. She asks herself how this can be, this state of abandonment. Where is the resignation and peace she is entitled to as an elder? The wisdom Hototo had spoken of so often? Perhaps her ears are plugged with age and her growing self-dissatisfaction? Or maybe plugged with the cotton of self-indulgence? The thought makes her smile despite her uneasiness.

She stands, stretches up to her full height of almost five feet, reaches her hands up higher yet and runs them across the oak beam that spans the length of the small log room. She has never wanted more than the one room. Not because she objects to convenience or is disdainful of creature comforts. She objects to the space things manage to displace inside her head, leaving no room for her thoughts. Besides, the roof obstructs her view of the sky, and a bigger roof would simply obstruct more of it. She has a good-sized woodstove against one wall. Her small hired-man's bed with the comfortable thick mattress Keane has given her is covered with a high-quality sleeping bag and on top of that the colorful quilt, the starburst of a lingering sexual ache he gave her long ago as well. Her body warms at the thought. Animal pelts are stuffed under edges of doors to stop windigo wind and other unseen enemies, though she knows the worst ones attack from inside. Tobacco pouches and bundles of sage hang from nails that have been pounded into overhead beams as a reminder to look up. And there are the rugs her grandmother Oneida made for her many years ago. Made of white wool dyed with chokecherries, black- or blueberries, pumpkin or butternut, in geometric patterns of red and black and orange. It's the red of our blood, she thinks, the blueness of our dreams, the blackness of our shame I keep with me daily and must keep under my feet.

Sometimes she hangs the rugs over the windows when the wind howls.

It had taken Keane three full days to make one window; she has two. He also made her the maple kitchen table she uses to chop meat and knead bread. He would have made more for her, but she wouldn't allow it. It isn't that she's been left behind in times of the world. Exactly the opposite. She knows Keane's world nearly as well as her own, her brain half soft and white soaked, something that used to worry her. Now, at last, much too late, she realizes that without the whiteness, the redness would have had no contrast.

She'll take the table when she goes, she thinks, and the wooden bowl that had been Izusa's, the rugs and the quilt, but not much else.

She runs her hands over the table, scarred now from years of wear, gashes made from hunting and fish-cleaning knives and the big mallet she uses to tenderize any meat she is lucky enough to come by, gashes that over time have filled with bits of dried flesh or soiled flour. A small packing crate that once transported rubber galoshes, marked "Goldfarb's" on the side, stands on one of several pine shelves on the kitchen side of her room. She rummages through it, through the hammers, hatchets, and screwdrivers, until she finds several grades of sandpaper. Enough to sand down the table. Ah! There's even a small piece of fine steel wool, just the thing. Kachina has taken it into her head to smooth out the top of the table a bit, remove the layer of grease and dirt, then see if she can find some good wax or linseed oil at the hardware store that might bring back the old luster.

Can these old hands manage some real work? She flexes them, squeezes them a few times, winces with pain. She won't sand *too* much, at any rate. She needs to see the egg-shaped burn mark—depressed and inky black—Topini had caused when her candle had burned too low several years back, the day Kachina had been next door helping Ruth Whitefeather bring her first child into the world. She needs to keep the teeth marks in the table leg put there by Kimi, a mongrel bitch they'd had ten years ago, now under the maple tree in the front yard. She needs to see the angry wound, the powerful gash Keane had once slammed into the wood with a butcher knife and all the force his weight and cold fury could muster, the last time Kachina had refused to marry him.

An answer given after the fourth request would stand; Keane had asked her only *three* times.

Yes, she'll keep the scars, she thinks. Her hand moves to her face, along the length of a gash that stretches from her right eye to the edge of her lips, then straight down for half an inch.

CHAPTER NINTEEN

The rain stops now, and the sun peaks through the east window. She pulls off the rug, opens the sash so she'll have air while she works. She lives alone in this cabin Keane built for her. Rather it is she and Topini. Here in the river bog that speaks to her, the place she can feel The Day best (or *could* feel it). People call her windigo and stay away from her most of the time, except the desperate ones—red or white, it doesn't matter—the ones with nothing to lose, the ones who will try anything. They shun her due to that colossal log sawyer Henry who raped her one night in the spring of 1920, down at Kingman's slough. Henry hadn't been alone. Other logmen were watching, and Kachina, who had left her knife at home, had known there was no stopping him. She had deserted her body to the leftover winter ice, abandoned it to Henry and departed to the steaming heat of her mind. The other men could see it, and they said that afterward she'd taken Henry's mind along, too. They said his saw whined war cries from then on whenever it sliced through the flesh of a tree and that he lost flesh himself and sat in bar corners stupefied and dribbling whiskey down parched gray lips and a quivering chin. That accounted for the whites. The Anishinaabek had their own reasons for considering her windigo.

But they all knew she had the touch.

Topini isn't awake yet.

She's always been a late riser unless you root her out with more than a bit of force. Since she's still sleeping, Kachina borrows Topini's red apron as it's larger than her cooking one. She knows Topini will complain, but she ties it on anyway, pushes the sandpaper along the old maple top, careful to move with the grain, moving slowly so as not to strain her shoulders.

There were never children of her own, as she knew there wouldn't be, though once she had carried Keane's for a short time. He never said anything, but she saw the accusation in his eyes. She knew he wondered if she'd used her emmenagogue concoctions or willed her womb to empty with what he suspected was the strangeness and relentlessness of her mind. But she hadn't. She'd simply known her body, and the red road would not support a child of her own issue.

Topini had been child enough.

The only time in all her sixty-two years she wasn't with Topini was when she went hunting. The odd hour in the evening when she'd gone searching for sweetgrass or dandelion root or comfrey and Izusa had taken over the watch. Consequently, Kachina couldn't do anything Topini couldn't do, go anywhere she couldn't go, and the child's every struggle had become Kachina's. As the seasons passed, their hours meshed: Kachina knew what it was like to swallow corn stew with a tongue that flapped like a blubbery lump of deer liver, what it was like to try to sit straight with a backbone like salt-soaked cartilage, to walk uneven trails with floppy joints and legs like conflicted rubbery snakes, knew what it was like to live in that swamp fog that kept Topini from being aware of how and where her body took up space.

Kachina knew the warmth inside when these adversities were finally conquered.

But she knows what it feels like to deal with the things that never can be. She strains sometimes, still, to hear intricate sounds with what feels like warm honey poured in her ears. She's jarred with hypersensitivity to sound the next moment. She knows what it's like to communicate a vast Sky Vault of ideas, even the simplest of wants and needs, with no more than a dozen words in her head, knows what it's like to focus on an object with her eyes roaming crazily in her head like darting fireflies, to struggle for domination over her fingers sufficient to eat with a utensil or weave a basket. And she's lived—what—nearly fifty years?—with the knowledge of what it's like to have few people ever touch her, or want to.

But no one had had to teach Topini to listen to The Day.

It surprised Kachina the first time she realized it. How the child would sit, head tilted to the side, eyes closed, a four-direction smile on her face as an evening breeze moved against her cheek or a bird warbled in the distance. When Kachina had trouble listening, she needed only to watch Topini to remember how, to remember that you hear The Day in the earth and the water and the sky and in everything you do.

The elders consider a child like her sister a gift. A special sign from the Creator that they are all to take note of and learn from. Not a punishment or a mistake or in any way a tragedy. Kachina knows this, has always believed it. But there had been other things in Kachina's life, things waiting for her, a direction that seemed familiar, destined pathways of knowledge. There had been the roots, plants, and herbs that only she knew how to arrange in healing order. An order she believed that she alone could interpret and, likewise, roads she knew they should never travel down. As a people, that is. It had been up to her to set up the kinawaa'chigan, the rocks that pointed their way, but in this she had failed as well. But Kachina loves Topini; she is too much a part of her not to. Kachina has always believed that Topini kept her from some of her destiny, had never believed the sign was meant for *her*.

Until now.

CHAPTER TWENTY

By the early 1900s, many of the Anishinaabek had become Christians, and/or given Gizhe Manido a new short white name. A few are Catholic, but in Elk Rapids, most are Methodist. Kachina walks beside her mother, Izusa, holding Topini's hand on their way to the morning service. The holes in Kachina's hand-me-down boots collect pebbles that jab into the bottoms of her feet. She stops every now and then to remove them. Izusa doesn't like it when she wears moccasins to church as Kachina prefers. So in deference to Izusa, she wears the simple cotton skirt and blouse, also hand-me-down, from the church. The ones she remembers seeing on Laura Martin not long ago. And everyone else remembers, too. Intricate beadwork she added herself lines the collar and the waistline of the skirt, which makes it seem more like hers.

Earlier that morning Kachina felt the familiar stabs across her middle that meant her moon cycle would begin soon. She's sorry it hasn't started already because then she could have stayed behind and been tended by Summer Laughingbrook and Little Quail instead of having to attend the service. Kachina thought the least they could do was attend church in Kewadin where the other Indians went, but Izusa said it was too far for Topini to walk. And she insisted it was a good thing to let the Chemokmon see them. "Stop brooding," she'd say.

But Izusa would have her think these were the only reasons she wanted to attend church in Elk Rapids. Izusa wanted them to become accustomed to the fact of *them,* believed that they would someday see that the Anishinaabek belonged here every bit as much as they did.

But it wasn't Izusa's stated reasons or even her perverseness that drove Izusa to this church every Sunday, Kachina knew. It was the *fear.* Izusa was afraid of many things, but it mostly had to do with Kachina's father, Nagani. Kachina remembered him as a wiry, compact man the color of bubbling, translucent maple. A gambler and a man who erupted. A man compelled to run in flashing, short, erratic sprints until he was spent, a man who exuded the smell of hardtack, whiskey, cigarettes, and a resentful cold sweat, the result of long winter days spent in the lumber camps, and with a nature as changeable as a false spring. Izusa claimed to have known it all along. And maybe she had known. He stayed long enough to teach Kachina to gamble, to play blackjack and cribbage. And he taught her how to use a knife.

"You'll always be fine," he'd told her, holding Izusa's cracked hand mirror up to her face. "That face will wear you well." She'd spent hours wondering how a face could wear a person and not the other way around. Nagani wouldn't say that if he could see her face now.

How many years since he left on that hunting trip in the year of the big drought? There had been word two years after he left that he was planning to find some of his people who were among the Pahouitingwach Irini, the people of the falls, somewhere in Wisconsin. They received word at one point that he was in Wagenagisi, a place white people call Cross Village, that he had another wife and family there, even spent some time in jail, but Izusa refused to comment. Then a few months back, Izusa tried locating him by the Tchissakiwin ceremony, and Tchissakiwinini, the great shaman from Peshabetown, told Izusa that Nagani would not be coming back. That same night Izusa had given Nagani his death name. He had become invisible, and Kachina spent no time wondering whether dead was a literal or figurative term.

Dead was dead.

And Kachina continued to brood.

But it was true that Izusa didn't find anything in the white church inconsistent with the old ways. For her they could exist side by side.

"How can too much wisdom be a problem?" she would ask.

But Kachina finds it hard to listen to The Day in the white man's church. Because of the noise. Izusa always said that if Kachina were listening properly, she'd be able to hear The Day anywhere. True? Possibly. But Kachina knows that the church service is one more thing that has come between the Anishinaabek and their wdjit dogs, or one more way to separate them from themselves.

She walks up the steps of the church, thinking for the hundredth time how white and sterile it is, wondering why the Chemokmon had to go to a place like this to talk to their god. Why did they choose to keep him separate and alone in this cold building when they could take him everywhere they went?

But in truth, it is not the God part that keeps her removed from the church. It's the people part. The way they talk like only they know the paths that could lead them to God.

Izusa and Topini and Kachina take a seat near the front of the church. Kachina looks down at her hands to keep from staring at Keane, who is sitting slightly in front of her. She can always feel his eyes on her, even when they aren't. She is aware of his whiteness, a whiteness made chalky by the almost blackness of his hair. But it is a whiteness that has no significance for her. He isn't loud like so many boys, white or Anishinaabek, and he laughs a lot. She can see him trying to gain balance and she likes the way he tends sick animals. He makes her feel peaceful in a way that no one else can. She finds nothing inconsistent about her feelings for Keane and her disdain for white ways. Mostly because Kachina never entertains the idea of *having* Keane.

The service has started, so Kachina uses all her energy to concentrate on The Day. But this doesn't last long because all at once she realizes that Luella Sharp is doing the scripture reading. She's reading from the book of Matthew. Chapter and verse don't register to Kachina, nor do the words, but it goes something like: "Jesus answered them, 'Truly I tell you, if you have faith and do not doubt . . . if you say to this mountain, 'Be lifted up and thrown into the sea,' it will be done. Whatever you ask for in faith, you will receive.'"

The scripture fails to fill Kachina with understanding, but nevertheless this is a day Kachina will not forget. Today is the day she realizes she will not be able to avoid this ordinary girl. And, moreover, that she is meant to be changed by her. The continual dancing around her, the moving aside while not being able to move away, the constant renegotiating of the path beneath her is beginning to change her already, affecting how high she lifts her feet, shortening the length of her stride, somehow remolding the shape of the journey. But mostly this is the day Kachina realizes Luella is *not* ordinary.

Her voice for one thing. Why had she not noticed before that Luella sounded as she did? The girl's voice is unlike any she's ever heard. Something like listening to the Maang clan, who have been powerful speakers since the beginning of time; it was said they had voices of the loon. But this is different even than that. The girl's words float around the church, vibrating softly at times, surging at others, lifting gently, rising and falling with the power of the wind. Separate from her body, the sound wings its way around the vaulted ceiling, whispers past stained glass, brushes close, next to her skin.

Moving the way The Day moves.

Luella begins reading again. "Chapter 17, verse 20. If you have faith the size of a mustard seed . . . say to this mountain, 'Move from here to there,' and it will move, and nothing will be impossible for you."

Though these thoughts are spinning through her head, Kachina notices again that the girl *looks* ordinary enough. Her straight brown hair, usually flying about, is pulled back in a limp pink ribbon, revealing strong features: nose and ears too large, forehead high, teeth small and even. Her face is broad, her cheekbones high. Her clavicle bone is more prominent than most people's, giving her a sturdy appearance, and her mouth has a straight, stubborn look to it. And though Kachina realizes all this is true, she is annoyed.

Then something strange happens. Kachina, though she isn't familiar with the ways of white churchgoing, knows it is strange. She tries once again to ignore the girl, like she's been doing for years, but finds she doesn't have the power. Luella has finished the scripture the reverend had prepared, the words surrounding them, holding them captive. Luella looks up at last and must have seen what Kachina saw, that every face was upturned to hers. It seems it's time for her to sit down now, but she doesn't. She keeps talking.

"I've been practicing this scripture Reverend Miller asked me to read and thinking about it. How it's all about God answering prayer, and I read something about prayer by Ralph Waldo Emerson." And now the girl is reciting, not reading. Kachina will look up the words in the school library several days later in "Self-Reliance," an essay from Emerson's first series of essays, and will commit them to memory. Years later, she will still remember the words:

> Prayer is the contemplation of the facts of life from the highest point of view. It is the soliloquy of a beholding and jubilant soul. It is the spirit of God pronouncing His works good. But prayer as a means to effect a private end is meanness and theft. It supposes dualism and not unity in nature and consciousness. As soon as the man is at one with God, he will not beg. He will then see prayer in all action. The prayer of the farmer kneeling in his field to weed it, the prayer of the rower kneeling with the stroke of his oar, are true prayers heard throughout nature. . . .

Then she stops talking, and a shocked silence fills the church. Kachina doesn't understand the words, but she knows how they make her feel, how Luella's voice makes her feel. She knows how unusual the whole event is, knows it upsets the white people in the church. But mostly she thinks about how the girl has been given a gift and about how wrong that seems, how unworthy for her to have received it.

How now Luella has at least two gifts she doesn't deserve.

When Luella finishes reading, she sits down. There is not a noise to be heard in the church. Though Luella's father, Cap, is sitting up front, he is off to the side far enough that Kachina can see the flush on his face, but he says nothing. Reverend Miller remains seated for what seems forever. At last he stands and walks to the podium.

"Thank you, Luella," he says. He looks solemn, though Kachina thinks she can see his eyes twinkle. "It's good to remember that God's words arrive from many different sources. We appreciate your bringing that to our attention this fine Sunday. Usually, though, we restrict the scripture readings to *God's* holy word. And we'll look forward to hearing you read more of *His* words in the future. Now if you'll turn to page 122 in your hymnals . . ."

Luella's head nods slightly. Kachina can see her well enough to notice that she doesn't seem embarrassed. When the service is over, they file out, and Kachina will never forget how Luella walks, Captain Sharp on one side of her, stiff like a stick, Keane on the other.

Kachina will think about the Methodist Church often as the years pass. About Luella's voice. About how if you move around and around and *away* from someone long enough, if it's done consistently and with *necessity,* the movement turns into an orbit, a polar attachment to the person being avoided. Her need to repel the girl would be the very thing that later held the two together.

And she will think about the fear.

The fear that made Izusa go to the church in the first place, the fear that made her send Hototo away. She remembers Izusa's face, the sad look on it, that is about more than Kachina's refusal to go to the school in Mount Pleasant. Kachina knows Izusa is worried about what will become of Kachina since Monato no longer wants her.

Izusa will never understand about the scars.

CHAPTER TWENTY-ONE

But at least Kachina had known who she was then. She pulls her gray wool sweater over her head and Topini's red one over hers. They will walk from Bass Lake into town and see if they can find some wax or an appropriate oil at the hardware store to refinish the old table. Nothing with any tint to it. Kachina wants the natural color of the wood to show through. And nothing with any lacquer, either. The wood must breathe as it was intended to.

Kachina pulls a blue mottled tin pot from the highest shelf. There's ten dollars and some odd change in the bottom. Kachina doesn't get paid much for teaching the children in Peshabetown, but it's enough. Sometimes people want to pay her for her touch, and occasionally she will accept a gift of chickens, eggs, and milk, even money, for her services as a medicine woman. Sometimes they bring bread, potatoes, even some beef. But should she *charge* a fee, Kachina knows the touch will desert her. Many white women visit with a variety of ailments and the belief that she can somehow fill the emptiness in their hearts.

Kachina and Topini don't move fast these days, but they get where they need to. They walk toward the village, along the banks of Elk River. The stumps look alive. Lonesome, shadowy figures in the late afternoon light.

Kachina feels that stiffness in her left hand again. So she flexes and kneads it as they walk along. The stiffness gets her thinking about the day they lost Topini. How rigid she had been back then.

Because of the hate.

Izusa was right about hate wearing away the part of you that was good.

KACHINA CAN HEAR A GENTLE rain falling on the tin roof. The roof had once been made of cedar bark and was much quieter, though undependable. She prefers the racket. She has growing pains in her young legs and she rubs them up and down, but the insistent throbbing pulls her from sleep. She isn't sure how long it's been raining. Long enough for water to seep into the corners of the shelter and drip onto her feet. She can see Izusa and Oneida asleep at the far side of the dwelling, resting on tanned deer hides thrown over layers of cedar boughs, which in turn cover handwoven reed mats. Her father should have had a place on the other side of the structure, but her father, that short distance runner, is long gone. Like lightning.

Hototo is gone as well.

Kachina's flow had begun late the day before, the day they had returned from the white church.

"Stay here," Izusa had told her. "Topini doesn't like it when you're gone. The others won't know." They'd know eventually, Kachina reasons. And there are matters of contagion to consider. To compensate, Kachina has kept her hair braided. Two braids means you walk in balance with Mother Earth and The Day. One braid means you walk in the very center of that balance. One braid always feels best to her.

Kachina feels the first signs of fall seeping through the wool blankets. Cold or not, Kachina often wakes with a feeling of dread. A result of the conviction that she must keep her people from disappearing. Not in a literal sense, though that seems a possibility. Kachina thinks it would be more tragic if the Anishinaabek were to *be here* and *be gone* at the same time. Kachina knows this is a great want. Which is why she knows she can have only *one* want. She has not tried to explain this to Monato. Instead she'd touched his hard body one night down by Jansen's corners, behind the old grain elevator. Her pulse had quickened as his hands moved over her bare breasts and down between her thighs. She'd pulled him on top of her, felt his quick release inside her. But his seed hadn't taken root in her heart. She never would have let it happen if she'd thought there was a chance of that. She hadn't repeated the act and she'd let him assume they would be married, but she had known all along it was impossible.

She thinks of Keane. And about love. Years later, she won't really understand the nature of it. Does it come for everyone just the one time? Or does it come with lesser intensity with each successive failure? She thinks that if she *could* ask for more than one thing, she would ask for Keane Mulcahey. She'd walk right up to him, move into him. Of course, once you move into a person, there is the chance you'll move right on through, like an eagle flying through a hailstorm, fly right out the other side as she'd done with Monato. And if that happens, who knows how many storms you might fly through after that? But she hadn't moved through Keane Mulcahey. Or even into him. She'd stopped on the front side of him instead.

But it isn't Keane or any of the usual thoughts that awaken her. Instead it's a feeling like the one she used to feel on hunting trips with her father, the feeling of waking up on unfamiliar ground, smelling foreign air, only to realize she was along a strange river or lake.

Then she realizes what is wrong: Topini isn't asleep beside her.

She decides not to wake Izusa or Oneida. Not yet anyway. There's only the one rubber coat to share between them, so Kachina pulls it around her as she leaves the dwelling.

The rain, which at times cools things off and refreshes her spirit, feels dank and cold. The wind blows sharply now from the northwest direction of the bay, and the birds seem preternaturally silent. The rubber coat keeps her head dry, but she isn't out more than a few minutes before she needs more newspaper in the bottoms of her shoes. Water is seeping through the holes, soaking her feet. Which reminds her that Topini sleeps with nothing more than socks. Would she even have those? Kachina decides it hasn't been raining long after all, because there is a slight frost on the tall grass, which is melting off in the drizzle.

One good thing, at least.

The child is nowhere in sight, but Kachina knows from listening to The Day that this will be the case. She walks in ever widening circles around the village to the shore of Bass Lake and the edge of the dunes.

Topini loves water.

Kachina has been walking nearly an hour and figures it must be eight o'clock, so she checks downtown to see if Topini might have gone to the bakery, the one inside the Mecca Cafe. There is an apple pastry Topini has eaten there a few times and never forgotten.

When she walks in, Mrs. Sheraton is frying crullers in a large cast-iron skillet, and the oily, doughy smell makes Kachina's stomach turn. Several noisy men sit at a long wooden counter eating bacon and drinking coffee. They leer at her sideways across their coffee cups with moist expressions on their faces. She makes it a point not to meet their eyes.

No one has seen Topini.

As she's leaving, she collides with Keane, who's headed in with Luella. The school year has not yet started so Kachina imagines they are heading out to help Captain Sharp on the *Mabel* for the morning run. No, it would be too late for that, she thinks. Luella looms tall suddenly, even next to Keane, but Kachina refuses to look up at her.

"What's wrong?" Keane asks her. It surprises her that he realizes something is wrong. But she doesn't want their help, doesn't want to waste time explaining.

"Topini's missing," she says anyway.

There is a small hole in the back of her rubber coat she hasn't realized was there, and Kachina feels water on the back of her neck. Coldness, excitement, dread. Fear would arrive there first and spread until her body felt like nothing but neck.

"Where have you looked?" Luella asks. Kachina looks up at the girl in spite of herself, startled by the quality in Luella's voice.

"Around the village, down by the lake, over by the sand dunes."

Keane asks Mrs. Sheraton for half a dozen crullers and a cup of black coffee, and Mrs. Sheraton, who has overheard the conversation, pours it into a tin cup, hands him the crullers in a small paper cornucopia. Keane puts the coffee into Kachina's hand.

"Drink this. Take it with you." He shoves a cruller into her other hand and opens the heavy oak door for her. "We'll help you look."

They separate, search the streets of Elk Rapids again, and meet at the bakery a half hour later. Keane searches the harbor, Luella the three streets closest to River Street, and Kachina the three farthest to the south. No one has seen or talked to Topini. There is only one other place Topini likes that Kachina can think to look, a place on the edge of Elk Lake where they often go berrying. Topini knows it well. "Bayyyy," she would say when she wanted to go there. The trail winds several miles through the woods. Kachina isn't sure Topini knows it well enough to make it there alone, but there is nowhere else she can think to look. She thinks about going back to tell Izusa, who will be furious that Kachina hasn't told her the child was missing in the first place, but Kachina decides she might as well check this one last place.

They walk the path in silence while the rain continues to fall in a fine mist. The temperature is dropping, and the wind has come up, making it colder than ever. Kachina can feel bad spirits, the manitous, huddling on the back of her neck, looking for weakness, points of entry.

Luella checks the ground for tracks. "These scuff marks could be Topini's."

"She's probably wearing only socks," Kachina answers.

"That could account for it then. I'm seeing something else here, too, maybe a red fox or small coyote. Don't see the bar on the heel pad for a red fox, but the rain could be wiping it away. Another half hour and there won't be tracks of any kind."

Kachina is impressed at how much Luella knows about tracking. About paths in general. There is no denying a path reveals much about a creature. Where it goes, where it doesn't. Only *being there* is important, too. Whites never understand that, constant motion being part of a white mentality.

Kachina wonders if Luella and Keane have heard the soft rattle of the massasaugas she'd heard a few steps back in the bushes. The weeds and brambles are high because trees are sparse here. On the next rise she sees the rock pile, the kinawaa'chigan, placed often as this one is, on a high place. It's not a kinawaa'chigan meant for a memorial or to warn against danger, though she can certainly feel it, but a kinawaa'chigan meant as a direction marker. She has a feeling it has been pointing her in this direction since the day she was born.

"We'll find her," Keane says. They walk, and bits of spray find its way into their eyes and keep them squinting, faces turned to the ground.

"What does Topini mean?"

Kachina knows Luella is attempting to distract her from the fear. She has no intention of talking. But the cold fingers reach down the back of her neck along with the rain, so she walks faster and begins spitting out words with each step.

"Do you know that when a child like Topini comes to a village that it is a sign, a message to all that live within it? It's a command that everyone must learn something. No one must turn from it."

Luella frowns. She looks confused, and that irritates Kachina. Whites are always confused when so much is perfectly clear.

"My uncle George says things like that," Luella says. "Kind of. He's not sure things don't happen by mistake, good or bad. Says he's not sure if there's a God up there or not, but if there is, he doesn't think he'd shove us around as if He were playing with paper dolls or chess pieces. But it's all grist, he says, regardless. Something we can learn from. Not that all of us do, he says. We just get the *chance* to. I guess that's not quite the same thing you're talking about?"

Luella is young, Kachina thinks, but an Indian would have known without being told. In fact, the Anishinaabek didn't need words to understand things or even to communicate with one another. They watched. Each other. Nature. Nearly every creature shows its young how to live. The Anishinaabek learn much from animals and teach their own children in much the same manner. Whites never seem to do that, she thinks. They are separated from even their children, something she hadn't realized before that moment. But she hasn't answered Luella, and when she looks at the girl's face, the fury she sees there surprises her because the words she has spoken sound so appeasing. It is the last time she will hear words like this from Luella, and even later, when it would seem Luella might understand she *owed* them to Kachina, she will not hear them. They will be replaced eventually by a stony silence and a line of demarcation, an attitude that suggested there were limits to what she'd take from Kachina, deserved or not. At any rate, Kachina is certain that Luella wants to throttle her now. She takes a step closer to Kachina, and Kachina steps a couple closer to Luella, but Keane interrupts.

"The path splits here," he says. "One way goes straight to the old lumber camp and the other down close to the lake. Both come out at the camp."

Luella and Keane have sturdy boots on their feet, and Kachina is sure theirs don't have holes in the bottom. She removes a piece of bark, like a reminder, from the bottom of her right boot. Keane steadies her arm but seems to realize there's no need and lets go.

"You two take the straight path to the camp. I'll head down by the water," Keane says. Kachina isn't happy about that, and she's sure Luella isn't either, but doesn't want to waste time arguing. Luella follows without a word. Every so often they call Topini's name. No answer.

The lumber camp is approximately halfway to the spot Kachina and Topini usually go to pick blueberries, which is a mile beyond the camp. The woods are denser through this section, more cedar and birch trees. Log drives begin anywhere from mid-April to early May and finish up by mid-July. As soon as the temperatures drop, the harvesting will start again.

Would Topini leave the path?

She didn't usually, but there are no guarantees she hasn't this time. If she has, she could be anywhere in this dense growth. Luella hasn't said a word since the fork, and they can see the lumber camp now. It sits next to a small stream that leads into Elk Lake, and they can see the van, or camp office, the bunkhouses in a row behind that. Tied to the dock on the river is a wanigan, or river raft, used during the log runs in the spring, a sort of floating bunkhouse.

Kachina stops instead of going into the camp because she's heard a noise in a group of cedars to the right. Two noises, actually. Distinctly different. One noise unmistakable: the *uh, uh, uh, uh* sound of Topini humming, which should have filled her with relief but doesn't. The other noise is one she can't identify but knows will be trouble, a low, guttural, growling that grows louder at each step they take.

Hauled up against the largest cedar tree is a small flat bateau, and underneath the boat, between it and the tree, sits Topini. She is humming, happy, though she has only socks on her feet and nothing but the red flannel shift around her. The nightshirt is streaked with mud, her hair a matted tangle, but the bateau is providing some protection from the rain. Topini's favorite spoons and tin cup sit on the ground beside her, and she has a stick in her hand that she's holding off at an angle to her face. Kachina can see her solitude, the circle inside her mind. She is floating free inside, at the center of the world, and Kachina wants to float, too.

But then Kachina sees the dog—wild, the color and size of a tawny wolf. Some sort of mixed shepherd maybe? Kachina can feel the dog's power, which chills her heart. But animals don't attack Topini.

Ever.

Kachina has seen this happen before, several times throughout the years. Mort Jacobs's hunting dog chained to a back gate. Everyone knew to stay away. Topini, before Kachina could stop her, had walked up and put her hand on the dog's head. Kachina was terrified, but nothing had happened. Instead the dog had seen inside the child, and that had been all there was to it.

This dog is doing the same, Kachina thinks.

The dog stands over Topini, growls. Takes a few steps toward them. Then he stops growling, but the hair is rigid along his neck for six inches, and every few seconds the dog shows Kachina his teeth. His coat is a brindled brown and gold that stands out from his body in a shimmery, dirty cloud. He smells of wet matted fur and things dead. And fear, Kachina thinks.

Kachina knows they won't be able to approach Topini. They're still a good thirty feet from the dog. She calls softly to the girl, which seems to amuse Topini. She smiles and waves her stick, but it's clear she has no intention of coming to them. Luella moves away from Kachina, closer to the dog, and the dog makes a sweeping pass at them. Kachina pulls her back by the arm.

"What are we going to do?" Luella's question annoys Kachina because she doesn't have the answer.

"I don't know. He's not going to let us get anywhere near her. I'll stay here, and you go get help. Tell them to bring a gun."

Even as she says this, she knows it won't happen. She can hear Keane coming along the trail from the other direction, the path leading from the river behind the lumber camp, the cedar tree between him and the bateau. It's unlikely he can see the child or the dog, and he hasn't yet heard or seen the girls. They call to him but not before he's stepped one step too close to the tree. Even before the dog lunges, Kachina knows the creature has been sent. She can see the trail of her footsteps in his windigo eyes and though she'd never seen the animal before, she recognizes him. The dog is connecting them, lining their spirits up.

The dog eats up the twenty feet in front of Keane in two devastating leaps. Keane leans backward, keeping his face away from the erupting fury. But not before the dog has sunk his teeth deep into his right side. Not before the force of the dog's power throws him off his feet, off the path, and into the tall weeds.

CHAPTER TWENTY-TWO

Kachina can feel the weight of the dog's body as if it is on top of her: teeth, flailing limbs, ripped clothing, sandy clay, and blood. Whose blood is it?

They pick up rocks, sticks, she and Luella, but they are useless because the two bodies are a continuous blur. Keane is big for his age and, incredibly, Kachina thinks, stronger than the dog. As they roll, Keane gets his hands around the dog's neck but can't get a firm grip. The rain has stopped. Kachina listens, but The Day leaves a gap, like a giant pause, over them all.

Kachina learned something when she was a child. Something from Hototo. The ability to make something smaller, externalize it. Shrink it until she could visualize it on the point of a beading needle, while she herself would grow large. Large enough to inhale the wind, radiate the sun, big enough to swallow the sea. Keane and the dog nearly disappear from her consciousness, and when she allows them to enlarge a hair, she can see that the gnashing teeth and reeling bodies are slowing to a point she can manage. What comes as a shock is that Keane is doing something that appears similar. Kachina can see his mind focus, but she can also hear what sounds like humming. A barely audible chanting noise, familiar to her but not familiar. A noise designed not to befriend the dog but to empower it.

Kachina moves closer to the dog, shrinking him more until the blood, matted fur, and flashing white teeth blur, run together in a muted, benign brown-pink color.

"There's a knife in my back pocket," Keane says, his voice sing-songy in her ears. "Don't come near until I get a better hold on him."

Keane's hands are slippery and red with his own blood, but he seems finally to have the animal in a tentative grip, so Kachina approaches slowly. When she does, she sees the dog look inside her, is sure he recognizes her as well, and he thrashes wildly in Keane's hands, forcing him to lose his grip. As she reaches for the knife in Keane's pocket, the dog sinks his teeth deep into Kachina's left hand.

But for Kachina the pain is small.

Keane twists the dog's neck until one shoulder and foreleg are in the dirt, hindquarters still raised, like he'd wrestle a steer to the ground. He adds a knee to the mangy shoulder, and the dog's legs slide from under him. Kachina grabs the fishing knife out of Keane's back pocket, glistening in refracted shades of lavender from its sheath. She adds the weight of her own knee to the dog's chest, grabs it by the scruff, ready to pull the knife across his throat. As her weight comes down on the animal, she feels its spirit come up, the searing heat of it rising against her thigh.

"Not yet," Keane says to her. His voice is low, but she can hear the urgency. "Wait until I tell you."

If she needs to kill the dog, she will.

The dog knows that, and she can see Keane knows it, too.

Keane continues to make the chanting noise in his throat. "Sit on him, Kachina, but don't kill him unless I tell you to."

Kachina sees he's willing to gamble. All the Anishinaabek know you must gamble. Otherwise, you lose anyway. You just lose sooner.

She sits lower on the animal's haunches while Keane keeps up a steady pressure on the dog's throat, forcing him close to unconsciousness, releasing his grip now and then to see if the dog is yet satisfied. But he's not. Whenever Keane loosens his grip, the dog resumes snarling. He squeezes tighter until the animal is hardly breathing.

Who sent him? Kachina wonders.

She'd seen a dog like this in a vision once, and he was carrying a large bundle wrapped in blankets on his back. I roam the world, the dog told her, picking up chances. My bundle will soon grow so large, I will no longer be able to move. Has the dog picked up her chances now?

"I don't think it's working," Kachina tells Keane. "You're bleeding, and so am I." She can see the exhaustion in Keane's face.

"Not yet," he says, and when he says it, Kachina knows the dog has taken some of her chances and some of Keane's and maybe some of Luella's. He's always had Topini's.

It seems hours since the dog first attacked Keane. The rain stops now, but the wind continues to howl. Or maybe it's Keane himself who is howling. And Kachina finds, surprisingly, that it's okay with her, this state of affairs. But how long can they remain this way without acknowledging the truth of it? Keane looks at her then, and this is when she realizes she can hold things—the dog, the rain, the frigid cold, life, death, all of it—longer than he can. And that is a thought she can hardly tolerate. But perhaps she won't have to.

Perhaps they'll be eaten together.

Keane opens his eyes and shakes his head, forbidding her to do what he knows she's capable of. What eventually she *will* do. Kachina feels as if she's holding the knife to Keane's throat, but then Keane is threatening her as well. Love is like that, she thinks. It can be wide and wonderful like the Sky Vault but a knife at the throat nevertheless.

More time passes. Kachina becomes aware that Luella and Topini are huddled under the bateau, but if they have uttered any sounds during this strange battle, Kachina will not recall them. She can hear nothing but her own heart beating and water from the trees dripping on Keane's rubber coat. The dog's raspy breathing. And the chanting. Kachina reaches for the dog's throat off and on, but Keane's eyes stop her each time. She begins to wonder if Keane is controlling her the way he's controlling the dog. Keane looks over his shoulder at one point and with an exhausted smile says, "Care to waltz?" She tries not to smile but can't stop herself. We're already dancing, she thinks. Can't you feel it? But Keane's eyes are glazed and hooded now, and the glints from the dog's eyes have turned blue.

Keane nods to her. Then he loosens his grip slightly, and the sounds become love talk. Kachina feels soothed like the dog does.

"He was protecting Topini, keeping her warm when we got here," Kachina says. Keane's shoulder is resting against hers, and she can feel his body heat through the rubber coat.

"It was worth a try." Keane runs his hands over the dog's body, and though the animal's flesh trembles and jumps, he allows it.

"Where did you learn it?" Kachina asks him.

Keane keeps murmuring to the dog, running his palms over the rough matted fur, shrugs.

Kachina can see it's time to gamble, time to find out which chances the dog has. Kachina knows Keane is too weak to resume the fight, and she's lost blood as well. If he lets go and the dog attacks him again, it will be nearly impossible for either Kachina or Keane to kill him. But Keane's mind is made up. He loosens his grip, removes his knee from the dog's chest, and in one movement tries to stand. As he does, he staggers, and Kachina feels the ground slide as she grabs him around the waist, holding him up. The dog lurches to his feet, shakes wildly, a mixture of water, mud, and blood, gives a low growl. He backs off toward the woods, then stops.

Keane doesn't move or talk. Then he takes a beef stick from his back pocket and holds it out while the dog advances warily toward him, gets within ten feet, and stops. Keane drops the beef on the ground at his feet, and the dog backs off, but Kachina can smell him still. Can smell Keane on him. And even her own smell. A bottomless, eternal smell she can't describe but will never forget.

"Let's go," Keane says.

Luella, carrying Topini and her toys, joins them now. Kachina tears cotton material from the bottom of Luella's skirt and ties it around Keane's middle, which has begun oozing blood steadily. His legs buckle, and Kachina wonders how she can support nearly his entire weight the distance they have yet to go. But she knows she will have to.

The dog inches forward and grabs the chunk of dried beef from the ground where Keane has dropped it.

CHAPTER TWENTY-THREE

Money. There hadn't been enough the other day to buy the oil to finish the table. Money doesn't go far these days, that's for sure. She was able to get the rest of the sandpaper she needed during yesterday's trip to the store, but that was all. Old John Quailfeather had been in the paint aisle, but when he saw her, he changed aisles. She knew what they said about her—how she had multiple lives like a cat and how when people came to her for her touch, she'd help them out, but only for a price. The story went that she healed you temporarily but bargained for years of your life or your soul, which was why she never aged, was probably centuries old. That's if she were ever going to die at all. They said she no longer walked in a life that belonged to her, which is why she no longer left footprints. She'd said good morning to John, who smiled warily at her from the garden section, then she paid for the sandpaper and left. There was plenty of work to do before she'd need the oil anyway.

The table was one of the first things Keane had made for her, right after Izusa died. Before that, they'd used a maple stump outside in the clearing for a worktable. Inside they had an old oak plank, nothing more than a shelf supported by two rough sawhorses, but it thumped up and down awkwardly, made carving meat or kneading bread cumbersome. In those days, they had eaten on their laps, huddled around the old woodstove or outside, if weather permitted, around an open fire. They used small tin plates, wooden bowls and spoons, some limited flatware they'd gotten from the church. They had Topini's emkwaanan, or spoons. They had knives and several tin cups between them, a cast-iron pot for cooking and a flat one for frying. The pots had been luxuries. At any rate, the fine color of the maple table is returning now. Kachina has been using only coarse sandpaper so far, which has turned the top from a greasy muskrat brown to a tamarack gold.

Topini comes in from outside, and she has Mary Crowfeather with her. Kachina is surprised as always that despite Topini's fifty-some years and the obvious changes in her body, she does not grow old.

Mary is maybe sixteen, lives in one of the neighboring shacks, and loves to play with Topini. She is round and firm like a hard brown chestnut and is carrying Topini's rubber ball in a tight hand, the red ball with the starlike chunk out of it. Topini is wearing the latest in a lifetime of red nightgowns, and Kachina feels guilty since it must be after noon and she has not reminded Topini to get dressed. That's strange, too, because Topini usually gets dressed each morning without being reminded. Today she wanders around the cabin with a bewildered look on her face, carrying a spoon in one hand and an aluminum saucepan in another. The spoon makes a bell-like clang when it hits the pan, which happens in the lull between Kachina's thoughts.

"Sit down, Topini," Kachina says when she can take it no longer. The woman sits in front of the maple table.

"Pop," she says as she bangs on the pan bottom with the spoon.

"Not yet," Kachina answers. "Orange juice and toast first."

"Hmmmmm," Topini says and bangs the pan bottom harder. "Hmmm" usually means Topini is displeased, usually something to do with food. But there are variations of "hmmm" that mean "well, okay, if you insist." There's a humming sound similar to the "hmmm," too, that means all is right with the world. This "hmmm" is gruntlike and means Topini is unhappy.

Kachina goes to the cupboard, cuts two slices of bread, and sticks them on the warming surface of the woodstove. She takes orange juice out of the icebox and pours Topini a glass, another for Mary, in tin cups she finds on a shelf over the sink.

"How is the day today, Mary?" Kachina asks.

"Cold, but the sun is out," she answers.

Kachina frowns. "And how do we say that in Anishinaabemowin? How do we say, 'The sun is out?"

The girl smiles at her, shrugs. Kachina tells her the Indian word, and it sounds strange even to her own ears, but the girl repeats the word slowly: "Zaagaate."

"Did you play ball?" Kachina asks. She nods. "Can you say, 'Throw the ball' for me?" This time the words roll off her tongue, but it is Kachina who has a hard time recognizing them. As if she has suddenly become Topini, and half the words that were once in her head no longer mean anything.

"Paagaadaan we pkwaakwat."

"Good," Kachina says. "Keep practicing now."

Topini continues to beat on her pot rhythmically until Kachina is sure it is her own head the child-woman is pounding on. "No pounding today, Topini, okay? Let's see, Mary. How do we say, 'Don't pound on the pot, *please.*'" The girl smiles but doesn't answer. "Keqwa weptowaake wakik," Kachina says. She reaches over and strokes Topini's face, moving her hair from her eyes and hooking it behind her ear. Topini pulls away, angry, begins to rock back and forth in her chair, but she stops pounding, for which Kachina feels profoundly grateful.

"Topini," Kachina says. "I'm making the table new . . . see, smooth." Kachina takes Topini's hand and rubs it on the tabletop. She takes a piece of fine sandpaper and moves it along the wood while Topini watches. After several minutes, Topini bends down, so her eyes are even with the plane of the table, and looks across the tabletop. The doctor prescribed glasses a couple years ago when Keane had suggested Topini's vision might be a problem, but she'd taken them off and looked sideways along the edge of the lenses. It became too hard to keep them on her, and eventually they'd disappeared, like everything else Topini wanted to get rid of.

"Help," Topini says, and Kachina gives Mary and Topini each a piece of fine steel wool.

"Like this, front to back. Don't go side to side."

Topini moves the steel wool as Kachina has shown her. Smiles. First at Mary, then at Kachina. Topini likes to help. She makes beds, does dishes, washes clothes. She never runs away like she did that day in the lumber camp.

Kachina finds herself musing about the dogfight all those years ago. Most people would find it surprising that a wild thing, obviously windigo, would develop an attachment for someone who'd so nearly taken his life. But Kachina has seen animals—even people—form attachments to someone or something undeserving. And in Keane's case it had to do with the chanting, something she'd witnessed only on occasion from her own people, and then not exactly that. The dog had followed them home that day, through the Indian camp where they'd left Topini, and then into town where Keane's father tended to their wounds.

The dog stayed a distance from them, but he stayed. Skulked around the edges of the trees that lined the perimeter of the island during Keane's illness. And Kachina knew why he stayed.

And she knew when he would go.

Keane had talked his mother into taking food out to the dog every night. After several weeks, the mongrel rounded out some, but Kachina didn't think it was the food that did it.

He was full, after all, of chances.

Keane got well, rounded out slightly, too, and over time the dog came closer. Not close enough for physical affection, but he was unwilling to let Keane get more than a hundred yards out of his sight, either. Keane said there was nothing to do but the obvious.

He named the dog Shadow.

CHAPTER TWENTY-FOUR

Kachina thinks spring will never come and she'll stay seventeen forever, but at last the days stretch out. The temperature reaches the high forties, and though her heart remains frozen, the maple starts to run. There are murky, watery-looking patches mixed with the charcoal gray ice in Bass Lake, which means Motchi Manitou is no longer hibernating. Kachina likes watching the process of what must happen.

Izusa, Topini, and Kachina cross the big road and walk down through the Anishinaabek village, or Sand Hill as the whites call it. There are maybe twenty wigwams next to the dunes, low dome-shaped dwellings no more than fifteen feet in diameter and formed of bent poles covered with either bark or reeds. There are two Indian boys, Anna Longbow's children, playing lacrosse in the snow as they approach, and an old, diminutive man, Lansing, who sits next to a fire playing a Jew's harp. Angela LaFontaine, who will one day marry Kachina's Monato, pushes firewood around with an elk scapula, and Binesi-kwe bends over the big iron kettle, stirring corn stew with a wooden spoon. In the summer, the Anishinaabek grow corn, beans, pumpkins, and squash on top of small hills, and the vegetables grow wild and run messily together in the valley. The hills stop the water from carrying away the power of the ground.

They reach the sugar shack and set to work. Izusa and Kachina carry the heavy wooden buckets from the trees to the shack. Topini darts between them, dodging patches of snow, jumping square into them with both feet. Topini is eight, small for her age, and round like a bullfrog. She has shoulder-length hair and unusually fair skin that's more a result of her affliction than heredity. Her shoulders are rounded because the muscles in her torso are weak. The strength that should be in her limbs has moved instead to her heart. But it is Topini's eyes that are special, a clear gray with white flecks around the rim of the iris—eyes like looking into a mirror.

Kachina catches sight of Luella. She's become a familiar sight in the village. Something that happened between them all the day Topini was lost accounts for the time Luella spends here, teaching the child to weave or eat with utensils, bringing her an occasional ball or a red scarf as a gift. As Luella walks to the shack, she grabs a bucket hanging from a wooden spile forced into a diagonal incision about three feet from the base of a tree. She carries it to the shack, careful not to spill any of the clear sap-water that threatens to slop over the sides.

"Thank you," Kachina says as she takes the bucket from her. "How's Keane?"

"Good," Luella answers. "Saw him out walking around with that mangy dog yesterday. We'll be catching brook trout in another month, so it's about time he was moving about."

Kachina nods toward the trees. "We tapped the ninautik two days ago." She explains that the maple moon had smiled upon them, the sugar content high due to the previous summer's warmth. "If it freezes tonight, then warms up like this tomorrow, we'll have another good day," Kachina says. Freezing would also mean they could scoop the chunks of ice out of the sap they'd already collected, and it would give them a head start on the boiling process.

"This is better than salt?" Luella asks.

The Anishinaabek boil meat in it, use it for healing purposes, drink raw sap every spring to clean out the bowels. The last few years they began using great iron cauldrons for boiling the sap the way the Chemokmon did. That way they could make it faster, bottle it quicker, and sell it if necessary.

It was always necessary.

Kachina nods. "It takes forty buckets of sap to make one bucket of syrup. We're low on soft sugar again, too, so we'll need even more than usual."

Topini sticks her fingers into the clear liquid, throws her red ball into one of the sap buckets to see it splash. It's clear she doesn't plan to stop, so Luella takes her down to play next to the lake while Izusa and Kachina finish hauling buckets into the shack. They'll pour the sap into the small wooden storage barrels and replace the buckets under each wooden spout. Luella, it appears, is willing to keep Topini busy while they do that. Kachina appreciates this.

And resents it, too.

When they finish storing the sap, Kachina walks down to join Luella and Topini. Since there is no way to avoid doing so, she sits next to Luella. She can feel the sun on her cheek, and the scar tingles, something that surprises her. Kachina had always thought a scar would feel numb. There's a hypersensitivity and an itch deep below the scar. Kachina can feel Luella's eyes on her face.

"You need us to see it," Luella says resentfully. "How did it happen?"

There were things about the scar Kachina was certain of and things she chose not to acknowledge. Someday, from the safety of years, Kachina will realize that Luella had seen the flaw that was more than the scar on her face: a terrifying single-mindedness that left no room for compromise and limited room for compassion. Even for herself.

Time stretches.

"It's mine," Kachina says finally.

Kachina smiles at the look of astonishment on Luella's face. Topini rushes up to her, hands her a twig, a few clinging red berries visible under the leaves. "We have a right to ask for only one thing," Kachina says, "and then we may not get it." She knows Luella has no idea what she's talking about. How could she? People like Luella want lots in life, and they get lots. What could this girl know about someone who wanted something so much that she couldn't conceive of more than one want?

"I would not make a good wife," Kachina says. She smoothes her hands across her flat abdomen as if she were smoothing wrinkles out of an apron. Topini throws stones out over the frigid water while the girls talk. The stones make plopping noises that echo in the stillness. Now she runs to Luella with the ball.

"Ba," she says and tosses it to her. Luella tosses it back with a smile.

"Tell me about Topini, Kachina," Luella says.

"Tell you what?" Kachina answers. What right did the girl have to answers of any kind?

"Anything. Tell me anything."

Kachina moves from the log she's been sitting on, squats on her heels, and draws lines in the sand with a stick. She draws a circle, then divides it into four equal spaces, traces several figures of animals: a loon, a bear, an eagle, and a short fat muskrat next to a raccoon.

"She is called Topini," Kachina says. "Did you notice that you can see your own scars in her eyes?" But Kachina doesn't tell her the rest—how if you look long enough, you begin to see *through* Topini's eyes and how that can shake your world.

"When we give a name to someone," Kachina says, "it's not simply because he's sly like a fox or wise like an owl or swift like a deer, though that might be true. A person's name is picked by someone important in the totem, always an elder, and always a powerful one, because a person's name becomes a type of power and a way for them to own that power. It's like writing your name in the sky. A person nearly always lives up to his name."

Kachina thinks about Luella's voice, has heard her in the church and telling stories to Topini.

"You, for instance. You would have been named after Nodin, the north wind, and if you were Anishinaabek, you would probably come from the Maang clan because no people can equal the power of their tongues. My people would call you Aansoke Niniikwe, the great storyteller. We would have recognized you when you were born, and you would now be living up to your name. You would not still be struggling to get them to understand." Luella's face radiates like the third moon phase in the evening light.

"What does Topini mean?" Luella asks.

"My grandmother, Oneida, named her. Izusa wanted her to be the one to name Topini because Oneida's sister Meemaca was a special child like Topini. She lived only twelve seasons because her breath was never strong, but she gave each person in the village a gift during the time she was alive. Meemaca ran away from her mother once. Early winter, I think it was, and already a hard one. The men hadn't returned from hunting, and there weren't enough furs and blankets to go around. Meemaca led the women down past the second fork, a place she knew she was not allowed to go, and there on the path lay a dead buck, freshly dead, killed by a pack of coyotes. The women chased them off with banging pots and long sticks. Finding the deer would mean venison stew and a fur coat. The Anishinaabek do not believe in accidents."

Topini climbs into her lap and plays with bits of Luella's hair.

Kachina continues. "Oneida had a vision about Topini, and the vision can never be told because that would destroy its potency and the potency of the name. 'Topini' means 'child of importance.' She is a gift from the Creator, a sign. There are always four people in charge of raising a child. Topini is being raised by Izusa, Oneida, Izusa's brother Kakagi, and me."

Kachina is moved by the roundness of Topini's cheek in the evening shadows. She hears the far papery laughter and sees the distant tears that have gone before. She smells the hard clean soapy smell. But the warmth has gone, or perhaps was never there at all. The tears have been gone a long time, too, and would not return simply because they were expected. There were things Kachina will not offer. Was Luella asking?

KACHINA WILL REMEMBER this day well. Everyone owns their own story, she'd wanted to say to Luella; it's not mine to give you.

I could as soon give you the Negwekigidki, the great sand dune, she'd wanted to say. Does it matter how the sun came to be here? It has always been here. If no one explained the sun to you, would you have failed to recognize it? Failed to understand its relationship to you? Remain untouched by its warmth? It will not disappear because you wish it.

Kachina will remember the sand dune, how it had loomed behind her, and she will remember wondering if Luella might like to take it home in her pocket, one grain at a time. Then maybe she'd reassemble it and examine it at her convenience. Is that how the truth works? Do you accumulate it bit by bit, a grain of it here, a crystal there, until you have it all? Then when you do, do you transfer it off into some dark corner and remold it like you would a sand castle, building it carefully away from prying eyes so no one can watch your expression as you recognize it? Would the truth be strong and steady like a castle or gray and hard and piercing like an arrowhead? She will remember how the sun had disappeared over the Negwekigidki that day, turning it to a mountain of shimmering gold.

CHAPTER TWENTY-FIVE

There is another day Kachina can't forget. Dark—1913 or 1914—
she isn't sure. Before the windigo dog.

She'd seated herself down by the bay in the shadows of the gijik,
the great medicine tree she likes to sit under to gather her strength.
Hototo told her how the roots of the gijik extend to the underworld
while its very tip breaks through the heavens. It has great power of
health and knowledge.

A storm is forming over the bay. Some say Motchi Manitou is
trying to get out of the water. But Kachina isn't afraid of drowning
and not going to heaven. Kachina knows that storms are part of The
Day's message. She can feel the power and stays to feel it swell to its
full height.

She's surprised to see Luella and Keane sitting on the beach. They
seem to be playing with sand and talking quietly. Concealed in the
shadow of the tree, Kachina knows she is stealing something private
between them but can't stop herself. The storm grows nearer and
stronger, but it doesn't chase Luella and Keane away. Time passes,
and she sees them run for the water and swim for the rock. She can
tell they are racing. When they reach the rock together, she sees
Keane pull Luella toward him. Lightning flashes, and the sky lights

up, and she sees their bodies close together. She hears the thunder echo across the bay.

Kachina stands. She walks out of the trees down to the water, the manitou wind whipping her hair from its braid and tangling it in the beads around her neck. Her feet are bare, her skirt dragging in the water. They don't see her.

At first.

He bends toward Luella and presses his mouth to hers, and when he does, Kachina feels the power and balance leave her, the emptiness invade, a void like the one she'd seen in Hototo's eyes the day he'd gone to the school, and for a moment she wants to keep walking into the waves. It seems the nothingness lasts for an eternity. But then—finally, thankfully—the pain enters, as strong as the emptiness had been an instant before, and that is all right.

She can live with the pain but not the emptiness.

Pieces of a canoe, a two-forked stick, and the wing of a dead gyashk-gull catch in her skirt. She lets the debris build up in front of her like a dam. She doesn't move, standing to her knees in water, the waves, and the debris.

Luella's back is to her, but Keane raises his head. She knows it's too far and too dark for him to see her face, and she can't see his clearly, but she knows he is watching her. Luella is close against his chest, but Keane continues to stare over her head at Kachina. No one moves for several minutes, and the agony, like exquisite piercing needles, intensifies with the storm.

Kachina stays until she sees Keane pull Luella on top of the rock, and then she turns and walks back into the trees.

CHAPTER TWENTY-SIX

Kachina adds a ham bone to the pot of stew, along with a bit of extra ham, a can of red beans, and then sliced potatoes, a satisfying meal to leave for Topini and Mary Crowfeather since she'll sit tonight with Keane. She gets out the measuring spoons and adds two teaspoons of dried sage and two of dried thyme, a tablespoon of salt, and a teaspoon of pepper. When did she start cooking like this? Measuring everything? Recipes are like road maps. She'd never used either in her youth. It had been seeing her own footprints, studying the way she'd come, that had pointed her way forward. She had walked through time instinctively, listening to The Day. But last winter that had all changed.

She'd had Keane to the doctor in Traverse, in Keane's gray Rambler. Dr. Glanville told them, in that routine way of doctors, that Keane's liver wasn't right anymore, and there wasn't going to be much he could do about it. He prescribed little white tablets. No alcohol or coffee, he'd said (which made Keane snort and say that would be the day). Lots of clean water. Adequate rest.

And that had been that.

Keane had talked on the way home about how he hoped for an early spring so he could get on the river and about how the new vet working with him, Dr. Allen, was coming along fine. And wasn't that fortunate, since it would give him more time for fishing?

She'd taken Keane home then. He told her he was feeling good but would nap a bit if she wouldn't mind. So she made him an infusion of dandelion root and licorice. He'd sipped it, set it on the bedside table, and closed his eyes, fingers interlaced across his chest.

It is early February, and they'd gotten a couple feet of snow in the last week, so she grabs Keane's snowshoes, tells Topini to stay put with Keane and the scrapbook Topini likes with the shiny photographs of Keane's animals in it. She heads north along the shoreline of the bay for nearly a mile, then straps on the shoes and heads east through the woods. The shoes are a new leather kind, a modified bear paw, more of a long crescent shape than she is used to, which makes lifting her feet easier than the old rounder, wider bear paw. But the leather causes her to sink some in the snow.

It has been a gray day, maybe thirty degrees. No wind. She walks two miles, a decent trek, focusing on each shoe as it slices through the snow, clearing her mind of every thought, listening to the sighs and the soft moans of the past, but finally thinking of nothing but her next shoe print in the powder. The synchronized motion, the thoughtless inertia of the shoes. *Shoosh, shoosh, shoosh, shoosh.* She pulls her hands out of her gloves and plays with what feels like pieces of corn in her pocket and some kind of tissue. She stops, pulls out the tissue, and wipes her nose. Then walks on.

And on.

Evening is fast approaching, and she'll need to think of dinner soon. She feels cold inside. These are paths she knows like the pathways to her heart, so why does she feel they have become hostile? She laughs and starts back along the tracks she'd made. Startled, she realizes she's been oblivious to the landmarks, focusing on the rhythmic propulsion through the snow. Nothing seems familiar. A rivulet she doesn't recognize, boulders and stumps she doesn't know, piled high with a couple feet of snow. She climbs over logs she doesn't remember, yet the evidence of the brushed snow testifies that she'd been there. Evening approaches faster, and Kachina, for the first time in her life, is truly lost. She tries to listen to The Day, but this is her first hint that He's turned His face from her.

Keep walking, she tells herself. The tracks are like bread crumbs, and if she follows them, she'll find her way back. But the wind has come up, blowing snow into her face with short blasts of frigid air. The snow has a rhythm, comes in waves of frozen fear, her tracks becoming fainter, disappearing from her along with The Day.

She starts across the clearing, wraps the black scarf she had in her pocket around her face to keep the blowing snow from stinging her cheeks, puts her gloves back on. The wind seems determined to erase any trace of her. Is she heading west? She must be, toward the water, but somehow it seems south. She passes a fallen log, the stump part of it covered in shadowy white. The stumps look like snow people. A rabbit runs out from behind the stump and away from her, to her right. Then next to her own tracks she can see others, snowshoe tracks that cross her own, perpendicular to hers. But which ones are hers? It's a stampede of footprints heading in all directions, her path obscured in the mess of them.

She sits down on the stump, squashing the snow person with her long fur coat, her breath snatched away on each gust of wind. She closes her eyes for a moment and wonders if she'll ever be herself again, if she'll make her way out of these woods she knows better than anyone could know them.

Then she opens her eyes and sees there are two sets of prints in the snow. Realizes the other set was made with older, heavier, wicker shoes, the kind with smaller webbing that makes less distinct markings in the snow. Why hadn't she seen that? *What is the matter with her?*

She gets to her feet, walking deliberately, putting the front of each snowshoe into the back of her earlier prints, concentrates on reforming each print, making them clear, whole, and distinct again.

THE GREAT WHITE BLIZZARD.

Kachina steadies herself, sits at the old table, and thinks back. It had been her mother, Izusa, who talked of the Great White Blizzard. Kachina had known Izusa was ready to return home as early as that February, though she tarried until late May 1955. Her face had been hollow and ghostlike, and she'd refused to rest, flitting around the woodstove or campfire, bad knees and all, like a dying moth. Airborne, she had ceased to leave footprints, and Kachina had known it was time, the weight of her words heavy in contrast to the lightness of her body.

But then Izusa did sit finally, at the end, close to a fire always, and close to Topini. Though there had continued to be rumors through the years that Nagani was still alive, Izusa had refused to speak even his death name after that day with the shaman. And Oneida had been gone now many years, as well. So it had been Topini who gave Izusa comfort. Words were unnecessary with Topini, and that seemed to give the old woman what she needed.

This was mid-May, during the hex hatch; the giant mayflies had seduced Keane, and he'd been fishing late into the night. Izusa had had a bad day, so Kachina had stayed with her, preparing her various herb tisanes and cups of sassafras tea. Kachina drank hers iced since it was unseasonably warm, but Izusa needed them hot. She sipped the tea in short, breathy gulps, holding the cup to her cheek, careful not to spill it on the black Bible she held on her lap. Topini sat next to the old woman, rolling a red ball between her hands and fetching lemon drops upon Izusa's request.

The sun had been lowering, and Kachina felt it moving away from her like she felt Izusa moving away, watched it dip over the edge of the earth. She remembered as a child feeling betrayed and bereft every night as The Day turned His face from her. She was comforted only by the shining dawn and the proof that He had not deserted her. She remembered how long it had taken her to have faith. Faith in the order and rightness, in the consistency and rhythm of nature, in the movement (it had been the motion that frightened her). But eventually she found peace in the change, even peace in the night. Knowing The Day trusted *her* to make it without Him for a few hours had equipped her for the times when she couldn't feel His warmth. It was the challenge of the night followed by each day that developed her strength.

Kachina had had a pot of whitefish stew bubbling over a fire outside, and Izusa and Topini were sitting around it in metal lawn chairs. Izusa had wanted Kachina to grow grass around the cabin, but she'd refused, though she kept the weeds trimmed back. There were wild daffodils growing under the trees at the edge of the clearing. Izusa had insisted they have a mailbox so she could receive letters from her sister who had long ago moved to Wisconsin with a French boat captain. The letters came weekly, and because Izusa had never learned to read, Kachina read them to her. She kept them in the corner of a Hoosier cupboard where they collected flour dust and grease stains.

She hadn't modernized the cabin, but she'd kept it in good repair, kept paint on the doors and creosote on the log walls to protect the wood. Some investors had wanted this property years ago for tourist cabins, but Keane had taken care of it, somehow, paying the back taxes.

Kachina went into the cabin and noticed that the screen door hinges had loosened over the winter. She'd need to get to that. She came back with a wool blanket Keane had given her years ago. It had a gold satin label stitched into the red-and-green plaid that read "Woolrich, since 1830, Woolrich, Penn." She wrapped the blanket around Izusa's shoulders and attempted to take her cup to get her more tea.

"No more," Izusa had said.

"The stew is almost ready," Kachina answered. Izusa waved her hand away and said she'd have a few more lemon drops after a while. But Kachina stirred the stew anyway.

"Have you seen anything of Oneida?" Izusa asked then. Only she didn't say Oneida's name; she used her death name, so as not to confuse Kachina's grandmother's spirit. Calling her name might cause her to hover around the living rather than rest in peace where she belonged.

"No," Kachina answered. "Though it's possible I won't see her at all. Maybe only you will."

"No," Izusa said. "You'll see her."

"Hototo has promised to come next week. Why don't we look

forward to that instead?" Hototo was taking a vacation from his job in the flour mill, bringing his son, Samuel, to see Izusa. Hototo had married a farm girl from Iowa and moved there in 1947. Izusa was sure he'd never forgiven her for making him go to the school. She frowned and stared at Kachina's face with the disapproval Kachina had seen so often through the years.

"You didn't have to do it, you know," Izusa said. "It had nothing to do with your calling. Nothing at all to do with the old road."

"I suppose not," Kachina said.

"I gave you that face."

Izusa's words startled her. She'd never known Izusa felt that way. As if she'd given Kachina a gift she hadn't appreciated. As if she'd rejected Izusa herself. As if her action had not been one of choosing a path, as Kachina was still certain it was, but the action of someone denying who she was.

"Fruitless gestures," Izusa said. "You're lost in the Great White Blizzard."

IZUSA DIED THAT SPRING of 1955. Oneida came to guide the way, and even Kachina had seen her. And Kachina had followed her own snowshoe prints out of the blizzard that day in 1962, thinking of Izusa's words. But she was still trapped inside the blizzard of her own mind, separated from The Day.

She leaves the stew simmering and returns her attention to the table. She's using a fine sandpaper and soon she'll use a fine steel wool with a diluted mixture of turpentine. The grain must close sufficiently before any wax or oil is rubbed into it. This is something that must be determined by feel. When it is time, the wood begins to feel silky smooth under your fingertips.

Like an eagle's feather.

When Kachina isn't working on the table, she organizes the belongings she'll be taking with her when she leaves this place: piles of clothing stacked unevenly by the door, cooking utensils, blankets, books. She'll leave a lot for Mary Crowfeather's family since she won't need much in the place she is headed.

The Chemokmon have the strangest ideas about place. Places to go to pray. Places to go to be healed. Places to go to learn. Places to go windigo in the head.

The Anishinaabek take all these places around with them or perhaps leave some of them behind when it's time. Places overlap in a person, and the Anishinaabek's goal is to join wisdom, health, and spirituality with all life. They leave the separate place for the sinsinawa, the grave.

CHAPTER TWENTY-SEVEN

Several weeks after Topini had been lost in the woods, they come for her. "For her own good," they say. It seems the "good" ladies of Elk Rapids are worried about Topini. Nothing that should be taken personally, they say. She is too much for one person to take care of properly. Surely Izusa can see that? Mrs. Campbell, spokeswoman for the group, is a small, fidgety woman with unusually large hands that she keeps clenched and hidden in the folds of her skirt. If she removes them from the skirt, it's to wave a handkerchief around for emphasis while she sniffs dramatically over what she calls "the situation." She has come with Dr. Jamison from the asylum, a gray man with a faded mustache, a small goatee, and an apologetic expression. In surprisingly uncertain fingers he holds papers made out by judges at the county seat in Bellaire. Kachina is surprised and optimistic at the uncertainty in his face. But she knows the time is not now; The Day has told her as much.

Izusa cries when they load a bewildered Topini into the buckboard wagon, but Kachina does not cry. Instead she sits stone-faced, and when the wagon leaves with Topini, who is also not crying but instead sucking her tongue as she does when she's anxious, Kachina simply begins walking without saying a word to Izusa, stopping long enough to pick up the rubber slicker with the hole in the neck and a couple slices of corn bread from the small plank table inside the wigwam.

It takes her seven hours to walk the seventeen miles into Traverse City from Elk Rapids. But there is no confusion; The Day presents no conflicting or alternative paths, and there is no fear like there had been the day Topini was lost. It's hot and dusty, so she walks along the edges of the road in the tall grasses to keep the stones from becoming lodged in her shoes and the dry wind from blowing dust into her eyes. It's midday when she starts and dusk as the hospital comes into view.

Gewnaadizii gamik. Asylum. Kachina has heard of it before. A place they'd taken several of the Anishinaabek men when they'd become liquored up one too many times in town, the result of "a continued public disturbance problem." It is an enormous yellow-brick building that stretches out for what seems miles, with pointy spires that pierce the sky surrounded by smaller buildings Kachina will hear called "cottages," which are also topped with imposing spires.

There's no iron gate around the front of the building. Instead there's evidence that they are replacing what appears to be a simple wooden farm fence with a low metal one. It winds along both sides of the entrance road around to the back of the property. But nothing prevents Kachina from making her way to the massive oak door of the main building. She doesn't knock but holds the latch down with her thumb and pushes, surprised when the door swings open. The hospital, at least here at the entryway, is not what she thinks a hospital should look like but is instead like pictures she's seen of a fancy hotel in Chicago. A woman seated at a large flat desk is the only indication otherwise. She is dressed all in white with a white pointed hat on her head. The only detail that isn't white (even the woman's skin and hair are white, almost gray, like a birch tree) is a single dark horizontal stripe toward the top of the pointy hat that matches the rest of the spires. The light is dim in the lobby. What color is the stripe? she wonders. It might be black or brown or slag blue. Or even an iron ore colored red.

"Can I help you?" the woman says. She is quickly joined by a young man also dressed in white who comes to stand next to her. Kachina has an urge to touch the woman's hand and then the white fabric.

"I want to see my sister," Kachina says. "A doctor came and took her away this afternoon. I want to see her."

"Visiting hours, upon Dr. Jamison's approval," says the woman, who Kachina realizes is much younger than she'd first thought, "are between one and three, Sundays and Wednesdays."

Tomorrow is Saturday.

"I'd like to see the doctor then," Kachina says.

"Dr. Jamison is gone for the day," the young man says. "He sees no one on Saturdays." Kachina gazes at the woman until she starts to move uncomfortably, glancing questioningly to the dark-haired man beside her.

"I'm taking my sister home," Kachina announces. The woman appears shocked, but the man smiles patronizingly at Kachina and says it would be best for her to return Monday when Dr. Jamison would answer all her questions. Kachina turns and walks back out the front door, pulls it closed behind her, walks down the brick steps.

It's dark now but unusually warm for April. To the right of the front door is a row of bushes Kachina can't identify that are just beginning to bud. Kachina wraps the rubber coat around her and squeezes beneath one of the bushes. Her last thought before she drifts off to sleep is that the young man's hands in the hospital had been pink and rough, as if they'd been scrubbed over and over with bristle brushes. As she'd closed the big door, she'd seen that hand grab the white-white-white woman's sleeve, urgently, Kachina thought.

The stripe is red, she thinks. On the woman's hat. Kachina is certain of it.

It's warm under the bush, and Kachina sleeps soundly and dreams of Izusa cooking hot bread in the new woodstove the church has given her. Izusa keeps closing the oven door over and over with loud clanking sounds that knock inside Kachina's head. It will be hard to get that bread to cook and rise properly if Izusa keeps opening the oven door like that. Then Kachina realizes it isn't the door making the intrusive sounds but a shovel against rock. A sturdy, black-haired man is repeatedly slamming one into the ground, the backside of it scraping down the side of the brick building. She sees that the sun has been long up.

"You're not allowed to make yourself a nest out of our grounds here, young woman," the man says, seeing she's awake and sitting upright. "If Dr. Jamison sees you, he'll notify the local jurisdiction."

"I want him to see me," says Kachina, who moves from underneath the bush onto the front walk, sitting squarely in the middle of it, where she will be visible from the upper windows of the enormous building.

"Suit yourself, young woman," says the man. "I have to get Dr. Jamison's new tree planted here."

Kachina figures it must be about eight thirty in the morning, but an unusually warm mid-April sun warms her backside. She reaches into the pocket of the rubber coat and pulls out a piece of corn bread she's brought with her. She eats slowly, watching the small man plant Dr. Jamison's new tree. It's not a tree she's familiar with, and she wonders how well it will do in Michigan's harsh climate. It's amazing to Kachina how a man could cart off a child one day and casually plant a tree the next.

A man dressed in a dark business suit walks past her without a word and enters the asylum, which is pretty much what happens the remainder of the day—people walking past her with curious faces, followed by more faces peering out various windows at her. There's one particular window from which eyes watch her closely, she knows. A dark form paces back and forth behind wooden shutters that blink open and closed as the day lengthens. No one challenges her for many hours, and Kachina watches the daily business of the asylum from her spot on the walk, watches as visitors and nurses and even a stray dog pass by. She watches people she imagines must be inmates who emerge from back or side doors and make their way to surrounding fields and barns, where they work with hoes or lead cattle about, lugging bales of hay or burlap bags of grain between buildings and animal shelters. Other inmates, those Kachina imagines to be the more unruly ones, enter gated courtyards and walk about aimlessly or sit in iron chairs under trees, the women in one great pen, the men in another at the opposite end. It's quiet for the most part, though she detects an occasional muffled cry emanating from inside or perhaps from around the back of the large institution.

What exactly is it, Kachina wonders, that qualifies someone as windigo in the white world? Among the Anishinaabek, there would occasionally be someone who was different in some way from the rest of them, "touched," as the white people call it. There were the whispers about Kachina herself. But even while the Anishinaabek feared people who were different, they nevertheless watched patiently for that person's special gift. The Day irrefutably imparted a message to people so afflicted, and the Anishinaabek in turn waited and watched to see what special message would come. There would always be one.

Kachina refuses to think about Topini and concentrates instead on listening to The Day. She stands when her backside becomes sore, sits when her feet tire. In midafternoon, she pulls the last piece of corn bread out of her pocket, eats most of it, and offers the remaining crumbs to several pigeons that have been fluttering about her. The gardener wordlessly offers her a tin cup of water about the time the sun slips behind a huge maple tree on her far left. Kachina smiles, but he doesn't wait for her to finish drinking, just shuffles off toward the stable, shaking his head slowly. Finally, the same woman Kachina had spoken to the night before comes out the front door and walks to Kachina's spot on the brick walk. She finishes the water and shoves the tin cup in her pocket.

"Dr. Jamison has asked me to tell you that you will not be allowed to sleep on the grounds tonight and that if you are still here past eight o'clock, the custodians will be forced to remove you."

Kachina is silent, and the woman walks back up the front steps of the building, pulling a dark blue sweater around her shoulders as she closes the massive door behind her. The sun disappears behind the great building, which brings the architecture sharply into focus. She can see the concrete crumbling in places between the brick. Like the lives of those within. About an hour later, Kachina sees Luella hurrying up the long front walk toward her.

"Izusa told me what happened," she says. "What in the world are you doing?"

"Nothing," Kachina answers.

"Have they let you in or talked to you or anything?"

"I went in the front door last night. Didn't try to go in today," Kachina answers.

"Holy Christ, come on. Uncle George is down by the livery with our democrat wagon." A lady passing by gives Luella a frown, but Luella pays her no mind.

"I'm not leaving," Kachina answers.

"We can sleep in it, for God's sake. They aren't going to let you keep sleeping here in the street, you know."

"I'm not in the street," Kachina says, but she stands and follows Luella, who keeps trying to get Kachina to tell her what in God's name she intends to do. Kachina follows silently, annoyed but grateful to find a soft straw pallet in the back of the democrat wagon and several wool horse blankets. Luella's uncle George, who apparently knows the livery people here in town, has pulled the wagon behind the stable, and there's a good fire going, a pot of hot coffee, and three large potatoes shoved up in the coals. They have ham sandwiches and pickles wrapped in paper and a mason jar filled with lemonade, all of which Luella pulls from a white pillowcase.

"We've only got food and money enough for tomorrow, and that's *it*," Luella says when they've finished eating. "And Uncle George will have to get back with the wagon."

Kachina nods.

"Well," Luella says, "don't you have anything to say about that? Aren't you planning to say anything about this at all?"

Kachina knows there are things to say where Luella is concerned, but she is possessed only with enough spiritual energy to deal with

Topini for now. Luella will have to wait. Kachina is tired, angry, and grateful all at the same time, but in order to have the focus she needs to listen to The Day, she needs sleep. And besides, she doesn't know what to say.

"No," Kachina answers.

"Okay, good," Luella says. "Go to sleep then. No one wants to hear you talk anyway." But Kachina finishes the last of her sandwich as Uncle George talks about the early spring, the value of a good horse blanket, and the condition of the road between Elk Rapids and Traverse City.

"I'm going for a newspaper," Uncle George announces. "I'll be back soon."

"Here," Luella says. She pulls the blanket around her shoulders, indicates that Kachina should gather close. "You'll have to share this with me, you know. That's all there is to it."

"You know," Luella goes on, "I'm getting sick and tired of that smug silence of yours. Sick and tired of it." Luella throws herself down next to Kachina, but instead of landing next to her, she barges hard into Kachina's hip. Kachina feels the weight, the intrusiveness of it. Despite her best efforts not to, she shoves the girl back slightly with her left shoulder. And then all at once they're both shoving.

"Goddamn it," says Luella. And then they are rolling around in the straw of the wagon bed in silent fury. Kachina is amazed at the girl's strength, at the wiriness of her body.

"Goddamn it," Luella says again. Kachina isn't really fighting, just defending the attack, and that seems to ignite Luella's fury even more. They roll around like a couple of logs caught behind an icy logjam for what seems forever. They roll one direction until they hit the side of the wagon, then roll the other. Luella's breath smells like coffee and dill pickles. Her eyes are not shut like Kachina expects but open and angry. Kachina wonders if they'll be stuck here forever rolling in the jam or if the spring thaw will finally turn them loose. Luella rolls on top of her, and she sees the girl is thinking of slapping her but instead rubs dusty straw in Kachina's face. It's started to rain, and the wind blows bits of damp straw in the air like soggy golden tears. Kachina can no longer hold back and grabs the girl's arms. She throws the full weight of her body against her, which causes the two of them to roll out of the wagon bed and land with a dull thud against the hard ground.

"Goddamn it," Luella says again. "Why don't you just goddamn say it, whatever the hell it is?" And now they're rolling in the dirt again, which is becoming more like mud as the rain comes down harder.

Kachina continues to hold her silence. But she knows, despite her own reluctance to do so, that they've connected at last; their two roads have converged.

As she pushes Luella off her, sits up, and starts fishing bits of straw from her mouth, she sees Uncle George's boots out of the corner of her eye, finds him holding the *Traverse City Eagle,* an amused expression on his face. He doesn't say a word, just pulls one of the canvas covers and several blankets from the wagon and begins making himself a bed next to the fire. *"Goddamn it,"* Kachina says then. "I need sleep."

"Okay," Luella answers.

They put one of the wool blankets over the remaining straw in the wagon bed and pull two of them over themselves followed by the canvas, though the rain has stopped. They begin the night on opposite sides of the wagon, but it's cold. Kachina wakes up once in the middle of the night to find a sky littered with stars and Luella's feet tucked neatly under her left leg.

CHAPTER TWENTY-EIGHT

On Sunday morning, Kachina refuses coffee but gratefully accepts one of the wool blankets. She nods her gratitude and leaves Luella shaking her head and Uncle George sipping coffee under another blessedly pleasant spring morning sky. When she reaches the walk, Kachina takes off the rubber coat and sits on it, pulling the blanket around her shoulders, which she knows gives an impression: Indian squaw. Indian squaw planted on the front walk. She sits very straight, as she supposes they expect of her, a hand on each folded knee. The day is much as the one before, the exception being that there is no gardener in evidence and no toiling in the fields, only a few workers tending to the animal stock. Like yesterday, Kachina is aware of the dark figure returning to a shuttered window on the second floor at the left of the front entrance. Kachina knows it could be one of the inmates but is fairly certain it's not.

At noon, Dr. Jamison himself walks down the front steps.

"Come with me, young woman," he says. Kachina follows him inside, where she sees a man polishing the grand stairway with what she'd call an abnormal zeal. Dr. Jamison doesn't lead her up it but to an office on the first floor. Several large desks are positioned around the room, numerous dark bookshelves line every wall, and there is a large multiglobed pewter light fixture hanging down from the thirty-foot ceiling. The window's open at the bottom, and the midday sun pours several feet into the gloom, a silty cone of light. Dr. Jamison points to a chair and sits down opposite her across one of the flat desks. A row of medical books on the back edge of the desk separates them. She doesn't attempt to see over them. Instead Dr. Jamison sits up taller in his chair.

"Now, tell me what this is about," Dr. Jamison says.

Kachina is surprised he can ask something that obvious, but she can't help noticing the weariness and even a bit of kindness in the doctor's eyes.

"I'll take Topini home now," Kachina says.

Dr. Jamison takes a labored breath. He doesn't say anything for a while. "You know this facility exists for numerous reasons. It exists not just to house those we consider dangerous to others but as a haven to protect those dangerous to themselves. For some it exists as an oasis in a vast desert, from which they can drink and restore their strength before having to return to that desert. Which, I might add, is often possible."

"It is better to take that oasis around with you everywhere," Kachina says, "than to leave it inside a building."

"Hm," Dr. Jamison answers. "It is unfortunately not possible for everyone to be possessed of that kind of inner reserve. There would be no mental problems if that were the case. Surely, you see that."

"My sister is a child. She's not crazy. And suppose she were? A human would probably seem a bit off in a squirrel's nest, don't you think?"

"Yes, but presumably another squirrel would fit in for the most part. But I know what you mean, I think. You mean, don't you, that perhaps we're all doing the fox-trot and 'they' are the only ones who have noticed that God's playing a waltz?"

Kachina smiles but does not comment.

"Believe me, the notion crosses my mind every day I walk in here. But still, the waltzers are in danger of being run down by the fox-trotters. Don't you see that?"

"I know that if the dancers aren't allowed to hear the music, pretty soon they will not dance at all. I can take care of my sister."

"It is plain," says Dr. Jamison, "that that is a difficult undertaking in a world as vast and unmanageable as yours. You may be expecting too much from yourself. You did lose her after all?"

Kachina is silent, but her eyes never leave Dr. Jamison's face as she knows he expects they will, the expected result of those particular words. He clears his throat at last.

"It is my job over the next week to determine if Topini should remain with us permanently. These are decisions I do not take lightly. You can be sure of that. Come. Let's see how she's doing."

Dr. Jamison walks Kachina down hallways that are decorated, she thinks again, like a grand hotel. Potted ferns stand on wooden pedestals; cupboards hold fresh linens and fine serving ware; cream-colored walls are stenciled with gay patterns near the ceiling; pictures of lighthouses, rivers, and monuments adorn walls; and gold tassels hang from the edges of gilt-covered frames. Tapestry carpets cover the dark oak floors, and Victorian curtains warm the enormous windows. Kachina walks past inmates dressed in their Sunday best sitting in comfortable rockers or on window seats. She passes a chapel. Along the hallway of the women's ward is a wall with the words "After Clouds, Sunshine" painted in blue amidst the shining rays of a hand-painted yellow sun. As they continue down the hallways, Kachina draws stares from inmates and soon she hears intermittent cries echoing incongruously through the gaily decorated halls.

"We have temporarily located Topini in Ward Five, the women's most disturbed ward, simply so she won't run away," Dr. Jamison says. "We expect this to be temporary." As they near Ward Five, Kachina sees a similarly decorated hallway with the words *"Veni, Vidi, Vici"* painted in bright red over a field of white daisies. Topini is not in the ward, and Kachina follows Dr. Jamison until they locate her in a patient dining room in which hover several men in white jackets. Topini sits across the room next to a window eating a bowl of ice cream. She's wearing a blue cotton dress with a white pinafore tied over it. At first there is no expression on the child's face, and then she smiles and offers Kachina a bite. A scream echoes from somewhere, and Topini abruptly stops eating and starts sucking her tongue. Kachina sits next to her without a word, and eventually the nurse and Dr. Jamison move away and into the hallway. Kachina doesn't want to talk to her of home, and she doesn't want to talk to her about the asylum. She finds it impossible to say a word to her, so she simply sits there for five minutes or so, and when she rejoins Dr. Jamison in the hallway, she notices Topini seems to have forgotten her, her head turned toward the window.

"I'm taking my sister home," Kachina says. She walks past Dr. Jamison and wanders around the hallways until she finds her way back out. She passes a clock on her way out the front door. It is 1:47 p.m. on April 10, 1917.

What happens after that Kachina will never remember clearly. She resumes her seat on the front walkway. Dr. Jamison continues to watch her and shake his head. Visitors continue to pass and watch her suspiciously, making a wide path around her and into the asylum yard. Luella brings her a sandwich and tells her that when it gets dark she should plan to come sleep another night in the democrat wagon and that if she isn't careful, they'll be shaking out linen and fixing her up her own little bed inside the asylum. But Kachina sits quietly and tries to feel what it's like to be windigo. Maybe she *is* windigo like they say. She wonders if a crazy person knows they're crazy. At about five o'clock, the sun dips behind the great yellow building. She sleeps another night in the wagon with Luella and Uncle George, another night spent mostly in silence. And when they leave Monday morning, Kachina refuses to go with them. She resumes her seat on the front walk and spends the next two days sitting there, spends the next two nights in the bushes. No policemen or orderlies remove her.

She's out of food.

The gardener brings her another cup of water and a slice of ham, shakes his head, and walks off carrying his shovel. Kachina will remember none of this clearly and thinks instead of days she'd once spent fasting, thinks of her vision of the windigo dog and about her chances disappearing. She thinks that if some chances disappear, others must appear to take their place. Did the windigo dog bring new chances, or did a person make them himself? She remembers that during the vision her eyesight seemed blurry, but her sense of smell had become acute. The air had smelled of matted fur and dead animals mixed with hope. What did hope smell like? She couldn't describe it, but she knew it was there.

Finally, on the sixth day, something happens that she does remember. A small old man walks out the front door of the hospital wearing a nightshirt tucked into a pair of unbuttoned dress pants, the ends of a belt flapping with each step he takes. Kachina watches him a moment, and soon he makes his way across the grounds. It's evident that Dr. Jamison has not given this man a "grounds pass." Kachina follows him to a pond, part of what she'd heard the staff refer to as the "beauty is therapy landscape," where a few ducks are swimming about lazily in the evening sun. The man kneels next to the pond and begins throwing small twigs toward the ducks. When Kachina approaches, the man says, "Get 'em, Henry. They've been in the orchard again."

"Yes," Kachina says. She assures the man that she'll be sure to "get 'em."

"They like the cherries best," he tells her.

"So do I," she says. "How 'bout dinner? I'll bet it's almost time. Should we go back?"

The man notices the beads on the front of Kachina's blouse and grabs for them, his hands flat against her breasts.

"Happy stones," he says.

Kachina removes the man's hands calmly and points again at the ducks when she sees Dr. Jamison headed her way with another man dressed in white. Kachina thinks Dr. Jamison seems old all of a sudden, older than before, and tired, so tired she isn't sure he'll be able to take another step. She wonders if he might reach them at all, but he does, finally. There is no need for either of them to speak. Dr. Jamison smiles the smallest of smiles, puts a hand on her shoulder.

"Mr. Benson, take Mr. Alanson to his room, please. And after you do, we'll need to round up an inmate and her belongings. This young woman has come to take her sister home."

The old man jumps up and down in excitement.

"They'll get the *cherries*, Henry," the inmate says to Kachina again.

"Oh, let them have them, Mr. Alanson," says Dr. Jamison. "It's been a very long winter."

CHAPTER TWENTY-NINE

It was unusual for her mood not to match that of The Day back then. It's something that won't occur for many years. She's not sure what's causing it now. But The Day seems almost to be teasing her. There is that unformed, cloying feeling, like awakening from a bad dream you can't quite recall, or would rather not. That vague feeling of dread. She chases the feelings around her head a few times until she catches a glimpse of the problem.

Luella.

Thinking of Luella has left her confused and irritable. She knows she'll feel better if she can find a place to put her. Somewhere she'll stay. But the trouble is, she doesn't stay. Kachina would stick her in the back corner of her mind, a place reserved for things she considers useless: umbrellas with holes, shoes with holes, trousers with holes—all that's unfit for the purposes for which they were intended. To Kachina, there is no greater crime than being useless, unnecessary, extra. Even evil has a purpose. Despite her conviction that Luella and Cap have earned their spot in her useless corner, the girl keeps sliding out.

The weather is good for early June, warm. Kachina needs some horsetail and nettle for a poultice for Izusa's knees. Though she's too young for symptoms like this, Izusa can hardly make it off her pallet, and she spends most of her time sitting on her stool near the fire, even in warmer weather like today. Kachina has dried herbs left from last summer, but she wants fresh horsetail and nettle. It's early to find them, but they will do Izusa more good if she's lucky enough to find them fresh. The poultice would help. Kachina will try hot castor oil packs if it doesn't.

Herbs and medicines are necessary to replace the vine that once connected heaven and earth, the vine that man severed in his conceit and stupidity. The concept of fluid, the proportion of blood in the body, equal to the proportion of water on earth—another example of balance.

As she walks, Kachina notices some chickweed in a clearing, which is good for the lungs, and a black walnut tree standing alone by a small creek that leads to the river. Walnuts are good in case of poison ivy or warts, but she sees no horsetail or nettle. Sage is an option for people of Izusa's age, but it's early in the season for that. It might have to be the cedar. It made excellent tea and was good for treating arthritis, and more importantly, Kachina knows she can find it. Cedars like low areas, and there's one particular tree that Kachina likes down on the north side of Elk River.

She walks up the north side of the rise where she and Topini go to pick morel mushrooms. It's been a rainy spring, excellent conditions for mushrooms, and they'd picked more than four hundred morels here several weeks ago. Izusa and Oneida loved to fry them in butter or lard along with a pinch of sage and a touch of raw sap or maple. Kachina notices some trillium left under the trees, but the mushrooms are long gone.

As Kachina nears Elk River, she sees overhanging willows, swamp cedars, and swales of tag alders, which line the banks and form secluded alcoves, common along the chain of lakes. A boat or canoe could duck into these alcoves anytime if a person didn't wish to be noticed. Many of the lakes are covered with white-and-yellow lily pads, but here in Elk River there are few due to the high frequency of boat traffic. The river is short but widens where it joins

Elk Lake, and then it empties into Grand Traverse Bay. Many years ago it was narrower, and there were stumps of dead white cedar and bog spruce. Since they added the dam, it appears more like a lake than a river, but it's necessary for boat traffic to adhere to the original narrows to avoid the hidden stumps.

Kachina carries a tin can filled with corn stew that Izusa had made for dinner. Food from her own portion, like in the old ways, an offering in return for the plants and herbs she intends to pick. This was one of the first lessons she'd learned when she was drawn to the art of healing, the Red Road. Though the lesson is true for everyone, it is especially important for Kachina: Giving is the only way to be sure there is never a lack, spiritual or otherwise.

The brambles bite into her legs, and she pushes the alders out of her face as she nears the edge of the river. A muskrat pokes its head down over the bank, and Kachina thinks he'd make a good addition to the stew for tomorrow but knows there isn't much chance of trapping him. Grasshoppers jump as she walks through the tall grass, filling the air with small clouds of motion and strident clicking noises. She makes the turn in the river, which moves her into a dense and more remote area few people venture into. She steps out to walk along the river when she sees Keane sitting on the bank, Shadow lying close by him. Keane is wearing ragged, chocolate-colored corduroy pants and a pair of tan suspenders. A white cotton shirt and a pair of boots and socks lie in the sand next to him, and the setting sun has turned his brown hair a russet red. Kachina has the impression that he's been swimming. He's tossing the dog bits of something, probably dried beef, and laughing as the yellow mongrel catches them in midair.

The Anishinaabek honor animals not just because they are good to eat but because they're good to think with. Animals are not always the product of original creation but are transformed in appearance and behavior by interaction with the spirits. Kachina knows that Keane understands this kind of power and its relationship to the dog, how the dog figures in the dynamics of the sacred and in the pattern of space and time. How had he managed to acquire the knowledge?

Kachina stops. For a moment, she thinks of stepping back into the dense overgrowth before Keane sees her, but it's too late. The call of a loon fills the air, and Kachina thinks of Luella, but there's no guilt attached.

Kachina doesn't think of people in terms of possessions.

It's the squeezing, the grasping that diminishes. For Kachina, owning a person is as impossible as owning the earth and sky. To hold on to something, you must make a fist. Only in an open, palms-up position can you be truly receptive to life.

Keane sees her.

It's too late to step back.

CHAPTER THIRTY

His hair is wet. He's been swimming in the river as she'd first supposed, up closer to the lake where it's deeper. On calm days like this, the upper levels of the lake will be warm, two feet or so of warm water. But down at the bottom, it's cold. A clear glaciated lake, spring fed. In about another month, it will turn upside down. Sometimes she would stand on the dune to see the concentric rings of color and watch them change, an effect made more dramatic if there were clouds, which formed dark shadows over the sandbars.

Keane watches her hesitate and then resume her path toward him. Shadow hovers near, making a small sound in his throat, not quite a growl, but a warning nevertheless. Keane reaches down, his fingers moving but not touching the dog. And that's really all there is to the story.

Except the sex, of course.

Keane will record his own version of this day in the years that follow, written on sheets of linen paper, offered to her when it's clear she will take nothing else, the letters smeared finally from years of her folding and unfolding them. She will keep them in a small drawstring pouch in one of the kitchen nooks where the logs meet behind the pump handle at the sink. She will take it out and read it occasionally until there is no longer any need to do that other than to see his handwriting, because she will have it committed to memory. Even the strange lilting slant of his hand will be imprinted on her mind permanently.

This is for you. I can't claim I thought these words at the time, but they came to me eventually.

You were beautiful, of course. I saw that, but it didn't hold my attention because all I could see was the damn line. Out in front of you several feet. A line in my mind, but it might have been a barbed fence; I could see it that clear. I thought about crossing it or climbing it and what would happen if I did. Who would I become? A man like my father? A man who owns things? A man who steals what doesn't belong to him?

You were close then, the scar on your face an omen.

Then I felt my word. Mine.

I let it bob around in my head. A word consumed already by the idea of itself. I was sitting in the sand, and as you got closer I decided to try my word out on you, tossed it toward you in my mind.

Mine.

I was surprised there was no change in your expression. I'd thrown it easy, though, a gentle underhand kind of toss. Perhaps it hadn't made it all the way to you and had dropped, instead, at your feet. Or perhaps you'd stepped aside, and it had gone sailing over your shoulder. It's true I lost sight of my word the second it left my mind.

You had plants in one hand, and the other seemed to hold food of some sort wrapped in a white handkerchief. Shadow moved closer to me. I reached over, and he let me touch him for the first time—strange it would be now.

I knew I could have sat there, greeted you casually, which would have kept things impersonal, and that's what I thought I wanted. But without deciding to, I stood.

Which of course changed everything.

The wind died then, and the river turned to glass, but I heard the sound of a tiny wave slapping the log I had been sitting on.

You stopped walking toward me, and Shadow moved between us, confused as to who to protect. You waited—something I knew was usual for you. For me a damned eternity passed.

I'd watched you like this before, maybe a year ago, saw you dance in the moonlight around a fire in a clearing. I thought maybe you saw me, and I imagined you were dancing for me. I watched you twirl in circles, a series of four, arms reaching up, hands full of some sort of moss. You threw it into a small fire, and I recognized the smell of tobacco. You reminded me of a bobcat I saw once. Your hair had slipped from the braid as you spun, parallel to the ground, and the moonlight made streaks of silver through it. Occasionally you would kneel, bend forward, face toward the ground, then you were twirling again.

I asked you later if you remembered that night.

You did.

Did you know I was watching?

Of course, you said.

There was about three feet between us.

That's when I realized I was wrong.

It wasn't a line in front of you, and it wasn't a fence, but space. Shadow was still standing between us, and it seemed to me as if the dog had personified the space, though I knew that was wrong; he could only be standing in it. I marveled that Shadow could exist there and wondered if I would be able to breathe in it or if it would be like being in outer space or under water.

What would it be like to touch you? There was nothing soft about you. You were spare, hard and brown, though from a distance you seemed slight, almost childlike, like Oriental women I'd seen pictures of. I was a head taller than you, and you made me feel large and clumsy and elongated in comparison. Shadow moved behind me, next to my right calf, touching me again, so strange for him. I was watching your face and doing my best to keep my word from you because I could see it would not fit in the space.

I turned to follow your gaze.

"You named him Shadow," you said, finally. Relief flooded through me at the sound. "The Anishinaabek believe there are three parts to a man," you said, "the body, the soul, and the shadow. The shadow is in the brain and is the perception and intuition that precedes logic. The soul lives in the heart and is the basis of intelligence and the source of the life force. Yet they can be separated. When you get a glimpse of someone you know is not there, it is their shadow you are seeing."

"Separated," I said.

"Yes," you continued, "but if the soul becomes separated from the body for any length of time, you will go mad." There was a half smile on your face, and I thought for a moment you were making fun of me. The scar on your face had turned into a question mark. The wind died completely, and the sun felt warm. I could hear what sounded like doves cooing near the edge of the thicket. The river had turned to glass. I knew I must fill the emptiness even if it meant leaving my word behind to do it.

Kachina is a dancer—one who joins the movement of the earth and stars, and the dance is part of her healing art; it is what her name means in Anishinaabemowin.

But this is before the letter, and they are still on the riverbank.

For Kachina there are two suns, the one in the sky and the one in the flat black glass of the water, an orange blaze mixed with inverted spiral shadows formed by the cedars, aspen, and poplars that line the riverbank. A gull lands near the blaze, feeds a few moments, lifts off again. The trees have stopped murmuring, and the sounds of birdcalls bounce around the water. There is the whine of mosquitoes and a distant buzz from what is probably a honeybee and a gentle rustle in the weeds near an alder, maybe a snake or a squirrel. She's lying next to Keane, floating on a cloud, with the water and that reciprocal sun suspended above, his curly hair spread over the cloud. Any attempt to talk about what has happened, to prolong or extend, would merely diminish it.

"I can picture you old," he says. He tells her that he can see her long black hair, how it would become white wisps of clouds, and how her face would become paler until her black eyes became the only contrast. He tells her that he can see where expression lines lead a person in thirty years. "Sometimes," he tells her, "I picture myself fleshless."

"I never think about being old at all," Kachina says.

"It doesn't matter," he says.

Kachina makes no attempt to cover herself, so Keane drapes his plaid shirt around her shoulders. She shrugs it off and dresses hurriedly.

"Come on," she says.

Keane tucks his shirt into his cutoff trousers, adjusts his suspenders. Shadow, lying in the cool water along the edge of the shoreline, moves next to him. As they walk, she searches for animal tracks in the dirt.

"Luella is teaching Topini to track deer in the woods," Kachina says. "Luella is an amazingly good tracker." They both know that what she means is that she is a good tracker for a white girl. "Topini is learning to see them. She sees better farther away than up close."

Kachina sees guilt on Keane's face when she mentions Luella, but Kachina knows better than to compromise with it.

"Where are we off to?" Keane is following along behind, watching her cotton skirt sway, catching in the fronds and what is left of the trillium.

"Gijik. I have to get some. There is one particular cedar tree that heals my people. Sweetgrass would be better, but I'll settle for cedar."

Keane reaches out and grabs the back of her skirt playfully, and she pushes his hands away.

"How did you learn it?" he asks.

How had she learned it? This trusting of The Day that had set rhythm to her days, balance to her soul, a raging thunderstorm or blinding blizzard that could impart something good and useful to someone who listens, a skill she was born with or one honed perfect from endless hours of practice? She has never known. But she's been doing it as long as she can remember. Long before Hototo went away.

"Oneida taught me some of it. Hototo taught me most of it. And some I have known since I was small. Before I was five, I would feel myself drawn to a plant and I would know what its strengths were, whether it was good for cleansing the blood, stopping pain, strengthening the heart, calming the spirit—things like that. I would just know. The way I know that I will be a mishkiikii ninii after my moon cycles end. The same way I know there are other things I must do."

He doesn't ask her what, as she expects he might. So she says it again.

Keane smiles at her. "There are things *I* must do, too," he says then. "Like being an animal doctor instead of a people doctor, not something my father thinks I must do. In fact, he will probably go into apoplexy when I do it. But there is no one good at tending animals around here. If I get good enough at it, I'll be able to help Morrisons and the other big farmers who lose many sheep and cattle each year to disease. I think they will even pay me to tend their stock, though Father doesn't think it will be enough."

Keane stops, pulls her toward him, runs a finger down the scar on her cheek. "There are other things I must do, too." What would his father think of this, Kachina wonders, seeing his son's arms around her?

"How did it happen?" he asks, finger still on her cheek.

She has never shared the truth about the scar with anyone or even discussed it with her own people.

"The Anishinaabek tell stories only in winter," she says. "The summer is for living, not storytelling."

They reach the gijik tree now, centered in a grove of cedars surrounding a small mound of earth, trunks curved and leaning from the accumulated effects of wind and rain. Kachina pulls the knife from the waistband of her skirt and makes careful cuts into one of the roots, and Shadow settles down again close to the river.

"You have to be careful not to take too much from any particular tree, especially in a drought or after a hard winter, or you'll kill the tree."

"You haven't seemed too happy lately," he says, ignoring her instruction. "When I see you in church anyway."

"It's the church, I suppose."

"If you dislike it so much, why do you go?"

"Because Izusa wishes it. Because I have disappointed her in so many other things. Izusa thinks of the church differently than I do," she says. "She thinks of the old ways and the Christian church as if they are each branches of the gijik tree. The same tree. The branches might run parallel sometimes, they might intersect, but they both reach toward the same God. There is nothing conflicting for Izusa in this. But for me, it is like hearing two people shouting at the same time." She finishes putting the cedar in the herb basket with the other plants, leans back against the largest tree. The river moves muddy now in the dark.

"We had long memories once," Kachina says. "We remembered the beginning of time. We taught our children to remember, but now we can't teach our children anything, because they're off in special schools, marching like tiny soldiers. They're learning to read, but they're forgetting their own fathers. Forgetting who they are. Forgetting how to listen to The Day. It makes Izusa sad to hear me talk this way. But I believe she has forgotten how to live *today*. She is too afraid of tomorrow."

Keane sits next to her between the tree trunks, his shoulder touching hers.

He wants to say something, she knows. Then she laughs. "Oneida told me that every morning Gizhe Manido sends an eagle across the world. As long as there is one of my people still performing healing ceremonies, He will let the world continue." She laughs again. "I am keeping your world together for you."

Mine.

Keane's word. Kachina sees it this time. Even before the letter. Though she doesn't know how she missed it. For a moment she feels angry, then sad. She picks up the basket, which swings between them in the space. She listens to the night fall, the birds going to bed, songbirds always before the gulls, so that even though the wind is soft, you can hear The Day in the treetops.

"I've got to go," she says. Shadow moves close to Keane's right calf. Kachina walks down the path toward home.

KACHINA PUTS A LID on the stew—her stew of 1962—thinks about Keane. *Stealing.* He'd used that word in the letter. He'd brought that word up often in relation to her, terrified it would become true of him as it had been true of his father. It was different with the girls at the sporting house in Aarwood that Kachina knew Keane frequented regularly. A girl named Angel (though Kachina had always pictured angels as ethereal, translucent, *white* creatures with a kind of temporary albino quality about them) had laughingly told Kachina all about Keane's visits to the establishment, at an Anishinaabek gathering they'd both attended. This Angel had nearly black hair, weighed probably twice what Keane did, and was far from ethereal. But she smelled of lilac soap. Kachina knew Keane was not "stealing" from Angel.

She'd left the tobacco and food beneath the gijik tree that night, as she'd planned. She's thought a lot about stealing and a lot about giving over the last fifty years and she's realized it's difficult sometimes to tell the difference.

There are seven wisdoms by which the Anishinaabek are meant to judge themselves, and it's clear that she has failed in most of them. She talked last week with the elders and the mishkiikii niini about the Red Road, told them maybe she wasn't meant to take that path after all. But the elders said that those possessed of great humility had doubts. They told her that they'd had visions of Kachina being a great teacher and healer and insisted it was a burden she was meant to carry.

But she's not sure they are right.

She has continued to teach the children Aninshinaabemowin as well as higher mathematics and advanced English that the segregated Indian schools and even the white schools around the state have neglected to teach them. They have not prepared her people for assimilation into white society as they promised. They have been assimilated instead into what Kachina thinks of as custodial America. Fit to do nothing but walk behind the great lady with giant brooms and dustcloths, garden hoes, or garbage trucks.

She hitchhikes twice weekly, or sometimes Keane drives her, to Peshabetown, where most of the Indians have settled now, straggled throughout the Leelanau Peninsula in old shacks and abandoned trailers. There is an old schoolhouse next to the bay, and it is there that she teaches the smallest children on Tuesdays. She comes on Saturdays to teach the older children, who spend weekdays in the white schools, but it's difficult to get them to learn after their long school week. She can't do much more than play games in Anishinaabemowin, but even this serves to remind them of who they are. She has gone through the motions, though she lives a kind of plastic existence these days, cloudy and claustrophobic. Hototo has moved to Wyoming, which is not better, he says, but quieter. Once you start moving, there's nothing to do but keep moving, he says.

Kachina had refused to move to the island with Keane years ago, refused also to marry him, though he'd asked her many times. Through the years, there were those who thought they could get Keane to marry them, and Kachina wondered once if one short dark-haired city girl might not get that arranged. Keane threatened once that he'd marry her if Kachina continued to be so stubborn, but she would not give in, and he had never followed through on the threat. No one seemed to mind their situation much except Keane's family, but after his mother died in 1940, it didn't seem to bother him again.

Keane worried about Kachina constantly. He replaced all the wood in her house—a house that was little more than a shack—with heavy logs, filled the cracks with cement, though she refused to let him run the electricity to her door and found no need of a telephone. He insisted on adding an icebox about ten years back, and soon after that he pumped water into her kitchen as well. Later, long after Izusa was gone, he built a separate room for Topini. Kachina hunts and fishes still, keeps a garden, though Keane, throughout the years, has brought flour, sugar, butter, milk, and eggs weekly to her house. And chocolate. Keane has brought so many boxes of chocolate that she can't understand why she's not as fat as old Angela LaFontaine, who now can't get out of a chair unless she's pulled out by her nearly as fat son, Oni.

Topini hovers around Kachina often now, sensing her loss of equilibrium, and needing her physical presence to reassure her. Kachina still thinks of life in terms of Topini's capabilities, but this no longer depresses her or makes her feel panicked, as it did when she was younger. Instead, she has the peculiar feeling that it is other people who lead handicapped lives and not the two of them.

Kachina's moon cycles have stopped at last (though they had lasted much longer than most women's, as if The Day were trying to prove a point). The scar on her face has turned pink again, perhaps out of embarrassment or maybe because her skin is becoming thinner with age.

Everyone who remembers about the scar is gone now.

CHAPTER THIRTY-ONE

Kachina and Topini walk into Morrison's Hardware, the years and chances settled now to where they belong. She needs that oil for the scars in the table, the ones she's decided to enhance. The man behind the counter wearing a cotton apron wipes his hands down the whiteness of it and greets her with a half smile. They are friendly enough, Kachina supposes. They count on her, after all. But they'll never understand everything.

A knife is an extension of your hand; it joins you with your actions, with the force of it, with the motion, with your victim, for that matter. It keeps you honest.

With a knife there is no distance, no indifference, no anonymity.

She guides Topini down the aisle, the one with the wood stains and lacquers, but there are too many choices.

She's always been good with a knife. Her people had had to be. The Chemokmon had taken all the guns.

She continues to search the shelves. She can always use a bit of corn oil or lard, but she has been hoping for better. Finally, she finds some boiled linseed oil and then she allows Topini to drag her back in her mind. Back and forth. Backward and forward.

The ceremony, in special recognition of Kachina's womanhood, turned out differently than Izusa had imagined.

Kachina remembers the ceremony from outside her body.

At midafternoon, Kachina heads to the lake to freshen up, accompanied by Nami Crowfeather and Wabisi. Since she won't be allowed to bathe in the lake, the young women will help sponge her back. Nami and Wabisi busy themselves in the thicket, gathering daisies for her hair. The lake is calm and the day bright, which gives her a good reflection. And that is a good thing. She'll need a good reflection.

A bit of red string catches Topini's eye, and she's motioning to Kachina to buy her some. Kachina agrees, but the red string forms a flowing crimson line behind her eyes.

The water moves in gentle ripples, enough so her face appears wavy and unreal before her eyes. For a moment she thinks she sees Hototo's face but decides it's simply her own resemblance to him. Then Hototo's face, or her own, disappears and she sees all the rest of their faces. She can't hear The Day, but she feels the energy move from Him to her, sees the years stretch out before her in one long line and her place, clearly, within the procession of them.

The knife is ten inches long and curved. It's the one she uses to kill and clean the animals she traps. She pulls it from between the folds of her skirt. It feels right in her hand, years of skinning everything from the doe her father had shot with his bow to the squirrels they ate regularly.

She hears Nami and Wabisi heading back through the woods toward her; she will have only one chance. They are not near enough to stop her yet, but she is out of time. She feels the power fill her mind, feels it infuse her body, encompassing every part of her. Her reflection is clear, her hand steady. . . .

Kachina has never seen red string before. She tucks the ball under her arm, then puts it on the counter along with the oil.

Kachina can hear Wabisi scream as she pulls the knife from her face. Blood mixes with the shiny glint of the sun and the knife itself, and she can see streaks of blue hard silver through the red. Sees the blood that will replace the blood of fertility as her destiny. Sees her new reflection in the gently rolling water, can feel her heart open at last to the seven great wisdoms: Truth, Honesty, Love, Bravery, Humility, Respect, and Wisdom.

Fifty-nine cents for the string.

That had been 1914. She had been careful, performed a nice even cut. Izusa had had no trouble joining the flaps of skin together. The damage had involved the muscle a little but not enough to drop the whole side of her face. But it was not her appearance that repelled them.

The oil is a little more than a dollar.

They believed she had conversed with the trickster.

The oil is expensive, but it will make all the difference.

And that was fine with her.

Luella

CHAPTER THIRTY-TWO

Other people's words, as Uncle George referred to them, poke at me. They drift along on the surface of my brain like jagged pieces of rotting driftwood. It's not the uttered words that stink; I can always skim those off and discard them like globs of congealing fat. It's the unuttered words that settle, the sedimentary words. How is it that "un" things take up space the way they do? Crazy dots in a dot-to-dot puzzle no one bothered to finish.

It's all about what gets left out.

Like I said before, Kachina and I didn't choose to be friends. But maybe choices are an illusion after all. Maybe our decisions are made on a primitive, cellular level, centuries before, a fateful blend of circumstance and heredity, all tied to a preexisting event or state of being like a link in some obscene collective chain.

No free will. No original thought. Nothing.

Paul Ree, Introduction to Philosophy, sophomore year, University of Michigan.

Anyway, it would be nice to know a pivotal day in the chain was coming so you could be ready for it.

The day Keane got bit was a pivotal day like that.

I WATCH AS EVERY MUSCLE in Kachina's body is flexed, poised, but on her face is a terrible calm as she waits for Keane to give her permission to end the dog's life. Kachina is like the wind and rain, the sun, the moon, the earth, and the sky all wrapped up in one, a force every bit as terrifying as that dog, because they're part of her.

They are all bleeding, even the dog, and they are in it together, the three of them. I can only watch. Should they invite me into their private battle, someone would still need to comfort Topini. She has become cold and confused, and there is nothing for me to do but pick her up. Her feet feel like ice, so I pull my coat around us both, hoping that will make her feel better, but the snarling dog frightens her now, and she continues to cry, her hands pushed tightly over her ears.

Topini has flat, undeveloped facial features, short wide hands that are dry and rough, like sandpaper against my skin, and as I enfold her in my arms, her limbs flop every which way. I try to gather her together, but it's like trying to gather up loose rubber bands. I notice her skin is fairer than mine, her eyes a nearly colorless gray with no depth to them, not so much an emptiness like you would expect from a lack of intelligence, but a quality produced by a sheer lack of color, white flecks around the edge of the irises. Her hair is a medium brown, brittle and stringy, so different from Kachina's. I wonder if she'd been born with errors in her pigment like Ghost, an albino mare Uncle George had a few years back, and I think that's part of it.

All at once I find my legs won't support me. I slide down in the mud, lean up against the tree so that the bateau keeps the rain, which has begun again, off our faces. It seems as if the struggle lasts forever—most of it going on between Keane and the dog, an interaction I don't understand, but Kachina seems to. Finally the dog gets up and moves away without Kachina having to slit his throat.

Have they both lost too much blood? I wonder if I'll have to go for help, but we start back, Kachina supporting Keane, me carrying Topini. It's over a mile and a half back to Kachina's village, but we have to get Keane to a doctor, which means another half mile farther. As we walk, I think about losing Keane or sharing him. I've never had to do that before. I want to keep thinking about Keane and Kachina because I need to find a place to store my thoughts, but I can't.

Because I think about Cap.

I think about what makes people do what they do and I remember Uncle George talking about paying the price. Mostly I think about tintypes. I have one of all of us that I keep in Mama's desk. Mabel, Cap, Mama (obviously pregnant), and me, standing in the front yard. Six, I might have been, so that would make it 1905 or so—no idea who took the picture. I've never seen a photograph where the people are so obviously posed yet standing so far apart. Most people stand or sit in a cozy group.

Not us.

We're each of us in our own corners, ramrod straight, like soldiers—Cap and Mabel on each end of the open front porch, Mama and me in the yard, close in the foreground. Me between Cap and Mabel, Mama at her post in the right front corner of the yard—all of us staggered like pieces on a checkerboard.

But it isn't the pose I'm thinking about as I carry Topini.

In the picture Mama is the closest to the camera, the rest of us farther away, visually higher in the picture, as if we were merely thoughts in her head. As I walk I can see that picture in my mind. Mama in her white dress, her good one, the one she wore to church on Sundays, the folds of it stretched from the child she carries. She holds a bonnet with a big white brim in her right hand, her hair swept up and back like she wore it, no smile on her face. The usual frozen expression of early photography. She's close in the foreground, as I said, and I can make out every detail of her wardrobe.

Even her jewelry.

I'm thinking about this jewelry as we're walking, Topini and me. The ground is muddy and uneven, though the rain has stopped some time ago. I slip occasionally as I walk. Every so often I peek down at Topini, quiet now, nearly asleep, snuggled against my shoulder. She's frail, cold, and wet. What must it be like to be her? Is she frustrated at how long it takes her to learn, or is it a way of life she's accepted as right and normal? Is she more or less afraid than the rest of us? Does she shield her eyes from an overbright and harsh existence, or is her world flat and gray and indistinct? Her red shift is streaked with mud, her face, too, and I worry about her catching cold.

And every step I take, a locket the child is wearing around her neck bounces in the corner of my visual field. It gleams bright gold against the red shift even though my day has become colorless. I first noticed the chain to it when I was holding Topini under the bateau. The locket had slipped beneath her nightgown, and I pulled it out to make sure it wasn't choking her. Now as I walk, I watch that locket bounce. My head moves slightly with each bounce, each step. Sometimes I forget to watch my step because I am busy watching that locket bounce.

Up and down, up and down.

Up and down.

Up and down.

Like the insides of my stomach. The outside has a finely engraved *S* on the front of it. No need to open it. I knew what I'd find there.

A picture of Cap on one side and a picture of Mama on the other.

CHAPTER THIRTY-THREE

Uncle George isn't there the night Mama dies. He's gone to Alden to try to find Doc Mulcahey and bring him back. It's snowing, the Torch River Bridge impassable, so he has to leave the team at Hendersons' farm and use snowshoes from there. Six hours in the blizzard, six hours back to the team once Uncle George finds Doc Mulcahey.

Mama is gone before they get back.

Lots of crying. Or did I dream that? It's impossible for me to separate what happened from the dreams, nor can I distinguish what happened those few days from the thoughts I've been thinking for fifty years.

For instance, the room doesn't seem square but cone shaped. Mama is down in the pointed end of the cone, and the closer I get, the farther away she seems—like looking the wrong way down a pair of field glasses. And that is the first time I notice my field of vision start to get cloudy.

Mama has always been one color, but now she's more so. Her hair and eyebrows—even her eyes, which are a light, light hazel—match the color of her skin, which is sand gray, but it's more like an absence of color, like the shells of snails I'd seen in the garden when I was worming. This lack makes the edges of her face fuzzy and indistinct. And this amazes me. Really amazes me. Because despite her coloring and until that night, Mama has always seemed overwhelmingly obtrusive to me, even at a distance.

I pick up her left hand. She has small hands with slender fingers. They'd always had round, clean, pink nails, though the skin was mostly chafed from the never-ending scrubbing she did. Now her nails are thick, dirty, and yellow, the fingers curled up like a claw instead of lying flat, the hand swollen and hot like she'd been sitting too close to the fire, her wedding ring seared into the flesh. But the room is cold. Mama doesn't wake up when I take her hand. Her hair is matted on the pillow, and she has furrows between her brows and a frown on her face, like she's ciphering. Mama was good with figures, could do complicated sums in her head, said she could see them in neat long columns, and she liked that. The same expression is on her face—like she's concentrating for all she's worth on the answer to one of those problems, as if it takes every ounce of her strength and focusing power to answer it.

I guess it takes a lot of ciphering to die.

I didn't plead with Him or bargain with Him the night Mama died or even ask Him why because I knew it wouldn't matter. I figured Elizabeth Hopkins had begged and pleaded when her father lay lingering for two weeks after that logging accident, and Mrs. Jacobs had done plenty of begging when little Adam died of the diphtheria the fall before. And Cap had been crying and asking Him to give Mama His grace and mercy these last two nights while we were waiting for little Emily to come. There were plenty of better people than me asking for God's help, but I don't think that's why I didn't ask. This is the part that's tough to separate out because I couldn't have been thinking all this at the time, being only seven.

I just never thought He ran the world that way.

Prayer isn't asking for stuff; it's conversation, back and forth, like Emerson said. So I'm not sure why, but whenever they'd let me in to see Mama, there was only one thought in my mind. I'd stand there and stand there and stand there, watching her concentrate, thinking how could I help her get this thing done?

CHAPTER THIRTY-FOUR

I turned eighteen years old this last January, which makes Keane nineteen, nearly, and Kachina seventeen. Topini is about eleven. Uncle George, despite being ill, has packed us all four, bag and baggage, into the democrat wagon and driven us to Suttons Bay for the opening couple days of the Redpath DeLuxe Seven-Day Circuit, the Big Chautauqua Special, which, according to the *Progress*, has arrived "triumphant from the great cities of South Bend, Indianapolis, Louisville, and Lansing" and is due, so they say, to open next week in Chicago. Uncle George has insisted we go (He purchased tickets himself.) because he says we must somehow find a glimmer of light peeking through this infernal gloom. Uncle George has been planning the trip for weeks, and from the manner in which he's been talking about it, I've begun to think of it as the pilgrimage. Or sometimes the quest.

Every detail has been thought of. There is a cover for the wagon that Kachina and Topini and I will share and sleep under. Uncle George and Keane will pitch a tent close, down by the bay. We have camping equipment, cookware, food supplies (perishables will be purchased in Suttons Bay), appropriate clothing, and headgear. We have Topini's other red dress and two red balls. And plenty of handkerchiefs.

As we approach Suttons Bay, I hear "Alexander's Ragtime Band" playing. The community band is positioned on the depot platform awaiting the crowds from Traverse City, Northport, and Omena. As Uncle George drives through town, I notice there are lumbermen, fishermen, storekeepers, farmers, teachers—people from all backgrounds. There are Norwegians, Germans, Swedes, Frenchmen, and plenty of Anishinaabek from Peshabetown. Wagons arrive all day carrying farmers and their families. Wealthy resorters drive brand-new Maxwells, REOs, and Model T Fords.

Suttons Bay merchants down the entire two blocks from Lars Sogge's grocery to Nixie Steimel's hotel have draped their stores with bunting, and along both sides of the street the Grand Army of the Republic and Spanish-American vets have set up poles with new American flags that wave in the breeze and startle the horses as they pass. The ladies have red-and-green felt hats, and printed on them are the words "Redpath Chautauqua."

The tent takes up the whole clearing near the town square. The sides of the tent are lifted, and two rows of plank-board seating surround it. With the sides of the tent up, I can see a xylophone and a piano next to a platform stage. The air hangs heavy with humidity, and I'm sure there will be an electrical storm before the end of our two-day stay. Uncle George reads my mind.

Let's get this tent pitched and the canvas cover set up on this wagon, he says. In case we get ourselves a storm tonight. Better safe than sorry.

We agree with him.

I'm not sure I should have come at all, and my mood is rubbing off on everyone, especially Topini. Little upsets her. Not getting what she had in mind for dinner, that upsets her, or not being able to locate her red ball or red dress or red pajamas, that upsets her. But we can change her disposition simply by laughing or teasing, or with nothing more than a hug or kiss. Most of the time she simply reflects our personalities right back at us, good or bad.

The reason I shouldn't have come is because of Cap. Uncle George wouldn't hear of me staying behind, even though I explained things weren't right with him. I did leave food for him, and as Uncle George pointed out, he was clearheaded when he was out on the *Mabel.* So far, nobody but Uncle George and I were aware that Cap was any different.

But Christmas 1916 had come and gone without Cap taking any notice at all. Maybe that was partly because Mabel didn't come home for the holidays—she'd gone to stay with friends in Oxford. She hadn't been home for a visit in a year. We got an occasional letter from her reporting the essentials of her life, but Elk Rapids was no longer home to Mabel.

I'd cut down a small spruce to serve as a Christmas tree, big enough for the top of the kitchen worktable. Decorated it, hung stockings, got a turkey from Tower & Cole, stuffed it with oyster-and-sage stuffing, and cooked the trimmings, but Cap didn't seem to notice the day was different from any other. Didn't come to himself even when I gave him his new captain's hat with the leather trim (though he had smiled his secret smile) and didn't seem to notice that he'd neglected to give me a present at all.

And three times in the last six months Cap had called me Emma.

The first couple times I didn't think much about it. Parents are famous for running through the whole list of their offspring, that's for certain. Mrs. McLaughlin, who had six boys and three girls, was known to run through every other kid's name in the family twice before hitting the right one. But this seemed different.

Even so, Cap had been fine for more than a month afterward. His mood continued to improve. He started to fish with me in the evenings, which he hadn't done in years. One day we were packing up the gear to do just that when it happened again. We'd eaten a quick sandwich left over from the box lunches so we could make it to the creek in time for the evening brown drake hatch, which would happen at dusk. Cap was getting his fly vest situated and was rounding up his fly box, net, and extra line.

You remember that time I hurt my back helping Nate Johnson lift those flour barrels? he asked me. Oh, must have been ten years ago or more, and old Joe Hawley decided I needed a few extra days to rest it? Guess he got tired of all my bellyaching. And ran the whole run, both ways, with the *Ruth*? It was darned nice of him, too, because that meant he'd have to spend the night on each end and couldn't stay at home on the odd night. It was late September, Indian summer, I think, and hotter than Hades, and we decided we'd take the *Mabel* on down to Clam Lake and camp out for a few days, stay on the water to get the breezes, and maybe do some fishing on Clam River. You remember that?

Actually, I did remember. It was a few months before Mama died. She was pregnant with Emily, so the heat was getting to her. Mama and Mabel slept in the wheelhouse where there was privacy, and Cap and I camped below. I've wondered often why Mama and Cap didn't sleep together up in the wheelhouse that trip. There was an abandoned cabin we camped in one night down by the water, with a woodstove to cook on and a brick fireplace but no water, and we had used kerosene lamps for light. It had seemed another world. Cap rested on a mattress or fished a little now and then. Of course, Mama didn't fish. She sat in the shade, dunked her feet in the water, and read Tennyson. She and I took a walk, just the two of us. Along the lakeshore it was hot even at night, and Mama would stop and splash her face and hands from time to time.

Days are sure getting shorter, Mama said to me. Always hate to see the summer go, even now, when I'm so hot I can't stand it. It's sad somehow. She stopped and sat on a big rock several feet into the lake, letting her bare feet dangle. She put her hand to her stomach. You were a feisty one, she said and smiled at me. This baby could use your energy, honey-babe. She sure doesn't kick like you and Mabel used to. Seems to stretch a lot. And hiccups all the time. About enough to drive me batty. I don't think this baby will be the boy your daddy's counting on, though. No, I think she's another girl. Nothing wrong with that.

Mama had a way of leaning away, standing just out of range from me. From all of us. I was never sure why but suspected it wasn't that she didn't want to be touched but that she possessed an acute need to be reached for.

But what bothered me most about that trip was that Mama should have talked, should have had some premonition about upcoming events and should have moved into range. Should have given me important advice and lessons to live by.

That was a great trip, Cap said to me then. I think we caught a mess of lake trout and some perch and bass, if my memory serves, and cooked it all under the fire hood. And it sure was a welcome rest for my backside not to have to pole that boat through the river. Cap had that same smile on his face, which gave me a cold feeling inside. Yes, I told him. I remember.

Darned near as hot now as it was then, he said. And you've been working way too hard again cleaning and cooking. I wish you would let some of that go. I've always said it wasn't necessary for you to work so hard to please me, Emma. Really.

I searched Cap's face that day for any sign that he realized he'd made a mistake, but this time there was no chance of any confusion, not for either of us. There was nothing to say.

CHAPTER THIRTY-FIVE

The next two days of the festival hold a big schedule of events. I had read in the newspaper about how the chautauqua festivals were first formed in New York thirty years ago for the purpose of improving schools, establishing libraries, and enlightening teachers. According to the *Progress*, they taught Hebrew, Greek, French, and German, classical history and literature.

But over the years, many of them had degenerated to circus-type atmospheres highlighting politics, evangelical oratory, and popular music with no intellectual focus to speak of. I'm interested to see if this festival proves to be one of the degenerate ones.

Uncle George has gotten the tent pitched, and as he begins on the cover for the wagon, I take Topini down to the bay to wash off the road dust. Kachina decides to do the same. There are several boats anchored in the harbor, and singing and laughter bounce around the water. Topini bounces, too.

I sit her down on a rock in shallow water and sponge off her face, neck, and hands. Kachina seems grateful these days for the help I give her with the child and seldom acts as she did that day I came upon them collecting sap. Topini gasps and giggles as the cold bay water splashes her face. Her nose is running again; she was sick most of last winter with chest colds and ear infections. Kachina hovers over her because she is not as strong as other children. I worry, too, that one day she'll become truly ill.

I make an inspection of my handiwork. A good brushing will take most of the road dust from the child's hair, and maybe tomorrow we can take an early morning swim to get rid of the rest of the grime. I must remember to put some extra handkerchiefs in my satchel before we head for the festival.

You are good to her, Kachina says to me. I lift my head in surprise. There's been much conflict between Kachina and me. Could it ever be significantly different? Not under the circumstances, I tell myself. She smiles at me, takes Topini by the hand, and leads her to the wagon.

I change into a fresh dress inside Uncle George's tent and I see Kachina has put on a clean skirt and blouse. We have only one change of clothes for Topini (her other red dress) and we decide it would be better to save it for tomorrow. There are plenty of bugs tonight, at least near the trees, so I bring along a light blouse to protect my arms.

Moo-sic, Topini says as we enter the chautauqua tent. I see the instruments belonging to the Bohemian Orchestra, which is due to start any moment. There aren't many folding chairs left, but Keane finds some near the back for us, and I sit gratefully.

The evening consists of a serious talk by the Reverend Martin D. Hardin, a talk I sleep through parts of, about Christianity and the war. Then there are some newsreels on the Grand Canyon that Uncle George likes. And finally, for those still awake (since it's nearly midnight), a lady from Massachusetts recites poetry. The young woman's name is Margaret Springsted. She's dressed in a loose-fitting oyster-colored chemise dress with a small maroon-flowered print pulled in high at the waist with a matching fabric belt. She isn't wearing a hat, just a simple red flower over her left ear, and her hair has been bobbed, and I suspect even permanently waved. Her shoes are oyster colored as well with matching rosettes. She starts by reading Longfellow, which is a disappointment because everybody reads Longfellow. I wonder what they'd think of Rilke but decide this isn't the right crowd.

She is a slim blonde woman with a pasty complexion but dramatic eyes. Predictably, she recites "The Song of Hiawatha" for her first selection, and her voice is melodious, though perhaps not powerful enough—not that she can't be heard, only that her voice lacks timbre. She talks with her hands to the point that I feel nauseous, so I close my eyes, which helps, and all at once the woman's voice sounds pleasant.

I drift along on the words and think about how much I like them. Anyone's words. How wonderful it must be to write them and have them be yours because they could be changed or improved or borrowed even, and if they aren't yours and don't sit right with you, they can be ignored.

Seeing is different. If you see something, like a locket, you're stuck with it.

For her next selection, the woman has picked another Longfellow poem called "The Rainy Day," one I had memorized years ago to recite for school. I open my eyes as the woman starts the piece.

> The day is cold, and dark, and dreary;
> It rains, and the wind is never weary;

The woman stops reading for a moment, and her pasty complexion becomes whiter still, with a big red splotch here and there. Perhaps the pilgrimage has been too much for her, or the heat has finally gotten to her, or maybe she didn't have time for supper. She starts reciting again, but this time slower than ever.

> The vine still clings to the moldering wall,
> But at every gust the dead leaves fall,
> And the day is dark and dreary.

I think the woman said dreary, though the word barely leaves her lips when she falls to the floor, head hanging off the edge of the platform. A few people rush to her aid, and within moments the

Redpath's doctor is with her. Several men help gather her up, and before you can blink an eye, they have spirited her away, leaving me, and no doubt every other person in the tent, to wonder if she'd been there at all, except that one oyster-colored shoe has gotten shoved under the edge of the platform.

Several of us make our way to the front. I pick up the shoe and sit in an empty chair in the front row. Some of the people are milling about the tent. Others are still in their seats. I can't help myself: I finish the piece, still seated in the chair, but at least a third of the audience stops to listen to me.

> My life is cold, and dark, and dreary;
> It rains, and the wind is never weary;
> My thoughts still cling to the moldering Past,
> But the hopes of youth fall thick in the blast,
> And the days are dark and dreary.
>
> Be still, sad heart! and cease repining;
> Behind the clouds is the sun still shining;
> Thy fate is the common fate of all,
> Into each life some rain must fall,
> Some days must be dark and dreary.

I hear my voice resonate inside my head, deep for a woman, even to my own ears. One middle-aged man with patchy yellow hair and a sunburned scalp insists that I recite more, and soon dozens join in with "yes," or "please," or "that was wonderful," and I can hear Keane's voice in my ear, urging me, and before long, the patchy-haired fellow has led me to the platform and left me standing there, a solitary figure in my second-best dress, hair flying every which way. I smooth it to my head, stand, and decide I can recite no more Longfellow (primarily because I have no more committed to memory) and consider for a moment Emily Dickinson but feel dreamier even than Emily and settle on Yeats, which comes to mind because I have lately had a sudden and irrational desire to be old. .

I know I have begun to recite, though I can't seem to hear the words.

When You Are Old by W.B. Yeats

When you are old and grey and full of sleep,
And nodding by the fire, take down this book,
And slowly read, and dream of the soft look
Your eyes had once, and of their shadows deep;

How many loved your moments of glad grace,
And loved your beauty with love false or true,
But one man loved the pilgrim soul in you,
And loved the sorrows of your changing face;

And bending down beside the glowing bars,
Murmur, a little sadly, how Love fled
And paced upon the mountains overhead
And hid his face amid a crowd of stars.

The words are in my head—I can feel the power of them—and I wish I were old already, like the woman in the poem, and that the disappointments waiting for me would have happened already, because then at least I wouldn't have to be such a coward.

Now the words have stopped, and I'm aware of the quiet in the tent. Not one person has made a sound. Then there's deafening applause, or so it seems to me. A man saying he is James Hurt, the Redpath superintendent, is congratulating me and asking if I'd like to recite again tomorrow, but I tell him no. People are shaking my hand and complimenting me. They are smiling, happy for me, charmed by me, dozens of beaming, expectant faces. They understand what lies ahead for me. All my attempts at holding things back have been useless. Perhaps if I hold my breath, I think. . . . I've never tried that. If I don't exhale, things will have to stay as they are.

But I can see they all know better.

CHAPTER THIRTY-SIX

I didn't need to see them. Partly because I could've done without it, and partly because I didn't need to see them to get it.

It happens the next night, after the Penobscot Indian princess has left the stage. I'd taken Topini to the outhouse. But instead of sitting down when we come back, I stand with the child at the entrance to the tent. The soft glow from the hanging lanterns turns Kachina's skin the color of cocoa or more like the maple syrup they collected. She's wearing a white cotton dress I've never seen before. It's slightly too big and carefully worked along the round neckline with red-and-black beadwork as usual, and it's belted at her narrow waist, which makes her figure appear fuller. Her long black hair is a single braid down her back, dividing her body into two equal configurations.

Kachina leans closer against Keane's arm and shoulder, like she knows they are stealing these few extra moments, and I know Kachina needs nothing more than the present, has no thought for down the road, a state of mind I've never been capable of and resent seeing in her. As if the next moment could possibly take care of itself when I know it can't. It must be maneuvered, angled into place, coaxed and wheedled, richly wagered for, none of which comes without a struggle or without some cost from today. I no more think these thoughts than I realize Kachina does pay. In order for me to accomplish thinking of this sort, I would have to stop caring. Kachina can care *and* let go of tomorrow. It's not the caring that makes you vulnerable; it's the wanting that does it.

The band is playing "I Want a Girl," and a few couples begin to move dreamily around the platform, imagining themselves dancing like Irene Castle and whatever her husband's name is.

Keane pulls Kachina up by the hand and close to his body.

Dancing is imperative.

Dance with me, he says. Or I imagine that's what his lips are saying as they move.

And she does.

KACHINA IS UNAPOLOGETIC about it all, which makes me feel better.

But the pilgrimage is, in a way, the culmination to all that has happened that summer. We'd found Topini alive in the woods, which, when you think about it, was nothing short of a miracle. And we didn't have to kill the dog, which would have upset Keane, so it would've upset me.

Kachina said *The Day* was *waiting*. She wouldn't tell me what she meant by that—and seemed sorry she'd mentioned it—or even what The Day was, but I thought I understood.

And I wondered if it was enough.

Uncle George used to say it didn't matter in the least what happened to you, what stuff you had or didn't have, or even where you ended up on this planet. He said that if you're here at all, it can only be your reaction to a circumstance that has validity, so in that sense it's important that *something happens,* that there are wants and things to not want, and happenings—good *and* bad, because otherwise we never find out who we are. I think that's what Kachina meant by The Day waiting. If certain things happened, we'd understand a bit.

CHAPTER THIRTY-SEVEN

Final day of the festival.

We stop, Kachina and me, next to a small tent the color of unbleached muslin, one of many located behind the larger chautauqua performance tent. A woman of about forty is sitting behind a dark mahogany table, and on that table rests a large doily, and on that sits a white, androgynous bust of the human head sculpted of clay and elaborately mapped out in a convolution of black intersecting lines. The woman isn't dressed in scarves and bold-colored peasant clothes like the fortune-teller in the adjoining tent but is wearing white—some type of Red Cross attire, minus the cross. Her blond hair is knotted severely, an affect suggesting things medical. A bald man sits in the chair on the opposite side of the table, and the woman is talking about "the moral sentiments—imitation and mirthfulness." The woman gives us a glance, so Kachina and I back away from the entrance, giving the little man privacy.

We'll wait a minute for him to leave, I say.

Kachina stares at me. She's close enough I can reach out and touch her cheek, but I've come to recognize this separation that appears out of nowhere, like she's standing behind a curtain of cascading water.

We'll wait, she agrees.

I kick stones around in the dirt with my shoe, but Kachina is motionless. Head tilted. Listening to The Day, as she calls it. I suppose she hears nothing less than the murmured confidences of God pouring from the sky. I tilt my head, too. I hear children screaming and the sound of wagon wheels sliding in the gravel. A boat whistle squalls from the direction of the harbor, and the band, which I'd seen earlier on the platform at the depot, is playing "Alexander's Ragtime Band" again. Someone in the brass section misses a note, and it collides in my head with the sound of Kachina's waterfall. But I hear no murmurs from God.

I glance up. The sky is enigmatic—shifting clouds one minute, brilliant sun the next. We share separateness, Kachina and me, but we share oneness, too. We share March winds and slow-flowing maple. Spring floods and August droughts. Bad medicine, good fishing. We share the knowledge of how difficult (and exquisitely beautiful) a day becomes for someone who struggles even to hold a spoon. The steady accumulation of days that in the end can only add up to zero.

But have we become friends, I wonder? Kachina and me?

Come in, the lady says to us. The man is gone, but it seems that instead of the false head, the man has left his bald dissected brain sitting on the table in front of us. Next to that sits an enormous fishbowl crammed full of quarters and dollar bills. I add one dollar bill more. The woman owes me seventy-five cents but makes no attempt at restitution.

We sit in the wooden folding chairs in front of the table and wait while the woman pulls out a couple two-dimensional maps of a head neatly drawn on pieces of white paper. Kachina pushes her chair back from the table and is leaning away from it, watching the woman as she runs bony fingers over my head, examining the contours of my scalp. Kachina catches my eye. The waterfall is gone, and her expression has the effect of a hard shove in the chest. I've miscalculated; I can feel it. It would be better, I think, to stand up and leave, but I can't move. Kachina mesmerizes coyotes and deer and people and the occasional reptile into compliance or, more usually, robust good health. It's a gift that terrifies me but leaves me transported, while I have a gift as a storyteller, a modest gift at that.

In order to tell someone else's story, you must disappear in it, Kachina would say. You must be willing to drown in it. Let go, she'd say. Let go of the edge. I can hear her saying something similar in my mind, and she seems to have me pinned in my seat by the sheer force of her will.

Aptitudes, the woman says now. Phrenology is particularly useful for discovering what strengths a person possesses. The bumps in the skull correspond to the development of the brain, which governs each personality characteristic. Three major groups—the propensities, the moral sentiments, and the intellectual faculties.

At no point does the woman address Kachina.

Instead she points to the front of my head. Broad forehead, she says. Of particular note is the atypical development of Area A. The Individuality organ controls power of observation and discrimination. Eventuality controls memory. The Comparison organ is large and controls reasoning and analysis. Speakers, lawyers, poets—all have highly developed Comparison organs. Language and Color, this area close to the eye—is enlarged as well. An extension of the Causality organ denotes great originality of mind. I will warn you that overmaturity or undermaturity of any organ transforms a virtue into a vice, in this case leading to hypercritical thinking and obsessive attention to irrelevant detail.

She points behind my ear. Vitativeness organ, she says, holds the zest for life. Very puzzling in this case. It's not clear in the configuration of the head whether this organ is overly large, displacing Combativeness, or whether one or the other is nonexistent. The woman sits, circles the areas of the head on the sheet of paper, areas that apparently correspond to my skull. She pulls out pertinent information, hands it to me. The diagram, I imagine, will enable me to carry my head around, refer to it in moments of crisis or concern. In this way one can never really lose one's head, not when it is conveniently tucked in one's pocket.

Now it's Kachina's turn. But the woman doesn't touch Kachina's hair, doesn't invade her scalp as she has done mine. Just walks around and around her chair for several minutes. Kachina doesn't watch her circling but instead sits rigid. She ignores me and stares at the blank muslin tent wall.

The woman stops orbiting. She doesn't point to Kachina's head. Instead she sits and points to the white dissected cranium on the table in front of her, to the very back part of the still, white head, Area F. She starts talking, circling various sections on the drawing, all sections located near the base of the skull. Inhabitiveness, the woman says. This organ is pronounced and indicates a person's love for his home or country. You have not the spirit of the gypsy. She points behind the ear. Combativeness organ reveals the power of resistance and courage, which in your case is extended, but it would do well for you to remember temperance as the Destruction organ immediately over the ear is large as well.

The sun disappears abruptly, and a gust of wind raises the hair on the back of my neck. The woman points to the top of the statue's head. The organs of Spirituality and Veneration, she says, somewhat overlarged, can sometimes lead to a refusal to accept new ideas simply because they're new, a tendency to idolizing without any attempt to discover if the idol is worthy of adoration.

The woman continues marking up the head on the sheet of paper, her bony fingers brutally squeezing ink from the fountain pen. When she's done, she retrieves more information from the drawer in front of her. I examine the white bust and wonder what has happened to the front part of Kachina's brain. Kachina seems to be wondering as well. Her fingers move to her forehead, then down, trace the scar on her right cheek. The woman's fingers hover over her forehead. Is her brain there, or has it shriveled like dried sage? Or perhaps she is wondering if her brain even belongs to her at all. Maybe it has become a collective brain existing not as a pulsating living brain but the diminutive perception of a thought.

I can see these thoughts occurring to Kachina, see her wondering if they might even try to remove her brain from her skull, send it off to some segregated Indian school, like the one they sent Hototo to, and return it to her only after it has become untainted and snowy white. Clean and empty. Like a new, dry sponge.

But this ridiculous woman is nothing to Kachina; I can see that. This is all about us, Kachina and me.

Kachina watches me, and I try to survive the shock, the brutal transition of dangling high above the swells in relative safety one moment only to be submerged in an icy sea of her the next. Then I realize friendship is like that: dangerous and messy and tentative in a way blood ties can never be.

You must be willing to drown.

Kachina's expression has once again become rapt, and I tilt my head to hear, too. The Day is quiet but audible to Kachina: soft soughing through the birch trees, the cedars and red pines, like a mother's sweet, crooning lullaby. Kachina has been listening to voices arising from generations gone long before, resonating down a funnel of years to generations yet to come, while I have only my own deaf ears.

I hear nothing except the river. The water tears at me, the current threatening to sweep me away, drag me with the undertow, a place I've been lodged all this time. I can taste Kachina's sweat on my upper lip, feel her perspiration drip down my armpits and between my breasts, feel the dampness even between my legs. I lick my lips, and my tongue feels the indentation of her scar.

I haven't let go of the edge, but I can feel my fingers start to open.

The woman's back is turned to me. My Destruction-Temperance organ runs crazy roughshod over my Comparison-Reasoning organ, and I pick up the cold stone head from the table. Using both hands, I bring it crashing to the seat of my wooden folding chair.

A dollar bill dances crazily in the breeze.

CHAPTER THIRTY-EIGHT

Trout don't like to feed in the middle of a drought. I've never understood that. Who has it better in the middle of a drought than a fish? If there wasn't so much as a damned olive hatching, you'd think the trout would be so hungry they'd take a chance, visible or not. But I'm not expecting to see flies coming off the water and I'm sure not expecting to see a fish.

In the fall of 1917 Keane and I fish together for the last time. Keane wants to go to our favorite fishing spot on the westerly end of Yuba Creek. It's dusk, unseasonably hot, with a bit of a breeze coming from the west. It's a long walk, and I'm thinking I'd rather swim than fish, and Shadow probably agrees with me, but Keane is ready.

Dry flies, he says then. That's what we need today. Something midsize. The mayflies are coming off like no tomorrow. Look at 'em.

He's right. I hadn't noticed, but that's what they are all right. A big fly for so late in the year, though not so large as a giant mayfly or even a brown drake. I can feel Keane's excitement because they provide a change from the tiny flies of late summer or the monotonous blue-winged olives that hatch several times throughout the season, starting in early spring.

The white mayfly has a white thorax during the dun stage then turns slightly darker, more gray, a couple days later in the spinner stage. It has three tails, like a tiny white fairy. All at once I'm envious of the gossamer-winged creatures, so virginal and colorless. So light. So directed. One purpose: *mate and die.*

You're right, I say. I search my box lunch container for a medium-size fly, a couple light-colored ones, and one a bit darker in case they're preferring the spinners. I hook several to my blouse pocket, tie the net to my belt loop and the wicker creel around my shoulder. I take off my shoes, roll up my pant legs and follow Keane, who has been making similar preparations, into the river. We can see jagged heat lightning several miles to the west, over the bay, and it reminds me of a newspaper article about several people who had been hit by lightning and killed at Sleeping Bear Dunes on a bright sunny day, which seemed to me to be a case of God really speaking to you.

We fish close together that night, which isn't usual. We make a few short side casts upriver to see how eager they're feeling. The water is cold. Our shoulders bump a few times as we negotiate toeholds. I notice Keane's face is filling out. There's something peaceful, but I see regret there as well.

There aren't many people like Kachina, I say to him. People who do what's necessary and never waste a moment with regret.

He nods. There's much in that space that surrounds Kachina, he says, but regret isn't one of them.

It was Keane who got me thinking about space. Space as Place. Over the years I've come to realize that space is not empty. People spend their whole lives trying to figure out what lies within it or trying desperately to fill it. But I've come to realize that certain amounts of space are necessary.

Kachina believes people are responsible for their own pain, Keane says, but with a question in his voice, as though he thinks she might be wrong, too. Was she? I thought she was wrong at the time, and there was more I couldn't articulate. Finally I got hold of one thought.

Don't you think it helps to understand why? I ask him. In order to plan?

What difference does it make? he answers.

That makes me angry, and we don't talk for a long time. Keane catches a fifteen-inch brookie and then maybe a thirteen-incher in spite of his halfhearted fishing. He fills his creel with wet grass and leaves before he puts the fish in, while I do nothing but move my line around. Flailing.

You have a gift, Welly.

He's referring to my voice, and we both know as well the topic he is avoiding. Though it has nothing to do with what is going on between us, I think about my voice for a few minutes, how it's like a shiny piece of expensive jewelry much too grand to wear. Once in a while you pull it out, polish it up, admire it for a bit, then put it back in the drawer along with the dream—fostered, protected, a prize, something I can retrieve someday and sell or hang around my neck for people to admire. But for now it's all the more special because I don't have to share it.

I might do something with it, I say.

Keane keeps talking. Shadow here made sure I'd never have to get involved in this war, but I'm going to medical school, he says. He says this as if there isn't much difference between the two. Though most animal doctors don't bother with school and learn by trial and error, he doesn't think that's right and says it won't be long before they need certification, the same as people doctors. He's saved enough money to go to school, whether his father helps him or not, and he will because there isn't a single veterinarian in all of Antrim County. He plans, he says, on coming back.

I'm glad you won't ever have to go, I say then. Wilson's War to End All Wars.

But I'm thinking of Cap's future, thinking that farming or fruit growing will be the only viable means of creating a livelihood here in Elk Rapids for some time to come for those too old or infirm to get into the war. Keane means to fit himself into that picture.

But Cap is no farmer.

Except for the special excursions, the steamboat runs have been empty this year, and there will be no winter work in the lumber camps again. Dexter & Noble closed four of their five camps after the spring log run, all but Pressy. And Goldfarb's Clothing Store closed in March along with one of the apothecary stores, two of the saloons, and all but one blacksmith shop. No one had opened another smithy shop after Grandpa Sharp died last year because it was clear there was no need for more than one.

We've all been doing our best to ignore the exodus.

Keane knows what's coming, and I realize there are decisions to be made. But even that is denied me in the end. Kachina said there was nothing to decide. It was as it had always been, as it should be, that my path was plain in front of me.

The words reverberate inside my head. I think I complain to Keane about this, though I don't remember if he makes any comment. I talk until the subject peters out.

Do I leave her? I ask him then. I'm pretty sure I ask him, but maybe not.

I think about Uncle George and the lessons he'd taught me, how he'd tell me to picture the words. I was good at that part. Open your mouth, he'd say to me.

The evening dissolves into night and then deeper night, but we are reluctant to leave the stream. I'm sure we talk about Keane's mother, his father, Cap's strangeness. Mostly we stand in the river, moving upstream, then down, neither of us pretending to cast anymore, carcasses of white mayflies strewn across the water's surface, the river carrying them past us in silent decorum. When it's done, we step out of the stream together, almost in unison, which is how I know Keane wants it.

As I think about that night, it reminds me of the day I guided for the Purple Gang, though I didn't realize that's who they were at the time. I recognized Bernstein's picture years later in the *Detroit Free Press*.

CHAPTER THIRTY-NINE

George Sharp is no longer with us. George had become a nuisance. With mind and health well gone, ambition vanished, he was derelict on a limitless sea. Saturday Super Maxwell took him to Bellaire and turned him over to the county authorities. Now it's the infirmary or the state hospital.

—*Elk Rapids Progress*, August 14, 1917

George Sharp committed to Northern Michigan Asylum by probate court.

—*Elk Rapids Progress*, August 18, 1917

I SEE DOZENS OF PEOPLE stooped over in the fields hoeing and picking vegetables in the hot sun: beans and corn from what I can see. Some are leading cattle toward the low white outbuildings in the back. Some are employees; others volunteer. (They understood the benefits of sweat back then. Therapy, they called it. I called it enterprising.)

Northern Michigan Asylum has been the largest employer in Grand Traverse County for some time, a place where the "therapeutic landscape" was an integral part of the "moral architecture" and where "moral treatment" was provided that could cure what had been "hitherto considered incurable." The hospital is directly across the street from another large employer, a whorehouse called the Swamp House. It's a toss-up, I think, which therapy would be most beneficial.

The main building is located on Gray Street, appropriate, though parts of the complex have more cheerful-sounding names running through them like Blue Street and Red Street.

I walk up the main walkway, past the spot Kachina sat last summer before they realized they needed to let Topini come home. Sitting there this time would do me no good.

The white concrete walls of the asylum close in on you despite the twenty-foot ceilings. The mammoth Victorian structure must have seemed enormous to the people who built it, but I can see it isn't big enough. Maybe it's due to the sheer number of unfortunates, upwards of three thousand, housed within its walls. But I don't think so.

I notice that the walls (twenty-one inches thick, I find out later) are all rounded and equipped with mahogany handrails. No corners or edges anywhere. Nothing sharp or distinct. Wire covers the windows, and the five-panel oak doors with transoms over them have circular peepholes for viewing inmates. The men occupy the section with even room numbers; the women's side has odd. There is a women's wing of equal proportion to the men's. I've often wondered if women were crazy in equal numbers or whether they were more easily discarded. All a man had to do was sign his name and drop her off. I read a few years later that "mental retardation, depression, barroom brawls, fear, business reversals, sadness, nostalgia" were among the maladies that could lead you here. There were other things, of course.

Being sick, drunk, and a public disturbance could do it.

How'd you get here? Uncle George asks me.

There is a painting of the lighthouse on Old Mission Peninsula a foot above his head. I can't make out the artist's signature. I think about standing to read it, then don't. They are into light and beacons.

The train, I say. Old Pere Marquette was how I'd gotten there, on the flyer. Changed trains at the Williamsburg spur.

A salmon-colored curtain, one of at least twelve, forms a rectangle around us. Tuneless humming noises come from one rectangle across the room, soft crying from another. The room smells like a mixture of hard cider and disinfectant.

You won't make the run back home in time, he says.

No, I say. I would spend most of my savings and stay in one of the hotels in Traverse.

A nurse materializes, then shifts about in the background, but we ignore her. We're good at ignoring.

Time passes while Uncle George dozes. Then he opens his eyes. He seems to have dropped half his weight since the chautauqua festival, though he's not pale. He's feverish, and there's a readiness to him. His arms are stiff and straight at his sides. He's using all his effort to keep from gripping the bedsheets. Instead, he pushes down with his palms with what looks like a Herculean effort, enough force to lift himself into the air or push the bed through the hardwood floor.

Mostly it's quiet here, he says. It's the quiet that gets to me. His copy of Rilke sits on the table next to the bed along with his reading glasses.

Go to school, he says. But don't teach. It drains you too much for thinking.

I won't, I answer him. I watch his face and think that he's fatherly, something that has never occurred to me before, and then I wonder why it hasn't.

What is it about a person that makes him fatherly? And why do so few men possess it, even though so many are fathers? Fatherly men lack that sharp, selfish, opportunistic edge of other men, and they invariably become teachers in one form or another.

Uncle George was a teacher.

Uncle George pulls himself up on the pillows and gestures toward the door.

You know, he says, someday there will be places like this everywhere, different kinds of them: places people go to recuperate, old folks' homes, poorhouses, stuff like that. Society's great anesthetizers. We'll pay our few pennies and watch poverty and sickness stare us in the face because we've already given our share. Their way might help a few people who need it. Problem is, the rest of us, we *need* the pain. Can't pay someone else to feel it for you. It's what makes us human. It's much harder to walk past suffering if you think you may be the only one who can alleviate it. We'll be numb, separated from ourselves. A few people will gain, but we'll *all* lose. It wasn't like that for your father.

No, it definitely wasn't like that for my father.

Uncle George's face glistens with sweat from the effort of talking. I turn my head to the right and stare at the salmon-colored curtain, but I can feel his eyes. I pick up the Rilke and start reading, though I've had the entire book memorized for years. As has he, I'm sure.

No, he says, and he takes the book from my hand, lays it across what's left of his chest. And I can hear the next words coming before he says them.

Close your eyes.

Picture the words.

UNCLE GEORGE WAS RIGHT. You *do* get sick of other people's words. Like that nurse after the cancer surgery, changing bandages on my violated chest five years ago, in 1957, patting my arm and saying over and over again, *You'll get used to it, honey.* Finally, when I could take it no longer, I asked her what they *did with it,* to which she replied that it never occurred to them that I might want it. No one ever had before. But *I do,* I told her. The Indians used to make *lovely* coin purses out of them. See if you can locate it for me.

I was only partially kidding. People kept fingers and buried limbs, didn't they?

Uncle George left me his collection of "other people's words": all his books. And ten thousand dollars in cash he had in a saddlebag at the livery stable, part of which I used to go to school.

He was the only father I ever knew.

One of the best-known characters of Elk Rapids passed away last Thursday night at the state asylum at Traverse City when George E. Sharp breathed his last. George Sharp owned the dray and bus line and livery in this village and a couple years ago was considered prosperous. His career since is too well known to our people to need comment. He was born in Wheatley, Canada, in 1865, and died when he should have been in the prime of his life. His brother Ira came to Traverse City and brought the remains to Elk Rapids for interment. Rev. Charles Daniels officiated at the grave.

—*Elk Rapids Progress,* August 31, 1917

Cap

CHAPTER FORTY

I got the dynamite from the old Dexter & Noble lumber camp at Grass River. They always keep enough to blow a hundred logjams to kingdom come, and I don't need much. I been workin' there winters so many years, I know nobody'll think twice 'bout seeing me round there or miss the little bit of blast I need for my purposes.

I don't need much 'cause it isn't 'bout makin' a big noise. No, not at all. Not 'bout goin' out with a bang. Nothin' like that—I never was one to bring attention to myself. On the other hand, if I see somethin' needs doin', I'm the one to step up. I've stepped up to do things nobody else wanted any truck with all my life.

And this is a thing needs doin'.

It was the sinkin' of the *Ida* give me the idea.

I was nothin' more'n a kid first time I worked as a deckhand aboard the *Ida* in 1880. She was one of the first steamers to run the inland waterway connecting Bellaire, Eastport, and Elk Rapids here in the north country of Michigan. It was bustling back then, a lumber town. Not friendly 'xactly 'cause even then it sat on the hard edge of things.

Nearly thirty years ago I learnt my shippin' trade from old John French, who wasn't a bad sort. I guess you'd have to know he weren't a bad sort since he'd been married once to my mother a few years before they'd decided things weren't workin' out, and then she married my father, George Sharp, the local blacksmith. But we got along pretty good, John and me, so much so that he took me on as junior partner in the endeavor and taught me most of what I know 'bout boats. It was my brother George took to the dray business, took to horses, and one of us in the business was enough for my pa.

That was what we Sharps did for nearly forty years—transport people. There was a need for that then. No automobiles, no private launches. It was simple, and in takin' people "somewhere," George and me, we'd be part of where they ended up.

But it was the water that was my callin'.

I s'pose I could have been a hand on an exotic ship bound for China, but I chose to stay inland. Em was the biggest reason for that choice, though I don't think I were ever made for big water. So it's been *Mabel* and me goin' on forty years, my good partner Joe Hawley performing half the inland route with her sister ship, *Ruth*.

Mabel is fifty-four feet in length overall, fourteen feet across the beam, and draws four feet, four inches of water. She's a passenger/light-freight steamer made of solid oak, built by George H. Notter Co., Buffalo, New York, in the year 1893. She weighs nineteen gross register tons, with a single screw rig of fifty indicated horsepower. That's the specs on her. She was first called the *Bellaire*, but me and Joe soon renamed both boats after our oldest daughters.

Mabel and Ruth.

And we had us a good run. I know I shouldn't complain 'bout that.

But the world's changin'.

There are private launches now, and they been buildin' roads round these lakes the last few years for motorin'. Maybe George saw it comin' 'fore I did, and that's why he took so to drinkin' and why they took him off to North'n Michigan Asylum. They're talkin' 'bout a thing called Prohibition, but I'm not sure I don't agree with George: you can't save people from themselves. And they're talkin' 'bout women votin'. And a world war that it seems President Wilson has seen fit to involve us in.

"You gotta face this," George said to me awhile back. But he didn't mean the steamboat business. We were close once, George and me, but I didn't answer him much in later days. He pounded and railed at me about this and that, seemed to think I didn't see life clearly.

"She's gone, Ira," he'd say to me. He means Em, of course. They all think my lovely wife's gone, but of course *I* see her. I know what they think. They think I mix her up with my daughter Welly, that I'm not quite right in the head, but it's them who's blind. It's me who sees things clearly, me who does things have to be done, as I said before, when I can see others aren't up to them. And I know Em understood some of those choices I made.

"It's what it is," she says to me. "You didn't have any choice."

There's prices to be paid for vision that clear.

I remember Em was sick and tired. She knew what it was lay in front of me, what prices it would mean to be paid by Mabel and Luella 'cause it was them would pay most. And I knew she didn't blame me.

George never understood. But it's not me lying in Elk Rapids Cemetery, like George.

Luella had been suspicious this mornin' when I showed up with the champagne in my best captain's uniform. And a whole load of groceries and other sundries.

"Where you goin', Cap?" she asked me. "You don't drink champagne."

"Got it for a private excursion today, Welly. Now don't you worry," I told her.

"You know we're going to have to do something different, don't you, Cap?" she'd said to me. And I'd nodded. There'd been talk of selling *Mabel* to East Jordan to make the Charlevoix tourist runs. People hintin' that I'd have to take up some other kind of trade. Sam in the dry goods store won't meet my eye, which is how most of 'em are round town. But it's them don't see clearly if they think that could happen. At least the *Mabel* part of that suggestion is plain foolishness.

I dumped the turkey and potatoes on the counter.

"Fix us a feast, Welly," I told her. "It's cool enough to cook, and it's a day for it. Do your magic."

Then I stopped down to the cemetery and talked a few minutes to Em, not that it was necessary. And I told her what I had in mind, not that that was necessary, either. And when I left, I tipped my cap to her like I done the first time I met her down in the square, right before we'd both watched as poor Charlie Spaulsbury got killed when the rope slipped off that capstan and—so much heart in her—he'd died right there in her arms. Like I might as well have done, too; she had that much effect on me. I knew George felt the same 'bout her, but it was Em and me from the start.

And it was Em and me now.

So that's what got me here now on this dock, the harbor quiet today, it bein' Sunday. I take off my good jacket and cap and start scrubbin' and polishin' inside the wheelhouse. Just as I'd done as a kid on the *Ida*, I get a broom, sweep the deck, then pour buckets of water from the lake on it, scrub some more, even a bit on hands and knees, which hurts but feels good, too. I grab a bottle of linseed oil and spend a good twenty minutes polishin' the two-foot railing inside the gangplank, where thousands of people have grabbed hold as they stepped on board the *Mabel* these many years. I give special care here and on the benches that line the lower deck, which is worn shiny in places.

We transport freight but mostly the fine tourist crowd, sometimes a private excursion. *Mabel's* decks hold upward of fifty people. But she was a tug once, and she and me still dredge the river to keep it runnin' free.

Mabel lists slightly, portside, and she has to be coaxed and wheedled off sandbars with barge poles and the right ballast. But just when you think you've had all you can take from her, she can rescue you, float you easy through reeds threatenin' to haul you aground.

It was the *Ida* sinkin' give me the idea, like I said. I'd been bringing *Ida* back from Clam River just last fall where she'd been dry-docked since '03, me intendin' to repair her and put her up for sale. Amos Martin had made a couple stopgap patches to the hull and slid her into the water for me, and when I showed up, we talked 'bout sea captains we knew once, captains that once piloted the *Jenny Silkman* or the elegant *Queen o' Lakes*, owned by Dexter & Noble. Talked 'bout the old days but nary a word 'bout times to come. Amos give me a quick salute then as I pulled out of harbor, towing the *Ida* behind the *Mabel*, and we both knew what that salute meant.

It was a hot Indian summer day, and I remember thinkin' how much Em liked those kinda days. My youngest daughter, Luella, was with me, and just as we entered the lower end of Clam Lake, she yelled out "Cap!" and pointed at the *Ida*. The old steamer had been listin' bad, but now she was buckin', a kind of gut-wrenchin' motion like someone havin' the dry heaves. We heard the sharp crack of wood splinterin', metal creakin', and the *Ida* broke into two massive chunks and disappeared faster than I could believe possible. There was a wall of water, a tidal wave hammerin' our faces caused by us still haulin' the front end of the *Ida*, so I jumped up to the wheelhouse and pulled the *Mabel* out of gear, water droppin' from roof to deck making sounds like cap guns goin' off, and it all happenin' so fast, as I said, it was almost like we'd been ambushed. I expected the water to turn rusty red, but there wasn't so much as a speck of rust, bubbles just risin' to the surface of the water, water icy green and then still like death.

At first we said nothin'. Then I'd nodded at Luella who looked shell-shocked, and I said to her, "Well, bless her heart." I pulled out a hatchet from the wheelhouse, and with two sharp cuts, I set *Ida* free.

It wasn't a bad day when all was said and done. Not a bad day. I could only hope for as much for myself.

The *Mabel*'s engine has been runnin' this last half hour, warmin' up while I work, and now I wipe the sweat off my brow with a kerchief, put my jacket and cap back on, and guide her away from the dock for the last time. For a minute, it looks like Luella watching me from across the street at Morrison's. But when I look more careful, I don't see no one. The *Mabel* chugs softly, sweetly, like she does on her good days, and the sound is one I won't never forget.

We pull into Elk River, and I remember again how many times *Mabel* and I dredged her, and I steer between the stumps, throw a bit more coal in the furnace, the steam chuggin' out like what was comin' out of the pipe I light for myself and let swirl 'round my head.

And we head out of the river and into the lake.

I need to get out far enough so there won't be no damage to limb or livelihood, but I fancy her in close enough, I can think of her just out of the river into Elk Lake. Not in a place she'd be obstructive. Not in the river but in a place they'll have to give her a wide berth.

It takes about ten minutes to chug out, and there isn't nobody else on the water.

I haven't had a sip of alcohol since I was twenty-four or so, 'bout the time I became so disgusted with George over it. But this is a special occasion. I open one of the bottles and pour some into a tin cup, take a nice big swallow. The other bottle I take up to the front of the *Mabel*'s hull and crack it over her bow, sharp, just like me and Joe Hawley did the day we bought her, back when she was the *Bellaire* and we first set her to work on the waterway. And then I sit and think for a while 'bout what decides a man to do a thing. Whether it's upbringin' or bad circumstance or some flaw of his nature when his decisions seem lackin'. Or just good luck when it seems he's lived a charmed life. Whether most men decide anythin' at all or mostly let life decide for 'em. And I think 'bout what decided me to do certain things in my life. How good a husband I'd been or a father. And I don't know, that's all I can say. I don't damned well know.

But what can be said is that I took things upon myself.

We reach the edge of Elk Lake, *Mabel* and me. I pull her out of gear, sit on the stool, and finish a couple glasses more of the champagne and listen as the first mosquitoes of the evenin' buzz past my ears. It's maybe six thirty or seven o'clock now and clear, sun low enough in the sky to make that rust glow in the water I'd expected to see when the *Ida* sank.

I take off my captain's uniform and hang it neatly on a hanger in the wheelhouse, put my captain's hat over the gear lever, peel down right to my skivvies. It seems a little warmer than it did, close to seventy degrees maybe, and the work of shinin' up the old steamer has brought some warmth to the old bones, too.

I haven't brought too much charge, not enough to blow her to smithereens. And then for a minute I'm sorry I haven't. I think maybe Em is wrong: maybe I did have other choices, and I feel sick down deep inside me like the devil is wringin' my soul out to dry, and there isn't nothin' left of me when he's done.

Smithereens.

George. George. George's gone to Alden to try to find Doc Mulcahey and bring 'im back. It's snowin', the Torch River Bridge impassable, so he has to leave the team at Hendersons' farm and use the snowshoes from there. Six hours in the blizzard, six hours back to the team once George finds Doc Mulcahey.

I know he won't make it.

The room don't seem plumb. The closer I get to Em, the less solid she seems.

Days of trying to birth my baby has sucked her dry. She'd managed to deliver without Doc, but there were nothin' left of her but heart.

She weren't conscious, but we talked it over mind-to-mind like we always done. I'd been prayin', but I was done with that now, and I didn't want nothin' comin' between Em and me and those moments we had left.

"She was your daughter," George said when he got back. "You have three daughters, not two."

Three daughters. Mabel and Luella. My two daughters, different from each other, but strong.

And then I can feel her in my arms. Frailer, smaller, wrong, like Morrisons' lamb that didn't make it.

For a minute I think of puttin' my uniform back on, endin' this a different way, but I see Luella now, standin' on the shore, wavin' at me. But no, it's not Luella. It's Em, after all, and she'll be waitin' dinner on me. So I light the charge, which I've put in the appropriate spot down in the hull, and dive into the water.

For a minute I wonder if I can swim fast enough to escape harm, and I think to myself that would be okay if I don't, but then it seems I swim and swim with nothin' happenin' at all. As I turn to see if maybe the charge has gone out, the orange blast lights up the dusky sky.

I watch as the *Mabel* slowly sinks into the sunset orange pool, and I tread water until I hear the engine choke and then I hear 'er die. I can't hear nothin' then but my hands treading that water, a gentle whooshing sound, and I smell somethin' hot, a smell like Em leavin' the iron too long on a wet shirt. I swim to shore where I can see she is waitin' for me. And we walk home together, me in my underclothes and she holdin' my arm like that first walk we took together in '99.

It's all about me and Em now. Like it's always been. I can feel her hand on my arm, her fingers light but insistent. She never turns her head to look at the people watchin' us go.

And I don't never again look back to'ard the water.

Luella

CHAPTER FORTY-ONE

We never found out where he got the dynamite. He had plenty of access to it around the lumber camps. We knew that. He wasn't so crazy that he didn't know the times were changing and there would be no place in it for him soon.

I think about all of us. Curiously, I think about Mabel a lot. Mabel and me. How she'd been excluded right along while I had not been so much included as made an accomplice. It wasn't my age, I don't think; it was my willingness to sacrifice that made me the one.

Through the years Mabel and I never discussed those early years in Elk Rapids, but we built a tortured kind of friendship. For a while, we both lived in Oxford, Michigan. Later, I moved to Birmingham, which was still close enough for frequent visits. But the spaces remained; Mabel made it clear she had no curiosity about what she might have suspected, and I've learned enough about spaces to know that they stay there as long as a person wants them to.

But this is what I do remember about Mabel the person: she was married for a brief time to a man named Taylor who died early of a stroke or heart attack. She didn't have children, which came as a relief to her, probably, because she got enough of them teaching all those years in Oxford. Did Mabel do justice to the slugs and misfits that I never could have? I hope so.

I remember she had a particular yen for peanut clusters and peppermint. That she was on the basketball team and won awards between the years 1910 and 1914. That she had busy hands like Mama and a dignified face like Cap's. That she hardly ever laughed, but if she did, tears ran down her face. I remember her face jumped. She had developed permanent ticks in it, an eye jumping one minute, a cheek the next. The jerks seemed to encompass her whole face and made it pretty hard to relax around her. She was taller than I was, thinner, too, with a straight back. She was not stylish and wore shoes appropriate for a woman on her feet all day. She liked stage door canteen music, maybe because she once dated a soldier right after she left Elk Rapids.

And she was always good with a needle.

She made me beautiful dresses, ones I'm sure she didn't approve of but which were appropriate in the twenties and thirties for recitations I did in speakeasies and university libraries. When I married Duke in 1928, in a small ceremony in front of the fireplace at his parents' home in Lake Orion, she made me a small pillbox hat with a short veil, in a champagne color to match the dress, with exquisitely embroidered detailing and delicate lace.

She stayed with me a few days when Dick was born.

Though she wasn't much of a cook, she was an immaculate housekeeper, like Mama. She died two years ago at her home in Clarkston. I found her in the bathtub having a good soak, eyes closed, her face calm and utterly relaxed for the first time in her life.

She taught me to play bridge.

I cooked for her often.

It was me that got her to laugh.

Anyway, Cap announced to us both, Mabel and me, right after the dynamite incident, that he intended to do carpentry downstate, close to where Mabel lived at the time. Mabel and I had no idea how lucid he was and whether he'd be able to pursue an endeavor like carpentry or whether we'd have to support him.

But it turned out Cap took great pride in his work, did rough framing for quick money. He soon became known as a fine finish carpenter, and in later years he made furniture—chairs and tables primarily—out of cherry or pine, sometimes beech. He made beds with backboards intricately carved in mahogany or oak, though he always said oak lacked subtlety. He liked to do the caning on the seats of chairs, and people came to him to do that right up until he died.

Cap lived with me awhile in Birmingham. He was not comfortable entertaining, so we rarely did, and then only with a visiting relative or two. He would walk downtown in the early evenings and peer in the store windows and then go inside, always wearing his captain's hat. He didn't buy anything. He tipped his hat in a courtly fashion, though conversation beyond the initial greeting was not part of the routine.

He was simply a man used to greeting people.

When I was small, I could picture Mama old, but not Cap.

It never stopped surprising me that it turned out the other way. He grew frail, and there was a kind of fleshless straightness about him. No roundness ever, though his full head of hair was whiter than ever. I wonder sometimes if it was me who was the crazy one, if it was me who'd imagined Cap's craziness.

Toward the end, Cap and I drove up to Oxford to see Mabel and to celebrate Cap's seventy-fifth birthday. Duke was tied up with a death in town and didn't come with us. We took Cap to a new fish restaurant Mabel had run across, and during dessert a man came to the table. Cap, he said, reaching out and touching him on the arm. Turned out to be John Fuller who'd crewed on the *Mabel* for us a couple summers, now living in Holly and working for one of the car companies.

They talked about the summer of 1911, when business was booming, both the tourist trade and the lumber business. And John remembered when I was no taller than the bottom of the ship's wheel. They talked about fishing brown trout and rainbows on the Boardman River and how long it'd been since they'd each been back. When John left, Cap was drinking coffee and finishing the last of his cherry pie, gazing out the window at M-24, which runs from Lapeer to Pontiac. Cap kept talking. It was a particularly lucid night for him. And while he talked, I could see Mabel the person would rather he didn't.

Em always wanted you kids, he said. But it was amazing she did when it took her so much work to clean up after you and she with such a need. All that cleaning wore her out. She thought I was disappointed at not having boys, but I was living proof that boys weren't good for much. Never bothered me in the slightest. Luella was as good a deckhand as any boy.

The waitress leaned over Cap and poured him more coffee, picked up the empty pie plate. She was slim and middle-aged, had a tiredness and hungriness about her yet a kindness, too. Cap kept watching her, and I wondered if there was something about her that reminded him of Mama. I was sure that was it, since Cap didn't make it a practice to watch women in any overt way.

He picked up his coffee cup in both hands, like a woman would.

You were always a fine one with a needle, Mabel, he said to her, and I could see by her face that she liked it.

Luella could cook, Mabel said then. Still can. Nobody can cook like Luella.

That was the only compliment I remember getting from Mabel.

She used to study that *Boston Cookbook* that belonged to your mama's mama, Cap said. Used to cook some mighty fine fare out of that old book. And the Indians, they taught her to make stews from practically nothing. I remember they got us through a few tight winters.

I watched their faces, Cap's and Mabel's both, to see if mentioning the Anishinaabek would register emotion in either of them. And the answer, even when I think about it today, is that I don't know. Mabel's face was guarded, yet I can't say it was in any way knowing, and there was always the fear, the possibility that pushing Cap could send him off the deep end. There had always been the fear.

Cap picked up his coffee cup and drained it, pushed his chair back, and rose to his feet. He picked up his cap from his lap and carried it against his chest as we started for the door. No, daughters were always fine by me, he said. Loved all of them.

All of them, he'd said.

CHAPTER FORTY-TWO

Several years back, I ran into Keane on one of my vacations. I came often to see Topini and would see him then, of course, but this time I ran into him alone near the island on a Saturday about noon. He was getting into a small dinghy and carrying a bag of groceries and some fishing gear, heading to his house. I joined him, helped him carry his gear. He made us a couple mint juleps, it being Derby Day, that we drank together on the wraparound porch of the old Victorian house. He said the Fairbanks (the people who had purchased it from the Nobles) had been pestering him to sell, presumably to get the island to themselves, but he had declined. Keane had bought the place from his father, who'd moved to Grand Rapids soon after the war started, and he didn't think he could get used to someplace else. Also, Shadow was buried in the old maple grove as well as a couple dogs he'd had since, and he liked being near them.

Kachina would never live with me, he said. Said it was for both our sakes, though she never did give a rip about the opinions of others.

I nodded, and he talked about his veterinary practice, which had been good. He might not have piled up the kind of money that would have satisfied Doc, but it'd been more than enough for him. He poured us each another mint julep, which we agreed tasted like mouthwash but drank anyway, and talked about fishing, fly hatches, the reemergence of the tourist trade, and which one of us today would win a race to the Johnny Rock.

Lumps, I said. I'm suddenly short of lumps. He grinned at me. And you would have unfair advantage, I went on. I'd have to keep making a circle due to one of my rudders being missing. And that caused us to laugh hysterically.

You must miss Duke, he said. Yes, I said. (And I miss sex. Not the act itself, but the possibility of it. But I didn't say that to Keane.)

What about your reading? he asked me.

I smiled at him.

Keane's dark wavy hair didn't yet have much gray, though it was slightly sparser, and his face had lost that furtive restlessness. He was a man at peace, yet for all that "finishedness," there was once again a temporariness about him. It was in his genes for him to be a big robust man like his father, but he'd never quite achieved that stature. Shadow had done permanent damage to his liver, though I didn't know this at the time. Looking back, I'm sure he'd always known it and wouldn't have lived differently.

What stood out about that day was the peacefulness. You'd think we'd be uncomfortable together, that his betrayal would have been a constant irritant between us, but it had always been conflict that held we three together. And the ability we had to transcend it. And besides, it was more than that. I was gratified that I could feel Keane's longing for me, a physical longing, even that day, both of us older than God, that had been there right along. It was a longing he'd never figured out what to do with, and I'd always known that.

And, yes, I visited him at the end. I helped him tie a Hendricks, or rather he showed me a new variation he'd created. Kachina left us alone then. I stayed an hour. And that hour is the one part of the story I'll take with me to the grave, the one conceit I'll allow myself.

But now I'm sick of funerals and the words that attend them. Last night, Reverend Alanson, a new young minister at the Elk Rapids Methodist Church, stood in the pulpit shifting from one foot to the other, spouting platitudes and reading the same tired scriptures. The Lord is my shepherd and all that.

I decided at the last minute not to wear the black dress. Decided instead on the red plaid pantsuit I bought last week, which drew surreptitious glances from most everyone as I entered. Topini greeted me with grins and drew me into the second pew next to Kachina and behind the immediate family. She kept giving me copious hugs throughout most of the service, despite my efforts to calm her, which seemed to annoy the family even more.

None of us qualified as "family," of course.

The packed church smelled of stale air and old wood mixed with the heavy aroma of flowers. Cloying.

The funeral was held at dusk. No one was sure why. Keane had been ill for some time, made a will, and instructed that it be opened immediately upon his death. Though they had never been legally married, Keane left all he had to Kachina, including his own remains (something I had never seen done before), with explicit instructions as to the service and later interment. The church service was in deference to his father and brother who were still living, though not in the area. His reasons for the time of service were known only to him (and possibly Kachina). Keane had declined to attend this portion of the proceedings, and the family had placed his picture on a small table amongst the flower arrangements. I was surprised at the photograph they'd chosen. The picture was taken sometime in his late twenties, and his young arrogant face gazed back at us with the hint of a smile. The arrogance was something he acquired, I imagined, when his decisions to become a veterinarian and not to marry some appropriate white woman had become abundantly clear.

The arrogance looked good on him.

People kept glancing toward Kachina, who'd fulfilled expectations and worn native dress. She was upright and still, and it was hard to see her breathing. If they expected to be gratified by a display of emotion from her, they would be sadly disappointed. Keane's brother, John, who'd become a lawyer to the great vindication of his father, turned once and gave me a pinched smile. He had a bloodless-looking woman to his right who I assumed was his wife and an earnest-looking young man next to her, presumably his son. Keane's father didn't acknowledge us at all.

Not much else to say about the ceremony because it had nothing to do with us. Or even Keane. I didn't help Kachina with any of the arrangements, despite my expertise in these matters, because it hadn't been necessary. The service didn't last more than twenty minutes, a stipulation outlined in Keane's will. There was a lady playing "Nearer My God to Thee" softly in the background. And then it was over.

CHAPTER FORTY-THREE

Kachina invites me to come out to the island after the funeral. Anytime I feel like it, she said. And I plan to do that. But I'm hungry for trout, and my first inclination is to fish for it.

I take Keane's Hendricks down to Yuba Creek. I haven't fished in ten years maybe. And probably shouldn't fish alone at my age. I have waders, which I never used in this creek in the old days, but the boots have felt on the bottoms, and I am, after all, alone. It's dusk, and I see a few small rises upstream. It feels awkward, my first few steps, and I'm careful to shuffle, watchful for holes, but the strangeness doesn't last long.

This is my stream.

You should never be overconfident; your own water can fool you. But I can feel Keane guiding my footsteps, and I think, *Someplace has to be home.*

I tie on the Hendricks, notice again Keane's slight variation in hackle, knew he'd made it just for me. I make a couple hesitant casts toward those rises I'd seen before, and before long I'm lost in the rhythm. I can't get a perfect drift under that snag of tag alders, but I'm close, close enough, and when I feel the tug, I set the hook.

I fish a couple hours, and though I'm hungry for fresh brook trout, I release half a dozen fish. I'd become a catch-and-release fisherman.

It's near dark, so I break down my rod and hook Keane's Hendricks fly to my vest. I sit upon a fallen beech log when I notice the trillium. It had recently finished flowering, which is always sad, but I'm interested in the flowers. I study the leaves, which should have been at the peak of their seasonal development. One plant has a few unusual leaves on the stalk that are undeveloped, smaller, paler in color, leaves that have remained that early spring green and are fragile, slightly curled still, while the rest are a deep lustrous green, stretched out full length to all they can and ever will be. The pale leaves remind me of Topini in their agreeable passivity, their willingness to be pushed aside by the vibrant vitality of bigger, healthier leaves. I think about digging up the plant, taking it home, and planting it in my own beech grove, tending it carefully with water and appropriate sun. But I know what will happen. The undeveloped leaves will shrivel away before they even turn brown.

One day they'll just be missing.

Though the words have been missing all these years, other things have been missing as well. The story has become, for me, about *places*. Cold places, hard places, desperate places like the Northern Michigan Asylum where Uncle George ended up, and some said Cap should have, too. Empty places, like they said about Topini's head.

But there are places *not* missing, like the one in which Topini grew up, here with the Anishinaabek. A relatively good place, I think.

Topini made the places around her her own.

Where in the world do we put you, Topini? Where do you belong? I mean that in a physical sense, of course, but not only that. Are you like those leaves, missing important stages in your life, or are the rest of us simply cursed with them? It seems at times that you have not been allowed to open to your full potential, and that you have been deprived of the slow, natural decline the rest of us feel is our due. You've gotten a bit gray at the temple, a little thick in the body, a little slower in your step, but otherwise you are the same. One day you will be gone, and it will be as if you were never here.

Or is it me who has never been here?

Perhaps your purpose in coming is not to be touched but to touch others. An opportunity for them to rise to the occasion or fall flat as some would think Cap has done. You're no different than any other circumstance that arrives in a person's life. You cry and laugh and moan and groan and breathe. We move around you, slowly, not able to escape you, though we'd like to, and we must inevitably make a decision about whether we will allow ourselves to feel your touch, draw the fact of you into our existence. *Be changed by you.*

Kachina is the lucky one.

Kachina will wake every morning ready to fry you flapjacks with sugar maple, even when you're no longer there to eat them. She'll be ready to button your red blouse with buttons you've never learned to negotiate and pull a comb through the tangle of your unruly hair. She'll listen for your twenty inarticulate words to give meaning to her already full life, and the day after you're gone, she'll watch the morning wake up, listen to the birds, and smile, as you taught her to. This sounds sad, but Kachina is full of dents and scars and depressions that will ever so slightly make up for losing you, will be testimony to the fact of you. Whereas I will still be wondering if you were really here at all. Or if I was.

Just like Cap.

CHAPTER FORTY-FOUR

I found something out early on when I first started writing in my journal that Uncle George gave me, something I've realized now about my life: without these words, *I cannot exist.*

Kachina would not agree. Kachina used to say that I write because we Chemokmon have no sense of family and therefore no one worth talking to. We've scattered like so much chaff in a high wind. We leave first, she says. In our hearts.

Later we just move.

Maybe she's right.

But the words matter.

I CHANGE INTO DENIM PANTS and a blue flannel shirt. Chilly this time of night on the island. The stiffness in my bones makes it difficult to pull pants over my hips, but I do. Then I pull white canvas shoes over gray wool socks and tie them.

Will Kachina be glad to see me? She's always been hard to read. Another of the unanswered questions of my life. There are answers I feel entitled to.

I wonder what possessed me to think I should pack it all in and move back here? I think of Uncle George and how he said it was all about pain, how Cap had spent his whole life trying to avoid it. And how I had, too. I'm tired of the numbness, the palliatives the world finds so attractive. But moving back can't possibly be a move forward? It suddenly seems ridiculous. I'll call Ken in the morning and have him take my house off the market, I think.

I grab my knapsack, put some tobacco in it, the red flannel nightgown I brought for Topini, the remainder of the blueberries, a wooden bowl, and the bottle of Irish whiskey I'd needed a sip from all day.

River Street stretches west through town, and the eight o'clock shadows drop off into the bay. The street winds around next to it for a while, past the cemetery, then joins up with US-31, crosses Yuba Creek, and heads south to Traverse City—roads that now provide Elk Rapids access to the world. How would this generation feel about growing up wearing bloomers and knickers, using woodstoves for heat, kerosene lanterns or candles for light, horses, steamboats, and trains for transportation, then adjusting to the industrial age with electricity, radios, TVs, automobiles, jet planes, and flights to the moon?

I walk out to the field next to the cemetery and pick a handful of wild yarrow, put the stalks into the knapsack, and draw it tight, with the flowers sticking out the top. The island sits out in the water just far enough to call it an island, nestled between the bay and the inlets where the Elk River dumps into it. I step into one of the two rowboats that Keane keeps on each side, put my sack in the bottom of the boat at my feet, and start rowing. The night is brisk, the moon waxing, and the breeze is enough to remind me to row. The songbirds are calling it a night, though cries of gulls and whip-poor-wills fill the air, mixed with the strident chorus of frogs and crickets. I wave away a mosquito that insists on whining in my ear. I can hear a dog barking as my boat approaches the shore.

The island is lined on the village side by a mixture of willows, cedars, and other conifers. It's open toward the bay side. There is, though, a small maple grove to the north of the house that provides a buffer from the wind. The house faces west and has a maple or two planted in front to protect the house from the afternoon sun. I step out of the boat and head for the house when I'm met by a wary mongrel, male, this one another gray-brown shepherd variety. I'm about to step back in the boat when I hear Kachina call him. *Wagi, come.* The dog backs off, and I can see Kachina walking toward me.

How was your dinner? Kachina asks. She's changed into brown denim pants and a rust-colored wool sweater. Several rows of turquoise beads line the neckline as always. The beads are assorted shapes: round ones, long cylindrical ones, some horizontal, some vertical, some crescent shaped like the moon with the open side facing up so none of her dreams will fall out. She has rust-colored moccasins on her feet with similar turquoise beadwork on the top. Her hair is braided in that single braid down her back. In the moonlight, I see a few gray strands in the black silk I could not see that afternoon in the church. Her figure is fuller, and there is an ageless maturity about her, the scar silvery now.

How was dinner? she asks again.

Didn't eat, I tell her. Did you get something?

She tells me she has rabbit stew on but hasn't eaten yet. We walk up the steps and in through the back door of the old house, though I see Wagi has made his way to a smudge fire Kachina has smoldering to the right of the house in the small maple grove. The smell of the rabbit stew pulls me in through the kitchen, awakens my stomach for the first time all day, maybe even in years. As we walk into the main living area, I notice Topini asleep in a brown leather chair in the corner. And I remember how Keane's mother, drained of life due to his father's behavior, had seemed to hover like a moth near the wide expanse of windows that overlook the bay. But Keane's mother had wanted *out*, not in.

I find I have more compassion for her passivity than I did back then.

It's obvious that Kachina hasn't yet spent much time in the island house. I doubt if she's slept overnight here. Keane's presence is everywhere, the room devoid of female touches. The woodstove still sits in the corner between the main room and the kitchen. Most people would have removed it when radiators for hot water heat were installed. It's clear that Keane used the stove for much of the year as there's a woodbox half full of split logs, an ironware coffeepot on the warming plate, and a few ashes on the bricks in front of the open door. A pair of well-worn snowshoes, a shotgun, and a pair of rubber boots are all piled haphazardly against the brick wall behind it, next to which is a tin matchbox on the floor. There is a wooden rocker to the right of the stove with an Indian blanket draped across one arm, probably a present from Kachina.

Several wicker fishing creels in assorted sizes sit next to the front door, along with several different-size fishing reels, all full of line. Keane had never carpeted the wide-planked pine floors, and several Indian rugs, all red, protect them. There is a mark partially revealed where an old painting had hung on the wall behind the couch, gone now and replaced by an enormous dream catcher. A harvest table of at least ten feet sits in the dining area between the main room and the kitchen, with an enormous duck decoy serving as a centerpiece. A fishing vest with several flies still hooked to it hangs over the back of one of at least ten Windsor chairs that surround the table. I notice several framed pictures of Keane's family on the coffee table, several of Kachina, and surprisingly there is one of myself I've never seen before. Next to them is a pair of reading glasses and a pile of books, the top one by William James.

I feel at home, a feeling I don't know if I've ever felt in my own immaculate house. I'm aware that Kachina is watching me and I wonder if my feelings have been too obvious, wonder if Kachina has ever resented my closeness with Keane. I see no sign of it on her face, but then when do you ever see a sign of emotion on Kachina's face? I'm suddenly irritated with her.

Why in the world did you never marry him? I ask. I'm gratified at seeing pain or guilt cross Kachina's face for the first time since I'd met her.

Mostly, she says, I never believed in it. Kachina points at her legs. I need both these legs because of the unique relationship between them, she says. They have respect for each other and work together well because they are free to do so, and there is a willingness for them to do so. And when they do, I can run like the wind. Bind them together, and all they will do is pull against one another at cross-purposes. Crippled. Were you to lose one under circumstances such as these, do you believe you would even miss it?

I laugh. Sounds to me as if someone has been hanging around *objects too flaccid,* to quote someone I know well. Kachina laughs with me. And anyway, I tell her, *some* people would miss the struggle.

Yes, some people would, she says. Kachina stands then, stirs the stew. Would you like some tea or maybe some coffee? she asks.

I shrug and pull the flowers out of the knapsack. I brought you some tobacco and Topini a new red nightgown. And this. I hand her the wooden bowl. The Anishinaabek give each other mourning blankets or dishes, a gesture of love, a custom that suggests "a little something to keep your mind off it." They would use them in the Niiaabwin ceremony anytime a loved one entered the spirit world.

But if that doesn't work, I tell her, I brought this as well. I pull the whiskey from the sack.

You know how I feel about booze, Kachina says. Next week I will officially become a mishkiikii ninii. It's wrong for a healer to distort the mind.

Well, good, I say. Then you have *a whole week left.*

Kachina laughs, puts the tobacco in her pocket along with some sage, grabs two tin cups from a mess kit on a shelf over the sink. Let me taste it out of this, then, she says. Keane swears whiskey only tastes right out of a tin cup. We'll take it out by the fire. Kachina reaches inside and wipes a dead fly from one of the cups.

I watch Kachina take sips of whiskey from Keane's tin cup. She acknowledges that it tastes good out of the tin, though she points out that she really has nothing to compare it to.

To the rest of it, I say then, clicking my cup to Kachina's. We're sitting on logs next to the fire, which is beginning to die down, the red coals snapping in the stillness. It's a clear night, and the full moon reminds me again of Topini's round face.

Come, Kachina says. We'll have stew later.

She heads over to the maple grove, and Wagi, who has been lying under the trees, rises to greet us. Kachina says she hopes he will begin eating again soon. The grove consists of eight sugar maples, trees that Keane still tapped every year. They're approximately one hundred yards from the house, and farther on there is another small grove of cedars. The maples are up on a small rise, the cedars down in the dip that stays marshier. There are four graves under the maples marked with simple stones. I can tell which one belongs to Keane only because it's the freshest.

Meenong, Kachina says, pointing to the grove on the hill. I wait for her to explain. That means *the place we pick blueberries,* but it stands like a symbol, a good high place.

I think of how many times Kachina has pointed out markers to me over the years. Kinawaa'chigan, she would say. Which could mean *danger* or *good hunting* or *in memory of* or the one I remember most: *this way; go this way.*

She walks up the hill, takes the tobacco and sage from her pocket, mixes them in the tin cup, now empty of whiskey, and lights a piece of the sage. Then begins her prayers.

I'll be right back, I say to her. I disappear into the house, return moments later with the wildflowers. We both crouch, ancient knees cramped beneath bodies that must belong to someone else.

All that time, Kachina says to me, I told myself I mustn't want anything except my teaching, because as soon as you want or need something, it owns you. I was afraid to let people come between me and my ability to listen to The Day, but what I was really afraid of was that my faith wasn't strong enough, that I would come between me and *myself.* Izusa told me all along that if I was listening clearly, I could hear anywhere, but I wasn't listening, even to her. I was too busy being angry at her for being afraid when *I* was the most afraid of all. Wisdoms were to be shared with everyone, and while I wasn't afraid to love white people, I was afraid of being lost in their whiteness. Izusa was comfortable with the giving; I never was. In order to gain all, you have to be willing to lose all.

Our eyes have become a bit too bright, too full.

I've lost my ability to listen anyway, she says, so it was all a lot of foolish posturing. A thought occurs to Kachina. Did you mind terribly? she asks.

I consider a moment. Yes, I answer, and we both laugh loudly. You're damned *right* I minded terribly. We fall back in the grass, laughing until our stomachs ache.

Well, Kachina tells me, wiping tears from her eyes, I can offer you Sam Wilkenson. Last week at the grocery store he offered to *help me out* anytime I'm feeling the need, now that Keane's gone. Kept asking me wasn't it pretty cold in that shack?

That got us laughing again.

The man must be ninety years old, I say.

Yes, she says, and nearly deaf. He shouted the question at me while he was picking out frozen peas, and I had to yell *no thank you* at him three times before he heard me, with half the town as an audience. I think he eats Wheaties, though. Runs up and down the street wearing those drawers his daughter sent him from Hawaii, the ones with the pineapples running right down the fifty yard line. As we laugh, I feel some sense of myself returning.

That won't be the last offer like *that* one you'll get, I say.

Imagine it won't, she tells me. If I thought that was *all* they wanted, I might consider it once in a while.

It's never all they want, I say. How about a swim? I ask her.

I gesture toward the bay, and Kachina answers, Do you have *any* idea how cold that water is, and have you completely lost your mind?

Let's do it, I say.

Topini is still asleep, and we can see her through the window, though she's curled into a fetal position despite her fifty-six years. Kachina goes into the house, grabs a couple towels, and we head for the bay.

Then I stop, so Kachina stops as well. Waits.

The guilt should have been spread out between us, but Cap had never allowed that. This may surprise you to hear me say, but he was equal to the burden, and he'd known also that Uncle George and I had not been equal to it.

Still he had not saved us from it.

I consider the ramifications of asking Kachina the truth at last. Or rather, how the truth came to be the truth. I'd known what the truth was a long time now.

But every nuance of my life has been based on not knowing the particulars of my situation. The inability to deal with the not knowing. The inability to ask questions about it. To ask now and to know the truth seemed to invalidate my existence. I thought coming back to Elk Rapids was movement out of the quagmire, but maybe it was more of the same. Could I move into this world finally and make myself useful in it? Or was I simply coming home to die?

I think of Topini lying asleep inside. A woman in her fifties, she is old and still young. Her hair is turning gray but is the same silky fine quality of my own. Her ears are too small for her face but stick out, protrude through the delicate hair. Though they are closed at the moment, her eyes will have the same mirrorlike quality they've always had. Her body has become lumpish. She seems to be losing the battle at last to keep a border, a distinct edge, as I had lost it long ago. Our flesh, hers and mine, seems to be diffusing into space, spreading, then dissolving, intermixing, even yearning to be part of the earth again. Or the water.

Kachina and I walk quietly toward the beach. The call of a hoot owl drowns out the insistent yammer of the crickets for a moment. A stick bumps against a large rock along the shore over and over again as the waves hold it captive. I gesture back toward the house.

What will you do with the place now that Keane has left it to you? I ask.

A school. Kachina seems surprised she knows the answer to the question. To replace what we've lost. Kachina stops walking. What about you teaching here? she asks.

I'm shocked at the question. What did I know about the Anishinaabek way of life, about children, about anything? What did either of us have to offer, women in our sixties? I say as much to Kachina.

English, history, literature, dramatics. You can teach that, she says. You're a damn University of Michigan graduate for God's sake.

I wonder what Uncle George (or Cap) would think about *this* teaching job. I had walked through the asylum, now called Traverse City State Hospital, a few years ago when I was here on a visit, astonished at how many children like Topini were being warehoused there. Surely, I think, I'm too old to adopt, but my new house is a big one.

I begin to run, and my old legs move me remarkably fast toward the water. Last one in is last, I say to Kachina. Shirts and socks are flying haphazardly about the beach now.

You haven't done this in a long time, Welly, she says. Your memory must be a little dim.

That will be good then, I tell her.

I make no attempt to hide what's left of my chest or what time and gravity have done to my body, but there's nothing about scars that Kachina will not understand.

Scars have become redundant.

We jump into the icy waves, screaming as the water steals our breath. There is a chop tonight, not too much, but enough. We bounce up and down, waiting for our bodies to adjust, know it will take a few minutes. But it happens, like it always happens. The water begins to feel warmer. Our blood begins to circulate.

The light from the moon, refracted in the coppery water, scatters across the surface, gets lost in the swales, pops up again on the crests of the waves.

We realize it at the same instant.

There is no Johnny Rock, nothing to swim to.

Our eyes meet, bewilderment on both our faces. We move off together, swimming deliberately out into the big lake.

EPILOGUE

We draw pictures when we're new. We draw them like you would. Houses and trees, stick people, stick dogs, empty clouds. Nothing unusual. But what surprises you all is that most of us fill up the whole page—the air, the sky—with shapes: circles and squares, often with dots or even a triangle. You spend all kinds of time trying to figure out why we would draw pictures like that, why we'd put all those shapes in the air when the answer is simple.

Because they're there.

After a while, when we aren't so new anymore, we stop drawing them. Or we simply stop drawing.

You think we're slow. But while you look at things straight on, we look at angles, sideways. In order to assimilate the total dimensions and then make the appropriate reaction to it, you must get down and look at things laterally.

I am extraordinarily peripheral.

The biggest mistake you make is that you believe in spaces when of course there aren't any. Space is filled up and all connected, orderly and harmonious. And all necessary. You don't want to give up the spaces because you're afraid of what it will be like not to have any. To be closed in. You believe you can't move without space, but you're wrong. We had none when we were in our mother's womb, and that is the best that it gets.

I've been here a long time: I'm very old for someone like me. We usually go sooner than you, which you think is a negative, but it's not. One of the best things about us is that we remember while you forget. The doctor knew about me right away, of course. That I wasn't like the rest of you.

A nurse, dressed in vibrant royal blue, bustles around my room now, as I am once again a ward at the Traverse City Rehabilitation Center as it's called now. An aide helps her pack my belongings into an old red American Tourister suitcase. It seems I am to move yet again.

"Must be fifty years old, this suitcase," the nurse says.

At least.

"When does she come for her?" the aide asks.

"Soon," the nurse answers.

It's always strange to hear people talking in front of you as if you speak a foreign language or as if you aren't there at all.

"It's amazing," the nurse says, "that someone should be coming for a woman with this kind of impairment, more amazing that a woman this handicapped should be alive after nearly a hundred years."

"How old is she?" asks the aide.

"We're just guessing at her age. There's no birth certificate or paperwork. She apparently lived with an old Indian woman until the woman's death in 1995, and after that she lived with an old white woman in Elk Rapids who had long been a teacher in the local Indian school, until this past February, when she passed away as well. But they think she might be a hundred years old."

A woman enters the room now. I judge her to be in her early forties. High cheekbones, determined jaw, wispy, hard-to-control hair, moon-shaped face. She's carrying a purse, and sticking out of the edges of it is a journal or diary covered in muslin on which you can make out the letter L embroidered in blue.

"She's all ready," the nurse says. "It's good of you to take her."

The young woman smiles and begins gathering my possessions while the aide goes in search of a wheelchair to transport me.

"I see you are from Elk Rapids," the nurse says, hoping to get at least one word out of the young woman who seems reluctant to part with any. "Did you know the old woman she lived with?"

"She was my grandmother," the girl says. "Luella Sharp Kimball."

The aide returns with the wheelchair, and the three of them help me into it. Before we leave, the young woman walks to an empty wooden chair by the window for a moment to look out at the view from the four-story building. She sees the pointed roof of Building 50 where they kept me those few days back in 1916, before Kachina came for me. Part of the building is abandoned now, but it still stands silhouetted against the skyline, the pointed Victorian roofs of all the other "cottages" nestled eerily around it.

The young woman turns with a sigh, wraps her fingers firmly around the handlebars of the wheelchair, and starts pushing. Good of her to take me. I've been fortunate that way.

I think back. I remember Emma, my mother, was sad to have to leave me so soon. I remember what her skin felt like and how wonderful she smelled even through the sticky sweet smell of sickness. Cap prayed a lot, and I cried a lot while Welly stood in the corner of the darkened room and stared at my mother. And then Welly stared at me. Strange that she didn't recognize me later on.

White candles glowed around my mother's bed, and the flames flickered in the cold draft that seeped in around the window sashes as my mother wavered in and out. As she grew dimmer and somehow smaller, the edges around her grew more distinct, seemed to draw into focus.

They blame him.

Almost all of them blame him, anyway. But I'd always wondered if they'd given him time if it would have turned out the way it did.

Midnight.

His hands, which were without gloves, were large, and I could feel the warmth of them through the blankets that were wrapped around my naked body. But that was all the warmth there was as he held me away from him, and the snow, coming straight at us, pelted us both in the face, making it harder to see the fast-disappearing path as he walked through the woods. He made groaning noises every few steps and what sounded like a whine as he took a misstep or two in the deep drifts. He kept saying "Em, Em" every few minutes.

I remember his hair was already turning white, like the snow that landed on his hatless head, but mostly I could see his chin, fleshless, bare, and trembling, wet from the driven snow or maybe it was from his tears, freezing in irregular crusty patches. Steam from his ragged breathing wafted over my head but didn't quite reach me, which might have kept me warm if it had.

He stopped and sat on the top of a fallen log, bending slowly as if his joints had begun to set up on him. There was a sheltering grove of cedars that protected us from the wind and snow. He stopped talking to Em, and he stopped making any noise at all, as if he were listening or maybe praying. He laid me across his lap then but moved his hands away from me. They were hanging lifelessly at his sides. He seemed to be looking off through the trees as if he were expecting someone. Em, maybe.

The snow changed direction and came at us again, and the wind as well, and when it blew, it blew the blankets from around my body, and I could feel time easing away from me. I kicked and screamed for a bit, but the cold was making me drowsy, and it seemed all at once like an awful effort when I could go on back with my mother as easy as not.

I could see his chin bobbing then, as if he were considering napping, and I wondered if time were easing away from him as well. I knew he was trying to come to a decision. Off and on I thought I could hear voices or footsteps, but by now I was dreaming.

I felt warmer, somehow. And blue. A warm blue. His head was bent over me now, his eyes closed, the steam from his nose and mouth on my face. Just as I felt myself slipping off his lap, she picked me up.

Izusa.

She wrapped the blankets tight, then placed a fur coat or blanket of some kind over that and pulled me close to her body. She pulled him to his feet then. "Go home," she said. That was all. Just "go home."

But I don't think he ever did.

AUTHOR'S NOTE

First a word about the name Kachina. The word in Ojibwe means "dancer" and in my mind seemed to fit my character so well, as a shaman would so often dance during prayer and healing ceremonies, a joining with the motion of the universe and with God. I was two years into this novel before I became aware of the Hopi kachina dolls usually associated with western Native American language. I checked the name with my Ojibwe language specialist, Kenny Neganigwane Pheasant, who has worked with both the Little River Band and the Grand Traverse Band of tribal Indians, both of the Aninshinaabek nation. (Aninshinaabe means "first good people.") Kenny continues to work tirelessly in an effort to retain the language and culture of his people and is responsible for a great portion of the background I used to create the Kachina section of the novel. He assured me that the name was fine, and since I'd grown so accustomed to it, I decided to leave it.

The historical background and setting in this story are accurate, with a few notable exceptions. Dexter & Noble Company built the island house (Keane's house) in 1865 and shortly afterward built a broad bridge across the river that connected the island to the town of Elk Rapids. In my story, there is no bridge. Also, the other two-story house I refer to on the island never existed as a separate house but was leveled off and converted into the single-story E. S.

Noble House, which now serves as the Elk Rapids Public Library.

Dr. Jamison never existed, though the background of Northern Michigan Asylum (later Traverse City Hospital) is accurate. The hospital was founded by Dr. James Decker Munson, but the events involving "Dr. Jamison" were completely invented by me.

Many of the people in this novel actually lived. My great grandfather, Ira Sharp, did indeed run the steamship *Mabel* (as well as a few other steamboats) for better than thirty-five years on the inland waterway between Elk Rapids and Bellaire, Michigan. He had three daughters, none of whom were handicapped and all of whom he kept. One was my grandmother, Luella, who did have an older sister named Mabel but also had a younger sister named Edna. (Ira Sharp also had one son, Bailey.) Ira was a fine and decent man and my decision to use his name would probably be considered by him to be a dubious honor. His wife Emma lived many years and did not die in childbirth.

My grandmother Luella graduated from the University of Michigan sometime in the early 1920s. She was a theater major and read poetry in restaurants and coffeehouses. Her husband, Duke, was Oakland County coroner for two years and had just begun his second term when he died at age thirty-five of Hodgkin's disease. Luella worked many years at White Chapel Cemetery in Troy, Michigan.

Luella's uncle George ran the livery service in Elk Rapids and died of alcoholism or perhaps complications from an influenza outbreak in 1918 in Northern Michigan Asylum.

And that is *all* about the people that is true.

As for the boats, the *Ida* sank in the lower end of Clam Lake sometime after 1898, pretty much as was described in this book. The *Ruth* was sold in 1917 to Sears Brothers in Charlevoix to run between Charlevoix and Boyne City. She burned to a total loss in 1933 in Detour, Michigan, where she had become part of the Drummond Island Ferry Service. The *Mabel* was sold in 1917 to E. Knight & Sons for the purpose of making the run between East Jordan and Charlevoix, though it is unclear how long she was employed in that capacity or what happened to her after that.